FULLY IGNITED

SHANNON STACEY

The Kowalski series from Shannon Stacey

Suggested reading order

Exclusively Yours
Undeniably Yours
Yours to Keep
All He Ever Needed
All He Ever Desired
All He Ever Dreamed
Love a Little Sideways
Taken with You
Falling for Max

Also available from Shannon Stacey and Carina Press

Holiday Sparks
Mistletoe & Margaritas
Slow Summer Kisses
Snowbound with the CEO
Her Holiday Man
Heat Exchange
Controlled Burn
A Fighting Chance

Also available from Shannon Stacey and Harlequin

Alone with You
Heart of the Storm

For Megan. As your oldest sister, I have to admit that seeing a photograph of you in your firefighting gear struck a little fear in my heart, but I am immensely proud of you. Be brave, be safe, and know that I love you.

And though she be but little, she is fierce.
—Shakespeare

Recycling programs for this product may not exist in your area.

ISBN-13: 978-0-373-00297-9

Fully Ignited

This edition published by arrangement with Harlequin Books S.A.

www.CarinaPress.com

Printed in U.S.A.

FULLY IGNITED

ONE

"THE STREET'S PROBABLY going to be full of people, so try not to run anybody over."

Scott Kincaid ignored the helpful instruction from Simmons since driving the big-ass fire engine through the narrow backstreets of Boston was hard enough without looking over to roll your eyes at the asshole officer riding shotgun.

Chemistry in a fire company mattered, and Engine 59 had it. Or they used to. And it wasn't a surprise they'd been a close group. Their lieutenant, Danny Walsh, was Scott's brother-in-law. Aidan Hunt, his best friend for years, was going to marry his other sister very soon. Even Grant Cutter, who was the kid of the bunch, had fit right in. And their pumper always rolled out with Ladder 37, and they meshed with that company, too, which was good since they shared the old brick fire station.

Things had gone south about six weeks ago, though, when Danny got hurt. Besides smoke inhalation, he'd suffered a concussion, a busted arm and a leg broken in two places. Having guys fill in here and there wasn't easy, even short term, and then they'd heard the news Danny needed surgery on the leg.

They'd found a temporary lieutenant solution with Simmons, but it wasn't really working out.

Mostly because Simmons was such an asshole.

Scott turned onto the side street and rolled up in front of the function hall that had called in the alarm. He didn't have to worry about running anybody over because there was nobody on the street.

"Did the Rapture come and nobody told us?" Grant asked, leaning between the front seats to peer out at the empty street.

Aidan snorted. "Shit, the Rapture could hit and it would probably be a month before Boston noticed."

"Hey, anybody seen Mrs. Broussard lately?" Scott joked.

"Maybe we can save the stand-up routine for after we clear the scene," Simmons barked.

"Do you think everybody went home?" Grant asked.

"Dispatch said it's a wedding reception and they weren't sure what set the alarm off, so it's more likely they're all still inside," Aidan said.

"I want this building cleared," Simmons said, and he gestured for Aidan to go first. Simmons was never first through any door.

Scott was familiar with feeling as if he'd just stepped through a door into hell. But walking into the function hall was a special kind of hell.

Unable to silence the fire alarm, it sounded as if they'd simply cranked the music higher and kept dancing. For a few seconds he wondered how they'd managed to dim the lights more than the code would allow, but then he figured out some genius had plugged in a smoke machine.

"They weren't sure what set the alarm off?" he asked Aidan, watching fake smoke billow up from the dance floor to hover at ceiling level. At least the sprinkler system hadn't gone off, since it was triggered by heat.

"Everybody out," Simmons tried to shout over the music. Everybody ignored him.

Welcome to the party, Scott thought. As Aidan went to deal with the alarm, Scott sent Grant over toward the corner to pull the plug on the smoke machine. They'd have to clear everybody out and do a quick sweep of the building, but it wouldn't take long.

The guys from Ladder 37 came in on their heels, with their lieutenant, Rick Gullotti, in front. Gavin Boudreau, who was only a little older than Grant, stood in the shadow of big Jeff Porter, and Chris Eriksson—the oldest of all of them, barring Chief Cobb—pulled up the rear.

"You owe me ten bucks, kid," Chris said.

Gavin rolled his eyes at Scott. "I bet him it was somebody smoking in the bathroom."

"Hell, half the people in here could be smoking right now and nobody would know." Scott shook his head. "Simmons wants us to get everybody outside."

Rick nodded. "I only saw one cruiser out there, so we'll have to send Cutter and Boudreau outside with them. As drunk as these people are, they'll want to play with the shiny fire trucks."

Before they could move, a woman in a frilly hot-pink dress clearly marking her as a bridesmaid stepped up to Scott and ran her hand down the front of his bunker coat. “Well, hello, sexy.”

“I’m going to have to ask you to go outside, ma’am,” he said, taking a step back.

Instead, she looked over her shoulder and waved at a friend. “I think they’re strippers!”

It wasn’t the first time they’d been mistaken for strippers, but it was the first time it had happened to Scott at a wedding reception. Who expected strippers to show up at a wedding? Luckily, the alarm and the music both cut off, and Simmons’s voice boomed through the speakers.

“Everybody needs to evacuate the building so we can do our jobs. The sooner we can verify there’s no threat to your safety, the sooner you can get back to your party.”

It didn’t take them long to sweep the building once everybody had cleared out, even with two of their guys tied up keeping drunk people from climbing on the trucks. Then they stood around while Simmons rounded up the people in charge and threatened them with all kinds of dire consequences if the smoke machine was turned back on.

“It’s too bad you swore off women,” Aidan said. “A drunk bridesmaid who thinks you’re a stripper is just your type.”

“*Was* my type.” Scott snorted. “Except the drunk part.”

“Lydia was just talking about how we should reconsider having a small wedding because there won't be any single bridesmaids. Just Ashley as her matron of honor."

"Oh, hell no. When the wedding's for your sister, you don't mess around with the bridesmaids."

"How long's it been since you went on a date?"

As his best friend, Aidan knew he hadn't been on a date in months. "Not long enough to tangle with a drunk bridesmaid."

After it had become clear his last girlfriend—who he'd actually felt something for—had been chasing his benefits and even hinted she might get pregnant so he'd have to marry her, Scott had decided to take a hiatus from the relationship scene. Seeing Aidan and Lydia together, as well as what Ashley and Danny had gone through—from their separation and reunion to his injuries—had just driven home that he wanted the real thing. Love, marriage and a baby carriage.

But he hadn't found the right woman and he didn't want to miss her because he was hooking up with women he knew weren't in it for the long run.

"We're outta here," Rick Gullotti yelled to them, and they all headed for the door.

By the time they were backing the engines under the brick arches at the station, Scott was feeling the exhaustion set in. Even though they only worked two shifts per week—barring extra time to cover for somebody or events like the St. Patrick's Day parade last week—twenty-four hours was a long time. Hopefully, even though it was Friday night, he'd have time to hit his bunk for a quick power nap.

"Who the hell gets married at the end of March, anyway?" Grant asked while they went through the process of checking over the engines and putting their turnout gear on the racks for the next run. "It's too cold for a nice wedding, but not cold enough to be a winter wedding. Maybe you get a discount if you get married when nobody else wants to."

"Judging by the bride's extreme lack of sobriety, I'm going to guess it wasn't a shotgun situation," Aidan said.

Scott snorted. "She was pretty near that tipping point where one drink makes the difference between the groom having the best wedding night ever or the worst wedding night ever."

They all laughed, which annoyed Simmons. They knew he didn't like chitchat when they were going through a procedure list because he thought things got missed when they were distracted. Like they weren't capable of lining their boots up in a neat row while telling a few jokes.

"I'm going upstairs," Simmons said, disgust practically dripping from his voice. "I'm so glad after tonight, you idiots will be somebody else's problem."

Nobody was as glad as they were, Scott thought, though he wasn't so much an idiot that he voiced the thought out loud. He felt bad for the guys at Simmons's usual house, who were stuck with him on a regular basis, unless they all had sticks up their asses, too.

They'd just finished up and were ready to head up to the third-floor living quarters when a woman walked through the open bay door. Scott, who'd been just about to hit the button to lower the big overhead, dropped his hand.

For a few seconds, all his mind registered was an attractive brunette who was a little on the tall side and had a smoking body, and he assumed she was stopping by to see one of the guys or bring baked goods. Homemade cookies and muffins, and even the occasional pie, were definitely perks of the job.

Then he noticed the Boston Fire logo on her T-shirt, peeking out from behind her unzipped sweatshirt. The folded papers in her hand. The way she stood with her feet slightly apart and her back straight, her gaze sweeping around the engine bays in a way that didn't strike him as curiosity. She was appraising. Judging.

She stared at Engine 59 for a long moment, her gaze sweeping over the apparatus. And then she turned that same steady scrutiny on the guys, looking each of them in the eye for a few seconds before moving on to the next.

When she got to Scott, he looked into eyes that were a pretty shade of green and found himself surprised. He was expecting them to be brown. He grinned, a reflexive reaction to making eye contact with a pretty woman.

"I'm looking for Chief Cobb," she said, and the truth of the situation hit Scott like a hydrant wrench.

Holy shit. The new guy wasn't a guy.

JAMIE RUTHERFORD KNEW that look, since she'd seen it a few times before. It was the look that said somebody hadn't gotten the memo that Jamie wasn't short for James, and that they were about to share their firehouse with a woman.

She'd been in this situation before and, as long as there wasn't a straight-up misogynistic jerk in the building, she'd be fine. The guys would be awkward and stiff around her for a few days, but once she'd been out on some runs with them and done her job, that would wear off.

And if there was a misogynistic jerk in the bunch, she'd deal with that, too.

Since there were still guys moving around on the other side of the truck marked Ladder 37, she'd guess these men in front of her were with Engine 59. While she'd probably crossed paths with all or some of them, there were almost fifteen hundred firefighters in Boston and she didn't recognize any of them. She'd been sent some basic information ahead of time, though, so she knew their names and didn't have any trouble matching the photographs to the real faces.

"Is he expecting you?"

It was Aidan Hunt who'd spoken, and she wasn't surprised to see he was standing next to Scott Kincaid. They'd been best friends for years, although the relationship had gotten rocky when Aidan started secretly dating Scott's sister. Scott and his sisters, Lydia and Ashley, were the kids of Tommy Kincaid, a retired firefighter who owned Kincaid's Pub, and Aidan was like a second son to Tommy.

None of that had been in the file she'd received, of course. But she'd been to Kincaid's a few times, with a group, and she'd heard some gossip. So she also knew that the guy who'd been hurt and whose job she was taking—even temporarily—was more than just a coworker to these guys. He was literally family.

"He said I could stop by tonight and look around," she said. "I'll be filling in for Walsh and I wanted to get the lay of the land before Tuesday. Jamie Rutherford, by the way."

They each said their name, stepping forward to shake her hand. Scott was last and maybe it was her imagination, but his touch seemed to linger for a few seconds longer than expected. "Welcome to E-59."

"Thanks." She'd heard he had a reputation for being a ladies' man, but if he thought he could charm his way into her good graces, he was wrong. His thick dark hair and dark eyes, with a little sexy scruff on his jaw, would have put him squarely in "her type" territory, but the E-59 logo on his T-shirt was like an electrified boundary fence.

The ladder company guys walked over and introduced themselves before heading upstairs, and Jamie was thankful she'd taken so much time memorizing the brief bios in the file. She'd probably be overwhelmed as hell if she hadn't had a head start on putting names with faces.

"I'll take you upstairs," Grant said. "Cobb's probably in his office."

After she'd met the older guy, whose job consisted mostly of running herd on a pack of firefighters while slowly drowning in paperwork, she was handed back over to Grant for the grand tour.

The narrow but tall brick station house was pretty typical for some parts of the city. The two engine bays and equipment and personnel lockers on the ground floor. The second floor was offices, a half bath and a small bunk room for the officers. The third floor was the living space. Two old couches and a couple of older chairs were in the main room, facing a big television. An open door led into a bigger bunk room, which was empty at the moment. There was a shower room and a couple of bathrooms in the back, along with a space for working out. The kitchen was big and she noticed right away how clean it was.

When she mentioned it, Grant opened the pantry door to show the sheets of paper tacked to the inside of it. "We have a pretty strict checklist now because one of the other companies was slacking. It still says Walsh because so many different guys were filling in for him, but I can change it and print new copies."

"No sense in wasting the time and paper," she said. "I'll just do the things with his name on them."

"Okay." He paused, and his eyebrows furrowed as if he was trying to figure out how to ask an awkward question. "Where will you sleep?"

"In a bunk downstairs. Probably in Walsh's until he's ready to take it back."

"What about the bathroom? Well, the bathroom's

separate, but we just have a big shower room, like a locker room type because the building's so old and they had to make it fit."

She liked the way the younger guy laid his concerns on the table so she could address them, rather than whispering with the other guys when they thought she couldn't hear them. "I'll probably use the half bath on the second floor most of the time. But if I want a shower, I'll make sure nobody needs it and then I have a hanger for the doorknob so you guys know I'm in there."

"Okay." He didn't seem to have any more questions. "Are you hungry?"

"No, but thanks."

Scott Kincaid walked into the kitchen, and looked at her before heading to the fridge. "What do you think?"

"Not too different from any other house, except a little cleaner."

"He show you the lists?"

"Yeah."

Jamie watched him pop open a soda and chug some of it, his throat working as he swallowed. She'd worked in this so-called man's field a long time and had had her share of attractive coworkers, so she knew her body language and expression remained totally neutral. But inside, she felt a sizzle of sexual attraction that was strong enough she knew she'd have to be careful around this guy.

He lowered the can and grimaced. "I hate this crap."

"So why are you drinking it?" She'd caught a

glimpse of the wide variety of beverages in the refrigerator, so his choice had been deliberate.

"Looking for a caffeine and sugar double whammy. I was going to hit the bunk room for a nap, but there's a fully involved commercial fire and if they strike more alarms, we'll have to go."

A sugar high wasn't going to sustain him long, but he already knew that and *den mother* wasn't the first impression she wanted to make. "I should probably get out of the way, then. I guess I'll see you guys Tuesday."

"How's your commute look?" Scott asked after suffering a few more gulps of the soda.

"Believe it or not, I found a place only a few blocks from here because the price was right. Boston's not cheap, but I didn't want roommates, so it's just a studio. I had a bitch of a commute at my last assignment, though, so I'd live in a closet to be able to walk to work."

"But just temporarily," Grant said. "Danny's coming back."

She didn't take any offense, since she knew he hadn't intended any. "The rent's month to month instead of a lease, so if I end up back across the city, I can move again."

Scott rinsed out his empty can and dumped it into the recycling bucket. "Guess I'll see you Tuesday."

"Yeah. See you then." Because Scott was walking away and Grant was behind her, Jamie let her gaze drop to Scott's ass.

Fortunately, she managed to stifle the sigh of appreciation before it escaped, but she had a feeling she'd be giving herself a stern talking-to in the mirror later. Scott Kincaid might not mind being known around the neighborhood as a ladies' man, but people tended to be harder on women. The only reputation she cared to have was the one she'd built—a damn good firefighter who showed up, did her job well and went home.

TWO

Scott pulled open the glass door of Kincaid's Pub and stepped inside. His dad had chosen not to update all the old brick and wood, and the building still had antique fixtures, so it took his eyes a few seconds to adjust to the dim lighting.

He wasn't surprised to see it was on the slow side for a Saturday night. Besides the fact everybody was still partied out from St. Patrick's Day, the bar didn't get a lot of off-the-street traffic. The plain brick building didn't look like much, there were no neon or beer signs in the two big windows, and the only sign was a small one screwed over the door. While anybody was welcome at Kincaid's, Scott had always gotten the feeling his dad preferred it the way it was—a local watering hole catering mostly to firefighters.

His sister Lydia was behind the U-shaped bar, and he didn't see any sign of Ashley. After she and Danny had gotten back together, they'd spent time rebuilding their marriage. Then, shortly after she found out she was expecting their first child, Danny had gotten hurt working a fire. It was no surprise she'd been spending less and less time at the bar.

Fortunately for their father, who believed a Kincaid should man the bar at Kincaid's Pub, but who also didn't want to work too hard, Lydia was not only great at it, but didn't mind the job. Because of Aidan's schedule, they were free to work around the bar's hours. Even those weren't set in stone, since they opened around lunchtime and were generally closing up by nine or ten. Tommy wasn't into the late-night bar-hopping crowd so if the locals went home early, so did they. Occasionally a big game would keep them in front of the television past close, but it was at the whim of whoever was working the bar.

His father's best friend, Fitz Fitzgibbon, sat on his usual stool in the back corner of the bar, near the ancient scanner that barely worked. Not only had Scott known the man his entire life—he'd even called him Uncle Fitz when he was a kid—but Fitz had retired from Ladder 37 a few years after Tommy Kincaid retired from Engine 59, so there was a sense of kinship that went beyond being family.

When Fitz waved him over, Scott didn't need a crystal ball to know what was on the guy's mind. He'd been hoping to have a beer first, but Lydia was delivering food to one of the tables. Just as he reached Fitz, his dad stepped out from the back room.

Tommy Kincaid had always been a big man, but now he was made up of a lot less muscle and not as strong as he used to be. He could be a real son of a bitch at times and had a temper—which he'd passed on to both Scott and Lydia—but he grinned when he saw Scott and joined them.

Fitz set his mug down on the bar with a thump.

"Scotty, what's this bullshit I hear about a girl being assigned to Engine 59?"

Tommy snorted. "Fitzy, as the father of two adult daughters, I can tell you they don't like being called *girls* these days."

"What the hell am I supposed to call them?"

"Women," Scott snapped. "Seriously. Have you moved off that stool in the last century at all? You know they can vote now, too, right?"

"I'll move off this stool and teach you a lesson about respect if you don't watch your tone, boy."

If any other old guy gathering moss on a bar stool threatened him, Scott would have laughed in his face. But when it was your old man's best friend, you had to watch your tone. He wasn't too worried about his physical well-being, but it would suck if his dad threw him out of the bar and he had to go somewhere else for a beer.

"It's bad luck to have a *woman* around," Fitz grumbled.

"I think that's only on ships," Scott said. He wasn't sure about bad luck, but he had a feeling having Jamie Rutherford around was going to be a distraction.

He couldn't quite put his finger on what it was about her that made him want to sit across a table from her and ask her a million questions about herself. The hard punch of sexual attraction had taken him by surprise with its intensity, but it was more than that. She had an air of calm confidence that intrigued him—like she was a woman who really had her shit together—and that was something he must find attractive because he'd thought about her more than a few times in the last twenty-four hours.

It was too bad that they not only worked together, but that she was his superior.

Fitz gave a mournful shake of his head. "Can't talk about stuff of a sexual nature with your buddy when there's a woman around, if you know what I mean."

"Since *my* buddy's doing stuff of a sexual nature with my *sister*, trust me, that ship has already sailed," Scott replied, trying to keep the annoyance he felt from creeping into his tone. The old guy was really scraping the bottom of the barrel looking for a reason to disapprove of a woman being on the job.

"What do you guys talk about, then?"

"Sports and how much taxes suck, like everybody else."

As intended, the mention of taxes set Fitz off like a wind-up toy. Once he got going, dragging Tommy into a tirade about the government, Scott made his escape. "I'm going to grab a beer. I'll be back."

Not any time soon, if he could help it, but they probably wouldn't even notice. He walked around to the other side of the bar, which had no stools. Tommy had figured out a long time ago nobody ever sat on that side, but would stand around and talk, so he'd taken the stools out to make more space.

Lydia set a mug on a napkin in front of him and smiled. "I would have brought one to you, but I thought you might need a reason to escape."

"Thanks." He took a long sip and sighed. "I

knew they'd have some opinions about a woman in the company, but I thought they'd go with PMS or women having less upper body strength or something, not the fact we can't indulge in locker room talk around her."

"Aidan said it kind of sucks that he can't talk to his best friend about his sex life ever again."

Scott grimaced. "I don't even want to talk *about* talking about Aidan's sex life."

"How do *you* feel about having a woman in the company?"

"I don't know." He shrugged. "It'll be weird, I guess. None of us have ever worked with a woman before. But she's not only a firefighter, she's an officer, so I guess she's probably good at the job."

"What's she like?"

"Don't really know yet. I talked to her for like maybe five minutes."

When his sister just looked at him, one eyebrow arched, he wondered what Aidan had said about Jamie. Or, more specifically, what Aidan had said about what Scott thought of Jamie. While he had no intention of sharing his reaction to her with anybody because he'd never hear the end of it, Aidan was like a brother to him. If anybody would pick up on a look or body language or any other sign Scott was attracted to their new lieutenant, it would be him.

"I'm going to need better gossip from you guys if I'm going to be stuck behind this bar all the time," she said, letting him off the hook for now. "Aidan's out back with Chris. I guess the mother-in-law's in town, so his wife let him sneak out for a few minutes."

Scott chuckled and carried his beer back to the small alcove that held a pool table and a few tables. Chris Eriksson had been married a long time and they'd all spent more than a few hours hanging around the station, listening to his mother-in-law war stories.

The room was empty except for the two guys, who were sitting at one of the tables with their feet up on empty chairs. "Well, this is one helluva party."

"If by *helluva party*," Chris said, "you mean quiet and nagging-free, then yes. Pull up a chair."

Scott had been thinking about playing a couple games of pool, but neither of them looked like they'd be able to muster enough ambition to stand that long, so he pulled over a chair and sat down. Then he put his feet up on the edge of the chair Aidan was using as an ottoman.

"Heard your mother-in-law's visiting," he said to Chris.

"Yeah. And guess what moron made the mistake of mentioning the fact our new lieutenant is a woman?"

"Why's that a big deal? It's not your wife or her mother who have to carry the line if she can't handle it. Which I'm pretty sure she can."

"They don't even care about her pulling her weight. They want to know how old she is and if she's married and what she looks like, and shit like that."

Aidan laughed. "I guess young, attractive and single didn't go over well."

"She's older than we are," Scott said.

"She ain't older than me," Chris said. "And she ain't older than my wife so, in her eyes, Jamie Rutherford is a pretty young thing. Probably wouldn't have been so bad if it was just Cindy, but her mom wouldn't let it go. Wanted to know if she sleeps with us—you know, in the same bunk room—and about the shower situation and shit."

It hadn't occurred to Scott that some of the wives or girlfriends might take issue with a woman being assigned to the company. It was tight quarters and they tended to form a strong bond, so he could see how some of them would be insecure about it.

"Lydia asked me what she's like," Scott said.

Aidan laughed. "Oh, she already interrogated the hell out of me, but she knows I'm not going home to anybody but her."

Since the guy had been willing to sacrifice their friendship, his relationship with Tommy Kincaid *and* his job for Lydia, Scott wasn't too worried about Aidan straying. "Plus, when your coworker and best friend is your future brother-in-law, you know that's a one-way street to getting your ass kicked."

Aidan lifted his beer in a mock toast. "True story."

Scott nodded and drank his own beer, listening as Chris went back to telling them how dinner with his mother-in-law had gone. But he was only partly paying attention because his mind kept wandering to Jamie Rutherford.

He wasn't sure how having a woman in the company was going to work out, but he had no doubt it was going to be interesting.

JAMIE PULLED OPEN the tucked flaps on another cardboard box with a weary sigh. She'd gotten pretty good at moving over the years, but this was her first time moving into a studio apartment that didn't feel a whole lot bigger than the box she was unpacking.

She'd already seen to the most important stuff. The television had cable. The Keurig was on the counter and her favorite mug was next to it. The modem was hooked up, her laptop was on the small kitchen table, and her phone charger was plugged in next to the bed.

The rest she was chipping away at a little bit at a time. Having very few cupboards and only one closet was a challenge, but she'd picked up some under-the-bed plastic bins at the store. She'd also grabbed some picnic hamper–style baskets at the same time. They'd be good for storing things in the living room area while being somewhat decorative. As long as she didn't have cardboard boxes or piles of stuff in corners, she'd be happy.

Her cell phone, which was sitting on the counter, chimed to let her know she had a new text message. After hitting the button to heat up water for a cup of decaf, she picked it up and smiled when she saw it was from Steph Lawson. She worked at her family's pizza place around the corner from Jamie's old station and was the closest friend she'd made in Boston.

According to my app, it will take me five hours to visit you.

Jamie laughed. Stop exaggerating.

At least she thought Steph was exaggerating. It was hard to tell with Boston. When she'd first arrived in the city, she'd felt like a rat in a maze tightly packed with cars, angry people, construction and one-way streets, and she still hadn't quite mastered driving there yet. She could do it, but her knuckles would ache for an hour after from clutching the steering wheel. And she still had no idea how to calculate how long it would take to get anywhere. Sometimes it took fifteen minutes to get to the dentist and sometimes it took an hour and twenty minutes.

At least she didn't have to drive the fire trucks. She was perfectly content to ride shotgun when it came to getting a thirty-five- to forty-five-foot-long truck through the rat maze.

I want to see your apartment but the only day I have off is Tuesday and you have to work every Tuesday.

There's not much to see. Literally.

Give me a tour. I'm on break.

Jamie made herself a coffee while her laptop booted up, and then she initiated a video chat with Steph. After doing one slow swivel with the computer's camera, she laughed and set it on the counter.

"That's it?"

"Yup." Jamie laughed at her friend's scowl. With her blond hair pulled back tightly into a bun for work and her glasses on because she'd once had an incident with contact lenses and hot pepper juice on her hands, the frown made Steph look like a disapproving school principal. "Easy to clean, though."

There was a blue leather love seat and a glass coffee table in the living room area. A small glass kitchen table with two chairs between that space and the kitchen space. And toward the back was the queen bed, with an oak dresser nearly hiding the door to the bathroom. She could have had more floor space if she got a smaller bed, but she refused to compromise when it came to sleeping and she'd spent a small fortune on the mattress set.

She didn't even want to think about how much it had cost her to have what little furniture she had carried up to the fourth floor. Hopefully her next assignment would be in commuting distance because she did *not* want to move again any time soon.

"Tell me more about the new job," Steph said. "I have five more minutes to kill."

"I told you everything. I got the tour, met the guys and left. I won't have anything more to add until after tomorrow, I guess."

"You didn't say much."

"Because you were working and I hate texting entire conversations."

Steph shrugged. Because she worked for the family business and hadn't yet fulfilled her mother's dream for her of marrying a nice man and bearing a pack of grandchildren, she worked long hours and texting was sometimes the only way she ever got to talk to people who weren't related to her or ordering food. "Are any of them hot?"

Yes. Actually, a few of them were, but it was Scott Kincaid's face that popped into her head. "I guess. I'm not there looking for a boyfriend."

Her own fire company was the *last* place she'd look for a boyfriend, even if she wanted one. She'd never experienced a workplace romance, but she could only imagine how messy they got. Gossip and tension and, God forbid, the potential for a sexual harassment situation. Everything she'd worked her ass off for could be gone, or at the very least tainted. She wanted nothing to do with any of that.

"You never know where you'll meet your true love," Steph said.

"I'm hanging up on you. Go back to work."

Once she'd ended the chat, Jamie looked at the boxes still remaining and then carried the laptop and her coffee to the table. Pulling up her Facebook account, she settled in to catch up on things. Her sisters' kids were all still being cute and her mother was still sharing every knitting joke that crossed her feed. Jamie's best friend from school was at Disney World with her family, and Jamie hit the like button on a few of those photos. Her aunt was really hitting some online game or another hard, and the rest of her feed was full of political memes she skimmed past.

After privately sending her mom a picture of the

apartment—which she'd taken from the door, so it showed almost the entire place—she closed the laptop and sighed. She really wanted to have everything in order before she left, but she'd also need to get to bed early. Nerves were always a bit of an issue before starting with a new company, and she knew she'd have trouble falling asleep, which would make the twenty-four hour shift even harder.

It was time to get up off her butt and get stuff done. Tomorrow would be a big day.

SCOTT SHOWED UP for his shift on Tuesday with his game face on. Jamie Rutherford was going to be working with them for at least six weeks, and probably longer, and he was going to treat her no differently than he'd treated any of the other temporary replacements for Danny Walsh. Scott might have a reputation for liking women a little too much and having a bad temper, but he was also a professional firefighter. He could handle having a woman in the company, whether he'd had a particularly steamy sex dream about her or not.

Thinking about that dream as he walked through the open bay door wasn't a good move, so Scott turned his attention to the truck. He knew the guys who'd just wrapped up their tour took good care of her, but looking over E-59 was how he started every day. She was one of the older trucks in service, since she took care of a primarily residential neighborhood without the industrial buildings or densely populated high-rises other areas did, and so got less of the budget. But she was solid and dependable and looking her over always calmed him down.

When he passed through the second floor, he resisted the urge to look through the open office door and see if Jamie was in there. He never stopped to say hello to Danny, knowing he'd see him upstairs at some point, so he wasn't going to stop and say hello to Jamie.

When he reached the third floor and heard a woman's laughter, he paused. She had a really great laugh, and he listened until whatever had been going on quieted before walking into the living room.

It looked like he was the last one there, which wasn't surprising. He was never late, but the other guys had an annoying tendency to be early, which just made him look late. Everybody had coffee, most of them still in the slow stages of coming fully awake.

"Hey, Scotty," Aidan said. "You awake yet?"

"Not by choice. I hope you guys didn't drink all the coffee."

"We did."

"But I made another pot," Gavin said, probably guessing it was his coffee Scott would steal.

Jamie was just finishing making her own coffee when he walked into the kitchen, so she left the stuff on the counter for him. Her hair was in a French braid—which he knew because every time the school had sent a lice notice around his mom had put his sisters' thick hair into French braids so tight they'd whine. He guessed Jamie wore it that way because it kept her hair out of the way while not making a ponytail lump under her helmet.

"Good morning," she said, and he realized he'd been staring at her hair.

"Morning. So it sounded like I missed the party." She frowned at him over the rim of her mug. "The laughing, I mean. I heard you laughing."

"Oh, I was laughing at Jeff's reaction to me telling the guys I'm a vegetarian."

Scott almost dropped his mug. "You are? Seriously?"

She laughed again, the sound seeming to fill the kitchen. "No, I'm not. I just wanted to see what they'd say about not having meat with any meals for the next two months or so."

"That's…wow, that's mean. What did Jeff say?"

"He said there was probably some law that said she had to be accommodated and then told Grant to put a dozen steaks and a bag of carrot sticks on the grocery list."

Scott laughed. "Yeah, nobody cares if you get the shower to yourself, but we're not giving up meat."

He probably shouldn't have brought up her in the shower if he was trying to stay in a purely professional head space, because his mind immediately wanted to picture her naked and covered in bubbly lather.

Rick Gullotti chose that moment to come in and wash out his empty mug. "Hey, Scotty, when you get home, do me a favor and ask Tommy if he knows anybody who wants to buy a snowblower. I know it's the wrong time of year and it's a bit of a beater, but we'll give somebody a good deal on it. Joe used it to do the walkways while I did the driveway with the bigger one, but now that he and Marie have moved into senior living with a grounds crew, I don't need two."

"I'll ask him. You and Jess move downstairs yet?"

Rick shook his head. "We're going to take our time and remodel it the way we want it, and with her still traveling between here and San Diego a lot, that's not high on our priority list."

"You live with your dad?" Jamie asked when Rick had gone back into the other room.

"Yes and no. I rent the apartment upstairs, so I'm around if he needs me and I get a family discount on the rent, but I still have my own space. There's no way we could actually live together."

"I've heard a lot about your dad, actually. He's pretty well respected."

"Yeah." He wasn't always the best father and he certainly hadn't been a great husband, but he'd been a damn good firefighter. "You should come to Kincaid's Pub sometime. It's where we hang out and relax. Drink a beer. Shoot some pool."

"That's your family's bar, right?"

"No, we just stuck our name on the sign for grins." When she rolled her eyes, he laughed. "Yeah, my old man owns it. My sisters, Lydia and Ashley, usually run the bar, though mostly Lydia these days."

"And Ashley's married to Danny Walsh."

"You're pretty well-informed."

She shrugged. “People talk. Especially Danny.”

“What do you mean?”

“He reached out to me last night to see if I had any questions or concerns, which was really nice. You can tell he’s bored and sick of being cooped up.”

“Talk for a while, did he?” She nodded. “He fill you in on everybody?”

Jamie smiled, her eyes crinkling at the corners. “Yeah, he did.”

He waited, but she didn’t say anything else. Usually he’d shrug it off, but for some reason he really wanted to know what Danny had told this woman about him. The seconds ticked by, and he was about to ask when the alarm sounded and everybody started toward the engine bays.

“Suspicious odor in a residential unit. Haz-Mat en route.”

Scott paused on his way to the racks holding their turnout gear and looked at Rick. “Tell me it’s not a damn meth lab.”

“Won’t know until Haz-Mat goes in.”

Once they were geared up, Scott climbed into the driver’s seat and fired the engine. As soon as he had confirmation they weren’t forgetting anybody, he hit the siren and waited a few seconds for pedestrians and drivers to catch on and get out of the way before rolling out.

Jamie was riding shotgun and she seemed calm as she monitored the radio while keeping an eye on any potential hazards on that side of the road, but he didn’t miss her sharp intakes of breath or her fingernails digging into her leg or her right hand tightening on the door handle as he navigated the narrow streets and tight corners.

"Somebody's double-parked," she said as he swung wide around a right hand turn. "Flashers on, but it looks like somebody's in it."

Scott laid on the horn, since the sirens obviously weren't enough, and slowed down enough to let the idiot move.

"Don't hit him," she warned. "I'm pretty brutal when it comes to payback for any extra paperwork."

He chuckled, but didn't respond as he squeezed the truck down a narrow one-way with parking on both sides. They arrived right after the Haz-Mat truck, with Ladder 37 right behind them.

They'd stage for now, ready to offer support if something went wrong—like, God forbid, the odor was some asshole cooking meth—but nobody would go in until Haz-Mat cleared it or there was a confirmed fire.

"I will *never* get used to these streets," Jamie said as they stood and waited, and he looked over at her. She wasn't shaken, exactly, but he could see that she was trying to relax.

"I was born and raised here, so if I didn't want to spend my life walking or taking the T, I had to learn to drive in it."

"You're pretty good at it," she said, and he felt a weird rush of pride. "I like that, because it lessens the paperwork load."

"Worst paperwork ever was probably the time

Gullotti moved a cruiser with L-37's front bumper. I'm still glad it was them and not us because the ass chewing lasted for *days*."

"I can't even imagine."

"Rookie cop thought he could do double the traffic control by blocking the road with his car and then going down to the other end of the street. There were kids trapped on the third floor and it was fully involved, so Gullotti moved it himself. Wrecked the hell out of it, too."

"And the kids?"

"Everybody got out. Jeff Porter, the big guy over there? He printed out a photograph of the kids being hugged by their mom that one of the news guys took, and pinned it to the bulletin board so every time somebody gave them shit about the police car, they could look at it and not give a shit."

She nodded, her lips curving into a smile. "I think I'm going to like you guys."

It was a simple, casual statement that anybody new to the company might have made, but something about the words coming out of Jamie's mouth seemed to set Scott's blood on fire. He wanted her to like him, and that was a problem.

He realized they'd gravitated toward each other while talking, slightly separated from the other guys. While nobody else probably even noticed, he was suddenly self-conscious about it and stepped away from Jamie. "I just remembered I wanted to talk to Grant about something."

She just nodded, her attention on the voices coming through her radio, and Scott walked all the way back to the end of Ladder 37, where Grant was talking to Gavin Boudreau, the youngest guy in the ladder company. But he'd been lying about needing to talk to the kid, so he just stood there and listened to them talk about a video game and waited for an update from Haz-Mat.

THREE

Jamie was relieved when the word came through that the second-floor residents were trying to strip the varnish from their old wooden floors without proper ventilation, which caused the chemical smell throughout the building. Everything was under control and the fire companies could return to quarters.

She liked having the opportunity to respond to a call with them and see how they did things outside of a critical life-or-death situation. Not that she was worried about being able to handle that. Her training and experience would get her through. But it was nice to get a feel for the company in action first.

Once the trucks were backed into the bays, Jamie quietly stowed her turnout gear while keeping an eye on the guys. There was obviously a strong sense of camaraderie, and a lot of banter and laugher went on, but she didn't see any of them slacking or trying to take shortcuts. She could see that they took the care of the trucks and their gear very seriously, which was a relief. It was hard enough being in charge when you were the "new guy" without having to crack down on lax procedures right off the bat.

She and Rick went into their shared office and went through some paperwork. Luckily it was all standardized stuff, which didn't vary much from station to station, and Walsh had been good about staying on top of it, so Jamie didn't have to do much in the way of catching up.

After glancing at the clock, she pulled out her cell phone and called her dad. Every time she moved to a new station, he worried about her having a new group of guys in her life, so she usually called to fill him in.

"Hi, Dad," she said when he answered.

"Hey, honey. How are you? I have a client coming in about five minutes, so I'll take the abridged version now and you can have a nice long chat with Mom later."

She laughed, leaning back in her chair. Her dad had always worked out of a home office, so his daughters had grown up having access to him all the time, but in quick bursts in between appointments. "I'm good. I'm working with great guys here, and it's probably been one of the smoothest transitions I've had."

"I'm glad to hear it. I know you haven't had many problems—that you've told me about, at least—but I always worry. How's your apartment? You haven't had any problems with the neighborhood, have you?"

If he had his way, she'd live in a place with security and a doorman, but those weren't easy to come by in that part of the city, especially if you didn't want roommates to help float the extra cost. "No problems. And there are two locked doors and three flights of stairs between me and the street, so I'm not worried."

"Your mom showed me the pictures you sent. You'll definitely get your exercise." She heard papers shuffling in the background, since he'd put her on speakerphone. "Tell me about your new coworkers."

She filled him in, giving him a very brief character sketch of each of the guys. He seemed impressed when she told him about the chore list, maybe because he remembered the long venting session she'd subjected him to when she'd been a rookie and got assigned to a company that assumed, because there was a woman on hand, they didn't have to make coffee or scrub toilets anymore.

"You sound happy," he said.

"I am." She chuckled. "Tentatively, of course. It's still early, but I have a good feeling about this company."

"You're a good judge of character, so I'm happy for you."

"It must be time for your client, so I'll let you go. Give my love to Mom and tell her I'll chat with her soon. Maybe tomorrow. Love you, Dad."

"Love you, too, honey. Talk to you soon."

Once the call ended, she went upstairs to find the guys scattered around the third floor, ticking things off the day's to-do list.

When she went into the kitchen, Gavin and Chris were in there. "Hey, guys."

"Hey," they said in unison.

She opened the pantry door and scanned for

Walsh's name on the list. "Food purge duty, huh? That sounds fun."

"You and I can do the fridge and Chris has the pantry," Gavin told her. "It doesn't take long, since we try to do it every week."

They started by putting a fresh trash bag in the garbage can, while Chris took a second bag into the pantry. Then Gavin, who had a better idea of how long things had been in there, opened the fridge and started on the top shelf.

"I'll hand off to you," he said. "Anything disposable, you can toss the whole thing. If something's in a dish or whatever, dump the contents and we'll wash the dishes after."

"I guess if you try to do it every week, there shouldn't be anything too bad in there."

"Are you married?" Gavin asked, handing her a plastic bag of fruit definitely past its prime to toss. "Have any kids?"

"Nope. You?"

"No. Jeff and Chris are both married. Aidan and Rick are both engaged, and Grant and I are single, so we date and stuff. He's been seeing this girl for like a month, so it might get serious." He paused. "And Scotty's on a break right now."

"A break?"

"Yeah, from dating. He's not seeing anybody right now, and hasn't for at least a couple of months, I think."

"Wow, a couple of months." He was practically

a monk, she thought, though she chose to keep that bit of sarcasm to herself.

"He's dated some real winners, let me tell ya. I guess now he's looking for somebody to marry, so he's not dating until he finds the right woman."

"How do you find out if you want to marry a woman if you don't date her first?"

Grant looked confused for a minute, and then he laughed. "No, if he meets a woman he thinks he might want to marry in the future, he'd probably date her a couple of times to see. But he's not dating women he knows he won't marry just to have a girlfriend anymore because then he might miss out on the right woman."

"I guess people reach a point in their lives when they know what they want and what they don't want and their priorities shift."

"Scotty definitely knows what he *doesn't* want now," Chris said, his deep voice startling Jamie. He was so quiet, she'd almost forgotten he was in the pantry. "Now he's looking for a TV wife."

She laughed. "He wants a wife on television? Like an actress?"

"No, like a wife from one of those old shows, with the wife in the apron and pearls, making dinner while helping the kids do their homework. Meeting him at the door with his slippers and all that."

"Probably going to be a long break for him, then." If Scott was holding out for some idealized Suzy Homemaker version of a wife, he'd be spending a lot of time alone.

"He's exaggerating," Gavin said. "A little. And I think that's everything from the fridge and freezer."

"Not much," Chris responded, pulling the full trash bag out of the can and tying it off.

"Are you guys making food?" Aidan asked, walking in with Scott and Jeff on his heels.

"No, we're throwing food away," Jamie said, gesturing to the garbage can.

"I was thinking about eating that leftover American chop suey," Scott said, peering over her shoulder.

He was close enough so she could smell his shampoo, and she tried to ignore the goose bumps that tickled her skin. "I opened the container and smelled it. Trust me when I tell you tossing it was for the best."

His laughter was almost a physical touch, and she picked up the garbage can so she had an excuse to step away from him. After putting it in its place, she pulled the bag out and shoved the contents down so she could tie it off.

"I'll take that for you," Scott said, reaching for it. His hand brushed hers and it took all of her willpower to simply let go and move her hand instead of yanking it back as though she'd been burned.

"Thanks."

"Nobody's making more dirty dishes until we're done in here," Gavin said, making a shooing motion back toward the living room.

Jamie was surprised when the other guys listened to him. He and Grant were not only the youngest, but the lowest on the seniority totem pole, so it was clear to her that everybody in both companies respected the chore list.

Scott was the last one to leave the kitchen, and he turned back as he reached the door, giving her a grin that threatened to short-circuit her common sense. "Thanks for saving me from the American chop suey."

She felt herself smiling back at him and could only hope the heat flooding her body didn't show on her face. "Can't be going a man down on my first tour."

Once he was gone, she started filling the sink with hot, soapy water to give herself a moment. She'd never been attracted to a guy she worked with before, and she had no coping skills for the way her pulse quickened every time she saw Scott.

Dumping the dishes they'd taken from the fridge into the sink, she turned the water off, wishing she could turn the attraction off just as easily. It was time to start exploring the neighborhood and finding good hangout places. Maybe she'd get lucky and feel that same zing for a guy she *didn't* work with.

"You okay?" Gavin asked, and she realized she'd been standing there, gripping the edge of the sink and staring at the soap bubbles.

"Yeah, I just got lost in thought. You drying?"

She'd just pulled the plug after washing the last dish when the alarm sounded.

SCOTT RANG THE doorbell of his sister's house and then waited, zipping his sweatshirt against the chill in the air. When Ashley opened the door, he couldn't help grinning at her. It had become a habit—almost an involuntary reflex—since she and Danny had told him she was pregnant.

That had been mere days before the fire they almost lost Danny to, and Scott would never forget the gut-wrenching fear that he was going to have to tell his sister her husband and the father of her unborn child had died.

That was behind them now, though, and every time he saw his sister, Scott had a *holy crap, she's having a baby* moment. She wasn't showing yet, and wouldn't for a while, but she was already glowing.

"Hey, you. Come on in."

He stepped into the house the couple had bought cheap and then remodeled over time. They'd planned ahead and now, while their first child was still just a speck of a thing, they had a nice home in a great neighborhood for a lot less than most of their neighbors had paid.

"Hey, Danny, Scotty's here," she called, and Scott heard what sounded like a recliner being folded back into a sitting position.

Danny was almost on his feet by the time Scott walked into the living room, and he was glad to see him moving with less pain than the last time he'd stopped by. His leg was in a cast, and he tucked crutches under his arm as he stood up on his good leg.

"You didn't have to get up."

"Yes, he did," Ashley said. "He's supposed to get

up and move around a lot, actually. He just can't put weight on the leg yet."

Danny rolled his eyes, but the warm smile he gave his wife made it more affectionate than annoying. "I have to stop taking her to my appointments."

"Good luck with that," Scott said. "How you doing?"

"Better."

"Want to get out of the house?"

Danny's face brightened, but then he looked at Ashley. "Is that okay with you? Just for a little while, maybe?"

She chuckled. "Who do you think called Scotty and told him to get you the hell out of the house before I smother you with a pillow?"

"We'll just go to the bar for a bit and hang out, since you can't wear real clothes," Scott told him.

Danny looked down at the sweatpants with one leg cut off above the cast. "Sounds good to me."

"No beer, though," Ashley said. "Decaf or soda or something. I know you haven't been taking the painkillers they gave you if you can help it, but going out and sitting in those chairs might be a lot and you'll want a pill to help you sleep."

"Yes, dear."

Scott found a fascinating spot on the wall to stare at, bracing himself for an awkward family moment. Their communication issues had been one of the biggest reasons their marriage had hit the skids and, while Ashley didn't have as hot a temper as he and Lydia did, that was exactly the kind of platitude that would make her pop off.

But then Danny slapped Ashley on the ass and they both laughed when the action made him wobble, almost falling off his crutches. Scott kept staring at that spot on the wall, though, because then there was kissing. He was happier for his sister than he'd been about almost anything in his life, but that didn't mean he wanted to watch the reconciliation in action.

"You're presentable enough for a bar," she said. "But you should at least brush your hair."

Scott chuckled when Danny ran his hands through his hair and grinned at his wife. "How's that?"

She gave him an affectionate eye roll, and then she smiled when Danny rested his hand on her stomach for a second. "I won't be too late."

Scott felt a pang of something—yearning, maybe—at the gesture and went back to the foyer to grab Danny's sweatshirt off the hook. There was a lot of love going on around him, what with Danny and Ashley making up, Aidan and Lydia falling in love, and then Rick Gullotti falling for his landlords' granddaughter.

He wanted it. All of it. The love, the having a person to go home to at the end of the day. The holding hands and secret glances. The babies. Not just because the people around him had it, but because when he lay down at night, he felt the emptiness. He felt incomplete.

"You're going to have to take my car," Ashley said, taking her keys out of a dish on a side table near the door. "Unless you think you can catch him when he falls out of your truck."

“I could just drop the tailgate and hoist him into the bed. It’s not far.”

“The seat’s all the way back on the passenger side, so he can get in okay. He’ll need a hand getting out, though. The crutches fit if you wedge them between the front seats and…you’ll figure it out.”

Scott figured it out without putting the end of the sticks through the car’s display console, which he considered a win. Then, after locking his truck, he slid into his sister’s car and started the engine.

“It’s a four-cylinder, so don’t try to beat any lights,” Danny warned. “You won’t make it.”

Scott laughed and backed out onto the street. “Too bad I don’t have long enough ramps. I could put you in this car, drive it up into the back of my truck and then drive that.”

“We’d be legendary.” Danny laughed and then looked over at him. “I really appreciate this, Scotty. I’m losing my freaking mind at home. I mean, I get out with Ashley, but I know she’d like a break and I need a break.”

“Hey, any time.”

It took longer to get Danny out of the car, onto his crutches and into the bar, and then to go park the car, than it had taken to drive there, and Scott managed to break a sweat despite the dropping temperature.

By the time he got back inside, Danny had disappeared, but Lydia waved him toward the back room. Danny was sitting at a table against the wall, with his leg propped up on a second chair. He was talking to Gavin, who seemed to be there alone.

"Hey, I was hoping you'd show up," he said to Scott. "I had some time to kill, so I figured I'd see if anybody was around for a game."

"Since you got me a beer, I guess it would be rude to say no."

"I got you two beers, since Danny can't drink his."

Danny held up a soda. "If I can get enough of a sugar rush, I might be able to lean against the table and shoot some pool. For now, I'll watch."

Scott broke and the game was on. He won the first game, pausing occasionally for a sip of beer while Gavin analyzed potential shots. The kid was a math whiz and sometimes mumbled to himself, as if he was doing fancy geometry equations in his head to line up his shots.

Scott happened to be standing at the end of the pool table that offered a view of the door when it opened and a woman walked in. It was Jamie, and he was glad she went the other way—toward the bar—because he couldn't take his eyes off of her.

"Hey, it's your shot," Gavin said just as Jamie passed beyond his view from the alcove.

"You got somewhere to be?" he asked, turning back to the table.

"Yeah, I've got a date tonight. I'm meeting her at nine."

Scott bent over the table and considered the angle. "Who goes on a date at nine o'clock on a Wednesday night?"

"Two people who have Thursdays off. Was that Jamie who walked in just now?"

He asked the question midshot and Scott swore as the ball rebounded off the bumper, a fraction of an inch from the pocket. "Yeah, I guess."

Gavin sank his last two balls, putting an end to the game. "You must have something on your mind tonight. You're not usually this easy to beat."

"I read somewhere you're supposed to allow kids to win things once in a while. Good for your self-esteem."

A few guys wandered in, each carrying a full mug of beer. Scott recognized two of them as firefighters from a nearby station, though not nearby enough so they were regulars at Kincaid's.

"Hey, boys. How's it going?"

Scott felt his temper rise at the arrogant tone, but he shrugged. "Just finishing up. Feel free."

Gavin was heading out anyway, and he had no desire to shoot pool with this group. They'd been at a table when he showed up, so he knew they'd had a head start on the drinking, and he didn't like the one guy very much. Randy, he thought his name was.

He joined Danny at the table and took a long swallow of his beer before grimacing. A fresh cold one would be nice, but Lydia didn't wait on him when he was in the back room, so he'd have to go to the bar. And Jamie was at the bar.

Danny leaned across the table so he could keep his voice low. "Speaking as both your brother-in-law and your lieutenant, you don't want to go there."

"Go where?"

"I saw you, man. It was pretty obvious you were

checking out a woman you thought was hot, and then a minute later Gavin says Jamie Rutherford had walked in."

Scott managed not to squirm on the chair, but he didn't look at Danny. Instead he watched Randy whatever-his-name-was breaking, and he winced. The guy was sloppy and if he ripped the felt, Tommy would tear him a new one.

"Scotty."

He shrugged. "Yeah, so I looked. Nothing wrong with that."

"You don't exactly have a reputation for self-control when it comes to women." His brother-in-law held up his hand when he turned to frown at him. "Yeah, I know you're reformed and all that happy horseshit. I'm just saying you shouldn't go there. It's a bad idea."

"I know that." He also knew that changing his ways as far as women were concerned wasn't just happy horseshit. He was serious about taking relationships more seriously and finding the woman he wanted to spend the rest of his life with.

That didn't mean he couldn't appreciate a beautiful woman, though, as long as he was more careful to keep his appreciation to himself.

JAMIE CALLED HERSELF every synonym for *idiot* she could think of as she walked across Kincaid's Pub to the bar.

Yesterday, she'd told herself she needed to find some hangout spots and meet a guy who wasn't a firefighter and would hopefully distract her from Scott Kincaid. Today, she was walking into his family's bar.

She knew it was stupid, but she'd done her best to rationalize the decision, anyway. What better way to get to know her coworkers than to have a beer with them?

As soon as she reached the bar, she would have guessed the woman behind it was one of Scott's sisters even if he hadn't told her they primarily did the bartending. The woman with the dark hair pulled into a thick ponytail gave her a polite smile, and then did a double-take when she saw the E-59 logo on Jamie's T-shirt.

"You must be Jamie," she said, extending her hand over the bar. "I'm Lydia, Scott's sister and Aidan's fiancée."

Jamie shook her hand, smiling. "Nice to meet you. I've been in with friends a couple of times, though it's been a while and I don't think you were here."

"I was living in New Hampshire for a while. What can I get you to drink?"

Jamie told her she'd take whatever Lydia recommended on tap, noticing there were no stools on her side of the bar, though a couple of guys were sitting on the other side. They were in business suits, so she guessed it was an after-work meet-up and their work wasn't fighting fires.

Lydia set a frosted mug on a paper coaster in front of her. "You're not a New Englander, judging by the accent. How'd you end up in Boston?"

She shrugged, swirling her drink in the glass. "Classic story, I guess. I moved here for a guy. Then the guy moved on and I didn't."

"Was he from here?"

"No. He got offered a job in pharmaceutical sales and we'd been together long enough so he asked me to go with him the first time. Once you do that, you're pretty much an official couple, so every time he moved to a bigger city and a bigger company for work, I moved, too. Things were going south between us about the time he realized he hated being away from his parents and I like Boston, so he went home without me."

"Where's home?"

Jamie hated this part—all the questions—though she knew there was no way around it. The firefighting community was close-knit, and she was going to be part of if whether she wanted to be or not. "Nebraska."

Lydia frowned. "Really?"

"Really."

"I don't think I've ever met anybody from Nebraska."

Jamie laughed. "You'd be surprised how often I hear that."

"You guys don't even have a hockey team, do you?"

"Not a professional one, no."

"Nothing to stop you from being a Bruins fan, then. Some of the guys are out back, playing pool. It's that room off to the side over there."

Wondering if one of the guys was Scott, Jamie

picked up her beer and looked in the direction Lydia pointed. "Thanks. I guess I'll say hi, at least."

As she walked across the bar, she took a few deep breaths. If Scott was in there, she'd be ready for that spark she felt every time she saw him and make sure she didn't look at him any differently than she looked at the other guys.

It wasn't easy, though. There were four guys around the pool table, none of whom she recognized. But there, at a table against the wall, was Scott. He was sitting with a guy in a cast who had to be Danny Walsh, and they both smiled when they saw her.

Her stomach did a little flip-flop at Scott's smile, so she focused on his companion. "You must be Danny."

"Nice to meet you in person. I'd get up, but..." He waved a hand at the cast. "You'd probably be gone by the time I managed it."

She stepped forward and shook his hand, before backing up. Unfortunately, in trying to put a little space between her and Scott, she backed up too far and bumped into one of the guys playing pool.

"Oh, sorry," she said, turning to apologize.

The guy's smile turned sleazy when he looked her over and his gaze caught on her T-shirt. "Who'd you sleep with to get the shirt, honey?"

"Excuse me?"

"Does he know you took it or did you sneak out in it?"

"The shirt belongs to me." She turned her back on him because he wasn't worth her time.

"Aw, don't be like that, honey. You can play with my hose if you want."

Jamie turned to give the guy *the look.* It was a look that had served her well over the years and, more often than not, ended with the person on the receiving end dropping his or her gaze and muttering an apology.

But the asshole wasn't looking at her. He was looking over her shoulder, and before she could grasp what that meant, somebody rushed by her to the right.

Jamie dropped her beer as she reached for Scott, but he was too fast. He grabbed the douche bag by the shirt, but the guy had seen him coming and managed to get his fist in Scott's face. It didn't slow him down, though, and Scott landed a punch of his own.

"Scotty!" Danny yelled, and through the corner of her eye, Jamie saw him trying to get his cast off the chair. "Goddammit, Kincaid!"

The two guys went to the ground and Jamie saw the douche bag's buddies moving in. This was going to get messy, especially if Danny decided to be a hero and wade in on his crutches.

"That's enough," she yelled, bending to grab the back of Scott's collar.

When the douche bag's arm flopped out for a second, she put her foot on it, pinning it to the floor. That put her slightly off balance, though, so pulling at Scott's collar didn't accomplish anything.

She threaded her hands into Scott's hair and yanked hard. "I said that's enough."

He let go of the douche bag to reach for her hand. "Ow. Let go."

"Get up." When he resisted, she pulled harder. "Get. Up."

He struggled to his feet as his sister rounded the corner, a softball bat in her hand. She looked at Jamie and, for a second, she thought Lydia was going to smile. Then she looked at the guy on the floor before narrowing her eyes at his friends.

"Get your buddy and get out of my bar."

"He started it."

"Yeah, but his name's over the door, so get out and don't bother coming back."

Once they were gone, Scott batted at Jamie's hand again. "You can let go now. And you didn't have to do that."

She released her grip on his hair. "I wouldn't have had to do that if you'd listened to me."

"This isn't the station."

"No, it's not," Lydia broke in, pointing the bat at him. "It's our bar and if you pull this stupid shit again, you can find another place to hang out. Now go put some ice on that eye for a few minutes and then clean up that beer."

"That's mine," Jamie said. "Just tell me where the mop is."

"He can do it."

Lydia walked away, and Jamie might have smiled at the exasperated look Scott sent after his older sister, but she was too annoyed with him. And with the way Danny was watching them.

"Show me where the mop is," she said. "I'll clean this up while you put ice on that eye."

"You okay for a few minutes, Danny?" he asked.

"I'm good."

Jamie followed him, her eyes on the back of his head. Because he'd gotten sweaty in the tussle with the douche bag, she could still see the ruffled area where her fingers had been buried in his hair.

It was tempting to reach out and smooth the strands so she wouldn't be distracted, but she curled her hands into fists instead. No more touching Scott Kincaid.

FOUR

SCOTT'S HEAD WAS POUNDING, his eye socket was throbbing, and he imagined he could still feel Jamie's fingers wrapped in his hair. Later, when he was alone, he might reimagine that scenario without the fight and her throwing her authority around. Just him and Jamie and her hand buried in his hair.

He walked into the back room and turned to face her. "You're not mopping the floor, dammit. I'll clean it up. And I don't need any ice."

"What the hell were you thinking?"

Even though she'd just dragged him to his feet by his hair, her anger set him back a step. "What do you mean?"

"Did I ask for your help?"

"Did you hear what that asshole said to you?"

"Yeah, I did. And I didn't give a shit. You think that's the first time I've heard sleazy comments about playing with hoses?" God, she was gorgeous when she was pissed. "If a guy puts his hands on me, then I'll take care of it. Otherwise, the shit coming out of their mouths isn't worth my time."

"I'm not letting some asshole talk to women like that in here."

"It's different, Scott. Because we work together."

"So? That's even more reason not to let somebody disrespect you."

She blew out an exasperated breath, which he knew was a woman's way of calling him an idiot without wasting words. "Everybody's going to assume you popped off on that guy because you and I are hooking up."

"Or maybe they'll assume I'm not going to stand there and let a woman be disrespected in my family's bar."

She cocked her head sideways, arching an eyebrow. "You really believe that's what they're going to think?"

No, they weren't. They were going to jump to the conclusion he was parking his boots under the hot lieutenant's bed. "The only guy in that room whose opinion matters is Danny's and he knows we're not hooking up."

"Does he?"

"Yeah, because I told him we're not."

She looked at him, her eyes narrowing. "And why would he ask?"

Busted. He didn't want to tell her Danny had warned him off after catching him watching her walk into the bar. "I guess I just have a reputation for not being able to resist a single woman."

"Sit down on that stepladder and look up at the light so I can see your eye."

"You're very bossy, you know that?"

"It came with the promotion. Sit."

He sat, and then he sucked in a breath when Jamie

stepped close and took his chin between her fingers. She tilted his head back, scowling at his eye under the glare of the bare bulb. Her hand was warm, and he reacted immediately to her touch. Trying not to shift around on the stool to ease the discomfort of his jeans, he dropped his gaze because meeting hers wasn't helping. But he found himself eye level with her breasts, which was even worse.

"For a guy who runs his mouth like that, he doesn't throw much of a punch," she said finally.

"He barely made contact. His hand glanced off, mostly."

She didn't let go of his chin, though. "As for your reputation, I heard you *are* resisting single women and have been for a while. So tell me again why your usual lieutenant would ask you if we're hooking up."

"He was asking as my brother-in-law. Mostly." Since her hand was still touching his face, he didn't feel it was too out of line to rest his hands on her hips as he raised his gaze back to hers. "Fine. He might have caught me looking at you a certain way."

"That's a bad idea." She let go of his chin, but her hand didn't fall away. Instead, her fingertips trailed over his jaw.

"It's a really bad idea," he agreed.

Without moving his hands, Scott stood. She didn't take a step back, so their bodies were so close one of them only had to shift and they'd be touching. Jamie's hand dropped from his face to his shoulder before trailing down his arm.

"I've never been involved with anybody at work. Ever."

He tightened his grip on her hips, his gaze on her mouth. "We're not *at* work."

"And when we are?"

"Then we do our jobs."

They were so close, he felt the rush of her sigh over his mouth. "You make it sound so simple."

"It doesn't have to be complicated."

The tightening of her fingers on his arm and the subtle lift of her chin were all the invitation he needed. He closed his mouth over hers, forcing himself to rein in the hunger he felt for her and be gentle.

Her lips were soft and he moved his hands from her hips to her waist so he wouldn't be tempted to pull her hard up against him as he kissed her.

When her fingers threaded through his hair again—not pulling this time, but not gentle, either—he deepened the kiss. Her lips parted as his tongue dipped between them, and he groaned as she pressed her body to his. Her breasts pressed against his chest and for one crazy second, he thought about kicking the door closed.

He felt her yank his T-shirt free of his jeans and her hands sliding up his naked back. Damn the door. Damn the bar. He wanted this woman so badly his entire body ached with it.

"Scotty, get the damn mop out here before somebody slips in that beer and sues Dad and I end up having to find a new job!"

Jamie jerked away from him, her chest rising and

falling as fast as his was. She raised her hand to her mouth, her eyes wide. "I forgot where we were for a minute."

"I forgot everything but you for a minute." It was the truth, and it made her cheeks turn pink.

"I can't believe this." She blew out a breath and ran her hands through her hair as if smoothing it, even though he hadn't even gotten a chance to mess it up yet. "There's no way we're getting out of here without them thinking we were up to no good."

"There's an employee bathroom across the hall. Go hang in there for a few minutes. I'll tell Lydia you helped me with the ice and that you're dumping the rest of it."

"Okay. I'm going to head out, by the way, so… good night."

He didn't want her to go yet. It felt as if there was still unfinished business between them. Not sexually, since that would be an incredibly stupid thing to do, but he wanted to get an idea of how she felt about the kiss. She'd obviously been as into it as he was, but that didn't mean she wouldn't be mad at herself—or both of them—or have regrets. Or maybe she'd decided it really wasn't that complicated and the incredibly sexy kiss was okay. Maybe they could even do it again.

He'd like to know what was going on in her head.

"Dammit, Scott!" Lydia bellowed again, and he sighed.

"Gimme a minute!" He turned to Jamie, but she

was already slipping across the hallway and into the staff bathroom. “Good night.”

Cursing under his breath, he grabbed the mop bucket. The mop and the cleaning spray they used were already in it, so he wheeled it down the hall and into the bar.

“Where’s Jamie?” Lydia asked as he passed by, because God forbid his sister should ever be too busy to be up his ass about every little thing.

“She’s taking care of the ice so I can wipe up the beer before we get sued and you have to find another job.” She arched an eyebrow at his tone and he wasn’t in the mood to get into a verbal tangle with her, so he moderated it. “She said she was going to dump the ice and then she’s leaving, and that’s all I know.”

Danny was still where they’d left him, sitting against the wall with his leg propped on a chair. “I was beginning to wonder if you forgot about me and went home.”

“I probably would have remembered when I got outside and didn’t have my truck because it’s parked in your driveway.”

“True. Where’s Jamie?”

“She’s heading out after she takes care of the ice pack.”

“Uh-huh.” Danny crunched his empty soda can and set it on the table. “You’re asking for trouble, Scotty.”

He bent to pick out the larger pieces of the broken mug. “What are you talking about?”

“You didn’t put any ice on that eye, your hair’s

even more messed up than it was, and now your shirt's untucked."

"You've been cooped up too long with bad detective shows, dude."

When Danny just made a noncommittal sound, Scott yanked the old metal dustpan off the hook of the mop bucket handle and dumped the glass into it. He wasn't very good at getting anything over on his family, so maybe that kiss was going to end up being more complicated than he'd thought.

JAMIE DABBED AT her face with a paper towel, staring at her reflection in the mirror. The cold water hadn't helped much and she still looked like a woman who'd just been kissed senseless in a supply room.

What were the chances she could walk through the bar and out the front door without Scott's sister seeing her face?

What a stupid thing to do, she told herself. After years of proving herself and building a reputation based on nothing but being good at fighting fires, she'd made it through one damn tour with Scott before her self-control crumpled like a napkin.

Balling up the paper towel and tossing it into the trash, Jamie took a deep breath and reached for the doorknob. There was nothing for it but to walk out there and hope Lydia was busy with a customer. At most she could offer a casual wave goodbye as she walked out the door.

She should have known better. Lydia was leaning against the bar, her eyes on the television screen when Jamie walked out into the main bar area. Obviously Tuesdays weren't their busy night.

"Hey, sorry tonight turned into a circus sideshow for you," Lydia said when she saw her. "We don't usually have problems in here, and very rarely are punches thrown. Leave it to Scotty."

"The other guy had it coming, though it should have been me who got to smack him one."

Lydia laughed. "You've gotta be pretty fast to beat Scotty's temper to the draw, though he's been a lot more mellow lately."

"I'm just glad it wasn't worse. I guess I'm going to head home."

"You sure you don't want a beer? You never got to drink yours."

"I'm all set. I'm actually not a big beer drinker, anyway. It's just the easiest thing to order in a bar."

"I hear you." Lydia picked up a towel and wiped at a spot on the bar. "I hate to pile on whatever impression we're making tonight, but you need to kiss Bobby Orr."

Jamie heard the word *kiss* and her stomach clenched, but then the rest of the words caught up. What the hell was Lydia talking about? "Who's Bobby Orr and why would I need to kiss him?"

"You don't know who… Oh, that's right. You're from Nebraska." She pointed to a huge photo of a guy in a hockey uniform. It was in a frame that was literally screwed to the wall, and a signature was scrawled near the bottom.

Jamie had noticed all of the sports paraphernalia-lia hanging around the bar when she walked in, but none of it really meant anything to her. Even if she were a big sports fan—which she wasn't—this was Boston and other than a vague recognition of the logos because she didn't live under a rock, she had no idea what any of it was.

"Bobby Orr is a Bruins legend," Lydia explained. "And if you break a dish or a glass, you have to kiss the picture. If you don't, you're jinxed and who knows what'll happen next."

Jamie stared at her, wondering if this was some kind of firehouse hazing ritual, but Lydia looked more embarrassed than expectant. "You're serious."

"Yeah. It's a tradition. Or a superstition. Whatever you want to call it."

"I've noticed that's a big thing in Boston." Lydia shrugged, not denying it. "As much as I'd like to be free of jinxes, I'm not kissing that picture. This is a bar and if somebody's lips are on that glass every time a glass breaks, mine won't be."

"You don't have to put your mouth on it. Just kiss your fingertips and touch the glass. That's close enough, and it's what most people do. The sober ones, anyway."

"You know, it was technically your brother who made the mug fall."

"It fell out of your hand." Lydia folded her arms, waiting. "But a woman who refused to do it a few years back tripped after she left here and needed stitches in her knee, but she couldn't get to the hospital because her car had been towed."

Laughing—though she wasn't sure if it was at the superstition or herself—Jamie walked around the bar to the photo. After kissing her fingertips, she reached up and pressed them to the glass covering the man's cheek.

"Boston's a strange place," she said.

Lydia nodded. "But you chose to stay because you fit right in."

Jamie smiled. "Good point. Is it safe for me to leave now?"

"Yeah. I'm sure I'll see you again, though, right? We didn't scare you off?"

If she was smart, she wouldn't come within a mile of Kincaid's Pub for the rest of her time with E-59. "I don't scare easily."

"I didn't think so. We'll have to drag you out for a girl's night sometime. Ashley and I. It's probably good to get away from the guys now and then."

"Yeah, maybe."

Jamie had walked to the bar, which meant she had plenty of cold, fresh air to help clear her head on the way back to her apartment. Her head refused to be cleared, however, and her thoughts ran in circles all the way home.

She was glad she'd kissed Scott because it was fun and hot and everything she wanted in a kiss. And there was no harm in it because her stay was temporary and he was killing time while on the lookout for his television wife, as Chris had called the future Mrs. Kincaid.

She shouldn't have kissed him because she was

going to have to show up at the station in a couple of days and not only work side by side with him, but be his superior. It wasn't 1955 anymore and her record was pretty impeccable, so her career would survive kissing a fellow firefighter. But she didn't need the side-eye looks and the snickers behind her back.

A mug of hot chocolate didn't help. Nor did repeats of one of her favorite shows, about dropping naked people into the jungle to test their survival skills. And when she finally gave up and went to bed, she wasn't surprised when closing her eyes turned her thoughts right back to Scott.

She wanted to kiss him again. She wanted to kiss him longer, somewhere his sister wasn't yelling for a mop and there was a soft surface for them to collapse onto when her knees finally gave out. That one kiss had been like running her finger through frosting. Now she wanted the whole slice of cake.

It was a long time before she finally drifted off.

Because it had been Danny's turn to go on a grocery store run, Jamie got up the next morning—usually an off day—and, after showering under cool water to force herself awake after a rough night of tossing and turning, headed to the station to meet Grant Cutter and one of the guys from another E-59 group, who typically worked Wednesdays and Saturdays. Grant had told her they could manage without her and she could have a pass, since she was new, but she not only didn't shirk her duties, she had nothing better to do. If nothing else, it would keep her from thinking too much about kissing Scott in the back room of the bar.

It was all she'd thought about since she walked out of Kincaid's Pub last night, including during the hours she should have been sleeping. Standing in front of him, she'd been stupid enough to think she could kiss him and then, curiosity satisfied, they could move on.

Instead, the kiss had jacked her sexual attraction up to sexual hunger and she didn't have a lot of willpower when it came to denying herself something she *really* wanted.

"Hey, Jamie." Grant waved to her from the back of the bay. "This is Derek Gilman."

"Nice to meet you," she said, extending her hand when she was close enough.

Tall and blond, with a scar down his jaw, the other man shook her hand. "Welcome to the house."

"Thanks." She didn't see any sign of him having a problem with her gender, which was a relief. "Are we ready?"

"In a sec." Grant looked over his shoulder. "I think I hear him coming now."

She frowned. "Who? I thought it was just the three of us."

"Oh, Scotty showed up because he got his wires crossed and thought you weren't going. Since he doesn't have anything better to do, he said he'd still tag along."

Shit. She'd thought she had another day before she'd have to see him again. Because his sister had yelled for the mop, there hadn't really been a resolution between them. No *hey, what are we going to do about this* conversation so she could be absolutely sure they were on the same page. And that page was nobody on the job knowing there might be something going on between her and one of the firefighters in her company.

When Scott stepped out of the stairwell and into the bay, she swallowed hard and focused on keeping her expression neutral. He stopped when he saw her and their eyes locked for a few seconds, but then he lifted in his chin in a casual nod. "Morning, Jamie."

"Good morning."

He turned to the other guys. "Hey, Gilman. Good to see you."

"You, too."

"I guess I'll drive," Scott said. "My truck will fit all four of us and it's a nice day, so we can throw the groceries in the back."

"Shotgun," Jamie said, smiling when Grant groaned.

She'd said it out of reflex, but it didn't seem like such a good idea when she was sitting next to Scott, separated only by a center console between the bucket seats. Grant and Derek were talking hockey in the backseats, while silence and classic rock reigned in the front seats. Through the corner of her eye, Jamie could see Scott's thumb tapping the steering wheel with the rhythm of the music, and she wondered if he was the kind to sing along if he'd been alone.

It took them almost forty minutes to drive to the big chain supermarket, but Jamie knew it would be worth the time. Supporting the local businesses and small markets in a fire station's neighborhood was something they all tried to do on a day-by-day basis, but when it came to stocking up for the month, they had to try to keep the prices down.

As they walked across the parking lot, Jamie asked, "So how do we do this? Is the list divided up?"

Scott shook his head. "That would be far too organized. We wander up and down the aisles together, looking for the stuff on the list, and then eventually we'll start splitting up as we remember things that aren't on the list and they're almost always back in aisles we already hit."

She laughed. "That explains why we volunteer to come on our own time."

"That and the probability we won't have to abandon the carts to put out a fire."

Scott and Derek each pushed a cart. Grant had the list, and he and Jamie kept an eye out for the items they were looking for. And she kept her mouth shut about the fact they were starting in the refrigeration section, which made no sense to her. But the fact they'd all turned to the left without a discussion told her it was just the backward way they always did it, and she didn't want to nag. After grabbing a variety of sliced and shredded cheeses, a product on the list caught her eye, and she lifted the box out of the cooler with a frown.

"What is this stuff? Yogurt in squeeze tubes?" She'd seen some odd snack requests on house grocery lists, but this stuff looked like it was meant for the kindergarten crowd. "For the firefighters too lazy to wash a spoon?"

"Oh, we're not getting those," Derek said. "Mikey G. is the only one who eats those. His kid got him hooked on them, I guess. But he's behind on throwing his share of money into the kitty, so if he wants them, he can bring them from home."

"Harsh," Grant said. "Poor guy won't have his squeeze yogurt."

"Third month in a row this has happened," Derek replied. After a short pause, he chuckled. "He's lucky we don't make him eat bread and water at mealtime."

"Is he doing okay?" Scott asked.

Jamie had been thinking the question, but she wasn't sure how to phrase it. She liked that Scott was concerned being late on his firehouse fund payments three months in a row might indicate Mike G. was in some financial trouble. If he was and could swallow his pride enough to admit it, there were ways for him to get help.

"Yeah. We let him slide when he went through the divorce because getting his own place was expensive and then the child support and everything. But we get the feeling he's taking advantage now, so we'll start small. No yogurt for Mikey."

Jamie put it back and leaned over Grant's shoulder to see how much stuff was left on the list. "Maybe I should have packed a lunch."

"We kill the supplies in March," Grant said. "A lot of slow cooker meals because we get so many nuisance calls. People forget in March that it's still winter and it can be slippery out there. Plus, around St. Patrick's Day we've got extra guys on hand and we're busy and the pantry suffers."

"We should split the list," Derek said. After scanning it, he carefully tore a chunk out of the side of the paper. "We'll take these staple-type items. Coffees, spices, flour, sugar and crap. Plus paper goods. You guys keep working on the rest of it and then we'll go from there."

When Derek handed the paper to her, Jamie realized he'd naturally drawn the teams based on where they were standing at the time. Grant was standing next to him, while Jamie was in front of Scott's cart.

Great. Unexpected alone time.

They made it to the cans of fruit, where they needed to grab pineapple rings for ham, according to the list. Then Scott leaned on the handle of the shopping cart while she was reading labels. "Hey, while we're alone, I wanted to say something to you."

She tensed, fighting an urge to look around and see if they really *were* alone. Just because Grant and Derek weren't in Scott's sight line didn't mean they weren't still in earshot. "In the grocery store?"

"Yeah. I wanted to apologize for losing my temper last night and hitting that guy."

She hadn't been expecting that, and had braced herself for talking about the kiss while standing in front of canned fruit. "Oh. I should probably apologize for pulling your hair, then."

"I've worked on controlling my temper, but the way he was talking to you was… I should have let you handle it." Then he looked sideways at her, grinning. "I didn't mind the hair pulling too much, though."

"Stop that," she said in an urgent whisper.

He leaned closer to her and her fingers itched to bury themselves in his hair again. "We're still not at work."

"We're here in a professional capacity, though." She needed a stronger argument because the kiss at the bar was pretty solid evidence her current tactics weren't working. "Besides, you're supposed to be on a break from dating, remember?"

He shrugged. "Maybe I need a break from taking a break. A temporary relapse, like six to eight weeks long."

It was incredibly tempting. And also incredibly risky, because that was treading dangerously close to real relationship territory. "There's no possible way we could keep even a supercasual relationship a secret for two months, and it won't be *you* who suffers the brunt of the gossip or ends up with the tarnished reputation. It'll be me because I'm the officer and, most importantly, because I'm a woman."

"You're not good at secrets?"

"*Me?* Your company is like the freaking Brady Bunch or something. One big happy family—literally, almost—and I'd bet you a hundred dollars right now that some combination of Danny, Ashley, Lydia or Aidan have already had a conversation about us. Your life's part of a family game of Telephone right now."

It seemed as though he wanted to deny it for a

few seconds, but then he gave her a chagrined look. "Yeah, secrets are tough. *But*, Aidan managed to date Lydia without me knowing for a while. It can be done."

"Would he have been able to if she'd been working at the station and sharing living quarters with you guys for twenty-four-hour tours?"

"No. Shit, all you did was walk by me in the bar and Danny's radar pinged."

"You said at the bar it doesn't have to be complicated, but it already *is*. We don't need to make our jobs complicated on top of it."

"But—"

"Hey, Kincaid! Catch!"

Scott turned and got his hands up in time to catch the bulk package of paper towels Grant threw at him.

"Did you hear me?" she asked quietly, while they still had a few seconds.

He looked at her, his gaze holding hers in an intense way that made her shiver. "Yeah, I heard you."

It was for the best, Jamie knew. Their relationship needed to go back to being strictly business. But that determination she was doing the right thing didn't stop her from sneaking a huge bag of chocolate candies into the cart. A woman could only deprive herself of so many delicious things.

FIVE

SCOTT USUALLY HUNG out with his dad in the evening if it wasn't a night Scott had anything going on and Tommy wasn't going to the bar to sit and swap the same old stories with Fitz. It seemed stupid for Tommy to sit and watch television alone while Scott was one floor up, watching the same shows alone.

But tonight, Scott felt restless and he lingered in his own apartment. It didn't have too much of a homey feel, with most of the personal touches being limited to the leather sofa and love seat in front of his enormous TV. But he'd redone the floors from carpet to wood laminate himself, and repainted the entire apartment. He'd also sunk a lot of money into the bathroom, but none of that made him feel particularly bonded to the place. It was just where he lived, and he got a great deal on the rent.

It wasn't a home, though, and he wondered if that's what was nagging at him. Was it stuff that made a home? Or was it the wife and kids he didn't have? He was only twenty-seven, so he wasn't sure why he felt such a strong desire to finally settle down, but he couldn't deny it was there.

Maybe he should buy some stuff. He wasn't sure what. Wicker baskets? Or maybe some plants. He'd get a pet, but it wasn't like he was asking a dog to make it through an eight-hour workday without him. He was gone twenty-four hours at a time, and that wouldn't be fair to anything except maybe a fish, and he didn't see the point in that.

When he realized his dad was probably scowling up at his ceiling, wondering why he hadn't come down, Scott stepped through the sliding glass doors onto his deck. One flight of stairs down, he walked through his dad's back door.

"I was beginning to wonder if you were coming down tonight," his dad called from his ancient recliner.

"Yeah, I was on the phone," he lied. As he walked through the kitchen toward the living room, Scott looked around him.

Was it the stuff that made it feel like home, or just the fact he'd grown up in this house? Unlike the second and third floors, nothing had changed in the three-bedroom first-floor apartment, and there was definitely an '80s feel about it.

He had really vague memories of his mom nagging his dad to start remodeling, room by room. He'd always promised he'd get around to it soon and she'd roll her eyes. Then she'd been diagnosed too late with breast cancer. Scott was nine when she died, and giving away her personal possessions had been heartbreaking enough. The remodeling never happened.

Scott plopped down on the sofa and put his feet up on the old wooden coffee table. "I'm beat. I almost went to bed instead of coming down. I volunteered for supermarket duty today."

"I'd rather scrub floors. Speaking of the house, how's Danny's fill-in doing?"

"Jamie? Okay, I guess." He wondered if his dad's curiosity was related to the job, or if one of his sisters had said something to him.

"Pulling her weight?"

"Yeah. There hasn't been much weight to pull, other than some odor and medical calls."

His dad shook his head. "It's never made sense to me for fire to respond to medical calls. Especially both trucks."

Scott knew that, since they'd had this conversation many times at the bar. "I know, but E-59 and L-37 roll together, and we can be almost anywhere in four minutes. More fire truck coverage than ambulance coverage, which you know. But anyway, we haven't worked an active fire yet, but I don't have any doubts about her ability to pull her weight."

"You sound pretty sure of that."

Scott shrugged. "If I was worried about her doing her job, everybody would know."

His dad chuckled. "Yeah, you've never been shy about giving your opinion. We should invite her over for dinner. I'd like to get to know her some."

Oh, there was no way in hell could Scott let that happen. Jamie had made it pretty clear in the grocery store that she wanted to keep a wall of professionalism between them. Turning around and inviting her home to meet the parent probably wasn't what she was going for.

"I'm sure she'll stop by the bar some night and you can meet her," he said.

"The bar's loud and people are always interrupting my conversations to talk to me. Here we can have a nice meal and relax."

"It's just not a good idea, Pop. And she won't be around long, anyway. Once Danny's cleared to come back, she'll be gone."

"So? She's here now. And I wouldn't mind meeting the woman, seeing as how my son started a brawl in my bar over her."

Dammit. Somebody—maybe Lydia, or maybe anybody else who'd been there that night—had ratted him out. "It wasn't a brawl."

"I told you what would happen if you started a fight in the bar again."

"Yeah. You'd throw me out. But that was years ago, and I didn't start the fight. He threw the first punch."

His dad turned the television down a couple of notches and turned to give him a stern look. "From what I heard, he threw the first punch because you went flying across the room, knocking Jamie's beer out of her hand, and grabbed hold of him."

Unless one of the douche bag's friends had gone back to the bar when Tommy was there and complained, the only people who knew that were Danny and Jamie. Since Danny hadn't ratted him out directly to the old man, he must have told Ashley the details. And either Ashley had told their dad, or Ashley had told Lydia, who told their dad. He was guessing the latter.

Jamie hadn't been wrong about his life being the subject of a family game of Telephone.

"He had it coming."

Tommy chuckled. "The only reason I'm not pissed is the sheer enjoyment I'm getting out of picturing you being hauled off the guy by a woman with a fistful of your hair."

There was a time Scott would have leaped to his own defense, trying to protect his ego. But he just laughed with his dad. "I'm glad those security cameras in the pool room are just for show."

"I'm not. I would have liked to see it." His dad nodded. "She sounds like quite a woman, which is why I want to meet her."

"Like I said, Pops, she'll probably show up at the bar some night."

"Okay." Tommy shrugged, and Scott felt a rush of relief. "I'll make it a group thing and tell your sister to have Aidan invite her."

Scott wasn't going to win this one. "Fine. Do what you want. You always do."

"I think I'm going to like her."

"You probably will, not that it matters one way or the other."

His dad shrugged. "You never know."

Scott wasn't sure what he meant by that, but he was damn sure his family was a pain in the ass. His brother-in-law was trying to warn him off getting involved with Jamie, while his father sure seemed to think Jamie would fit right in. But whether he thought she'd fit in the company or in the family, Scott wasn't sure. And if he pushed the subject, he was going to look like he was protesting too much and Tommy Kincaid would latch on to that like a dog with a bone.

The cop show they both liked started, and that ended the conversation. By the time a commercial break rolled around, Jamie would be forgotten and his dad would move on to something else.

She'd be forgotten by Tommy, anyway. The episode wasn't good enough to keep Scott's attention and his mind wandered to earlier, in the supermarket. Obviously she'd been right about his family's inability to keep a secret.

Was she right about the fact she'd be the only one to face repercussions if their relationship became the talk of the station, too? He didn't like to think so, but he'd heard enough talk about women in general and female firefighters in particular over the years to know there would be dirt flung and none of it would hit him. Or if it did, it wouldn't stick. He was one of them—sixth-generation Boston Fire.

No matter how much he wanted her, he needed to pull back and leave Jamie Rutherford alone.

JAMIE SWUNG THE AX, punching a hole to vent the roof of the two-story single-family home, cringing as she did it. It was a nice house, or had been, and she didn't like inflicting even more damage on it. What the fire didn't ruin, the water would, but at least nobody would get hurt and their neighbors would be spared.

The cause had come through with the call, since the homeowner watched the fire start. The origin was an overloaded power strip plugged into an overloaded circuit, and the strip had been sitting along the edge of the wall, under the long drapes.

The woman had grabbed her kids and her purse and run, which was the right thing to do. She'd called 911 from across the street and help had arrived a few minutes later. Unfortunately, it was a fast-moving fire thanks to flammable decor and an open floor plan, and all they could hope to do was knock it down before it spread. There wouldn't be much left inside for the family to salvage.

"I don't know what the hell they insulated the walls with, but the fire keeps popping up in random spots," she heard over the radio. There were multiple companies on the scene now, so containment wouldn't be an issue, but it was going to be a long day.

It took them hours to knock down the flames enough to sweep for hot spots and refires. It was hot, dirty work and there was a lot of climbing in and around charred piles of rubble. She knew, out on the street, there would be news cameras and cell phones capturing the drama. Their support volunteers with their truck stocked with beverages and high-energy snacks to keep the firefighters going. A cluster of guys around the incident command vehicle. None of that was her problem. Making sure there were no hot spots that would reignite when they turned their backs was her problem.

She did hope, however, that the Red Cross had already taken the family to the home of family or friends, or helped them find temporary shelter. They'd lost everything, and watching the firefighters poke around the remains of their home wouldn't help them feel any better.

Her guys had done a damn fine job, though, she thought as she took her helmet off to wipe at the sweat gathered across her hairline. She and Rick worked well together, so there were no bumps in the road when it came to the two companies' teamwork. While the majority of their calls might be medical or motor vehicle accidents, their first fire together was the true test, and she thought she'd passed it.

"We're about done here," Rick said from just behind her, and she turned to face him. "We'll keep at it while the other companies clear out, since the trucks are blocked in anyway, but there's nothing else we can do at this point."

She nodded and looked around the mess. "We should probably check that south wall one more time and then we'll start packing up."

It was a quiet ride back to the house, but she wasn't surprised. It had been a hot one, and between the sweat and the grime of crawling through a charred house, they were all pretty wiped out. When the trucks were parked and tended to and the gear stowed, they all trudged up the stairs.

"You want to shower first?" Rick asked her, but she shook her head.

"No sense in everybody sitting around getting the furniture dirty waiting on me. I'll throw that chicken stew in the freezer into the pot and get it started. When you guys are done, you can take over and it should be hot just about the time I'm done."

"Sounds like a plan."

She washed her hands and arms before taking a couple of containers of the stew out of the freezer. Jamie had been told they were a gift from Chris's wife, who would sometimes make extra of something and send it in for the station.

It took a long time for the guys to all shower, and she hoped there would be hot water left. She also felt as if every minute that went by increased the chances of the alarm sounding while she was in the shower. She'd gone on a call once, years before, with clothes yanked onto her wet body and the shampoo only half rinsed out of her hair. Her scalp had itched the entire afternoon.

When it was her turn, she hung the pink fabric wreath on the door of the shower room and went inside. She'd had it for so long she couldn't even remember where she'd gotten it, but it had come in handy over the course of her career. After showering as quickly as possible, she put on a clean uniform and dumped the dirty stuff into her basket.

They were serving the stew when she walked into the kitchen, and she took a bowl from Gavin. "Thanks. It smells delicious."

Since the seats around the table were full, she took her stew into the living room and sat in one of the chairs. Jeff had the other, and Aidan and Scott were on the couch. There was an old back-and-white Western on the television, which she'd already learned meant Jeff had the remote control.

"Glad you're here, Lieutenant Rutherford," Jeff said. "It was good today."

Jamie let the warm rush of pride she felt show in her smile. "Thank you. It *was* good today, and I feel pretty lucky to work with you guys."

"You fit in."

"With this bunch I don't know if that's a compliment or not," Scott said, and Jeff chuckled.

"Speaking of fitting in, Jamie," Aidan said, "Lydia wanted me to pass along an invitation to her dad's for dinner. Maybe Sunday. Tommy wants to meet you."

She wasn't sure what to say. Scott was focused on his chicken stew, and Jamie wasn't sure if it was because he didn't care that she'd been invited to his dad's, or if he was uncomfortable with the idea and didn't want to say it.

It wasn't quite a royal decree, but she knew Tommy was important to the local firefighters and she didn't really want to decline his invitation. And while Scott technically lived in the house, he had an apartment upstairs, so it really wasn't any of his business.

"Who will be there?" she asked, when she realized Aidan was waiting for her to say something.

"Tommy, me, Lydia, Danny and Ashley that I know of for sure. And you'll be there, Scotty?"

Scott lifted his gaze to meet Jamie's for a few seconds, his expression unreadable. "Yeah. I'll be there."

"It sounds like fun," she said to Aidan, since Scott was giving her nothing to work with as far as his thoughts on the matter. "Sunday works for me."

"We eat about five when we do family dinners. I'll text you the address later, and I think you're in easy walking distance."

"You guys in Boston have a weird sense of walking distance, though. Driving here is such a nightmare I think you've all convinced yourself that 'easy walking distance' and 'would be considered a marathon if you jogged it' are the same thing."

They all laughed, and then they watched some cowboys riding around fake cacti while they finished their stew. Chris walked in a little while later and took their bowls, since he was doing the dishes.

"You need help?" Jamie asked. She'd noticed some of the other guys going through to the bunk room or to the weight equipment, so he might be alone.

"After I wash these bowls, I'm taking a power nap. You can dry them and put them away if you want, or they can sit and drip dry. Either way."

"It would be nice to have a dishwasher," she said.

"Budget," all the guys said at the same time, and she laughed.

Old Westerns weren't her cup of tea, so she followed Chris into the kitchen and pulled a clean dish towel out of the drawer. After he'd pulled the plug in the sink, he gave her a mock salute and went to take his nap, leaving her alone with a pile of dishes and the sound of Hollywood gunfire from the other room.

She wasn't alone very long, though. Scott came in, and judging by how close he stood and the fact he was practically staring at the door, she knew he had something to say he didn't want anybody else overhearing.

Jamie hoped whatever it was wasn't very important, since she had trouble concentrating when he was so close to her. She could smell the soap and shampoo that all the guys used, but there was something about smelling it on him that made her want to tousle his hair and bury her face in his neck.

"You don't have to go to my dad's for dinner if you don't want to," he said in a low voice.

"I wouldn't have said yes if I didn't want to go. Do *you* not want me to go?"

"What do you mean?"

She kept wiping the bowl in her hand, even though it was already dry. "You didn't look too thrilled when Aidan offered the invitation, that's all."

"I just… I don't know. I'm not sure if the old man's up to something, that's all. Like maybe he has the wrong idea."

"Where would he get the wrong idea?"

"Because of the fight at the bar. Because I got so pissed that guy was disrespecting you, and then he thinks it's funny that you broke it up by pulling my hair, so who knows what thoughts he's got in his head."

"You're never going to live the hair thing down, are you?"

He grinned, which made her feel better. "Never."

"Maybe he just wants to meet me because you have a dangerous job and I'm a big part of it and of helping you go home safely at the end of each tour, so he wants to make sure I'm up to it."

"Maybe."

It was the nature of a firehouse that they weren't going to be alone very much longer, so she cut to the chase. "If you don't want me to go, I'll tell Aidan I just remembered something else I had to do. No hard feelings."

"No, I *do* want you to go, which is part of the problem. You know I'm attracted to you, and I'm doing my best to bury that. Us being possibly set up by my father for a family dinner makes that a little messy for me, but I'll handle it."

She looked into his dark eyes, surprised by his candor. He wasn't playing games, and she appreciated that. He wanted her, she'd told him why she didn't think it was a good idea, and he was trying to respect that. "I won't go. It's really not a big deal."

"I want you to go more than I don't want you to go." He ran a hand through his hair. "How's that for messed up?"

"I understand." She sighed and set the bowl on the counter to pick up another from the dish rack. "Trust me, I know what you mean."

Grant walked in then, rubbing his stomach. "Is there any stew left? I'm still hungry."

"You're *always* hungry," Scott said, picking the dried bowl up off the counter and turning toward the cabinet as if he'd been standing so close to her because he was putting the dishes away. "And no, there isn't any left."

"Should I bring anything Sunday?" she asked Scott while Grant rummaged around in the fridge. She was going to go because she *did* know exactly what he meant. She wanted to see him more than she feared what would happen if she saw him.

It was a mess, and all they'd done was kiss one time. But she didn't have the willpower to turn down an invitation to spend more time with him.

SIX

Scott slapped the puck, and then groaned when it bounced off the goal crossbar with a solid and unmistakable clang.

"You are seriously off your game tonight, Kincaid."

"Screw you, Hunt." He flipped Aidan off as he skated by.

"Got something on your mind?" his friend called back to him. "Or somebody?"

The same somebody who'd been on his mind since the night of the wedding reception smoke machine, when Jamie had walked into the engine bay. "Just keeping Gullotti on his toes."

"On my toes?" Rick called from the net. "I could sit here on my ass and you couldn't get that puck by me tonight."

Trash-talking wasn't as fun when it was almost the truth. Not quite the truth, though. He wasn't on his game, but if Rick sat down, he could probably score on him. Thankfully they weren't playing a game tonight. Grabbing some ice time was simply their favorite kind of workout and a bunch of them often got together to play outside of the fire department league. Tonight, only three of them had been able to make it but they were playing anyway because they had the ice, taking turns in the goal.

"How's the dating break going?" Rick asked when Aidan pointed at the clock to signal their time was up.

"I haven't been on a date, so I guess it's a big success," Scott said. He'd date Jamie in a second, of course, but since she was off-limits, the break lived on. "How are things with you?"

"Good. I'll be happy when Jessica's here for good and doesn't have to go back and forth to San Diego, but it's worth the separations. *She's* worth it. And this way she's building a great relationship with her grandparents without bailing on her relationship with her dad."

"You set a date yet?"

"Not yet. Once Danny's back, she and I will take Joe and Marie to California to see Davey. They've been estranged for so long, it won't be an easy reconciliation, but she wants them all there when we get married."

They sat on the bench to unlace their skates. "There's only one of him. Wouldn't it be easier for him to come here?"

"It would. And cheaper. But there are so many memories here and so many people who know them that it'll be easier on his turf. More neutral, especially since we'll all stay at a hotel. And Joe and Marie have never been to California, so at the very least, it'll be a nice vacation."

"How about you and Lydia?" Scott asked Aidan. "Set a date yet?"

"Soon. Maybe as soon as Danny gets his cast off and can be in the wedding photos without the crutches."

"Really?" Scott paused with one skate in his hand. "Is there a reason for that?"

Aidan laughed. "If Lydia gets pregnant, you'll be the second to know. Trust me."

"Who's going to be first?"

"Hopefully me." Aidan shrugged. "But with your family, I can never be sure."

"So why the rush?"

"I don't think it's a rush, exactly. She doesn't want a big, fancy wedding. Maybe because she doesn't have her mom…your mom. You know?"

Scott nodded, reaching down for his other skate. Losing their mom touched them all in a thousand different ways, but he'd always thought it was a little harder on his sisters. There were so many milestones and occasions a girl needed her mother for, and Tommy wasn't the kind of dad who could fill that role.

"Anyway," Aidan continued, "we want to be married more than we want to plan a wedding, so we're thinking of a civil ceremony at the bar with just family."

"Hey," Rick said.

"*All* of our family. You know we wouldn't get married without you guys."

They walked toward the locker rooms, Scott listening to the two guys talking about getting married. He didn't feel left out, exactly. He genuinely loved both guys and couldn't be happier for them. But before long he'd be choosing between being an extra wheel to the married couples or hanging out with Grant and Gavin, and he was over the club scene.

"I'm going to grab a shower at home," Rick said. "Jess sold her place so she stays at a hotel when she's in San Diego. The Wi-Fi's better at the office, so we usually chat before she leaves there and I'm already cutting it close."

"I'm going to shower at home because I forgot to throw clean clothes in my bag," Aidan said and they all laughed. "Scott?"

"I'm going to shower before I leave. I walked and you never know who you might run into on the way home."

"Hey, you could bump into your television wife," Rick said.

"My television wife? What the hell is that supposed to mean?"

"Oh, that's what Eriksson calls the woman you stopped dating to meet. Like an old sitcom wife or whatever. Aprons and baking and perfect children."

That made him laugh. "Perfect children? It would take one hell of a woman to bring perfect Kincaids into the world."

"I've been your best friend since we were teenagers and the fact my children will each have one foot in the same gene pool as you scares the crap out of me. I mean, think about it. Me and the Kincaid

DNA means there's a possibility I'll have gorgeous, perfect daughters—like their mother—and then very attractive sons with bad tempers who kind of suck at hockey."

"Or they might take after me," Scott shot back.

The other two were still laughing when they left the rink, and Scott shook his head. It still blew his mind that Aidan was going to be his brother-in-law, but once he'd gotten over the initial shock, he had to admit he couldn't have picked a better husband for Lydia even if she'd let him.

He hit the shower before getting dressed and then slung his hockey bag over his shoulder. Maybe he should have done like the other guys and just showered at home, but the last time he'd done that, he'd run into some old friends and ended up in a bar in smelly workout clothes.

Walking was the right choice, though, he thought. Mother Nature had opted for a warm spring night, though there was another cold snap in the long-range forecast. A lot of people waved to him, and a couple of kids even recognized him from a Fire Prevention Week program he'd done with Chris and a few other guys at the elementary school. He talked to them for a few minutes.

After a couple of blocks, he turned down a side street to take a shortcut. The bag was heavy and he shifted it from one shoulder to the other. Sometimes he was tempted to drive to the rink because it was a long walk with a hockey bag, but he liked to think of each trek to the rink and back as one less hour he had to feel guilty about not being in the gym.

"Scott."

He looked to his left, at the woman he'd been about to pass by without really noticing, and stopped short. His tired legs and shoulders were forgotten as every nerve in his body seemed to spring to life.

She was wearing a long gray sweatshirt over black leggings or yoga pants or whatever they called those things. Her feet were shoved bare into sneakers and her hair was caught in a messy knot on top of her head by one of those clips with the painful-looking teeth.

God, he wanted her. He wanted to squeeze the clip so it opened, watch her hair tumble down around her shoulders in waves, and then bury his face in it. "Hey, Jamie. What are you doing here?"

She nodded her head toward the building they were standing in front of. "I live here."

"Oh. That makes sense then."

"Had a craving for chocolate pudding." She held up a folded-over paper bag. "They sell this pudding at the corner that's amazing. The owner's wife makes it, I guess. Have you ever had it?"

"Nope."

She peered around his shoulder. "That's a pretty big bag."

"Hockey stuff," he said, and then he smiled. "And some free life advice—don't ever open a guy's hockey bag without a gas mask or a clothespin for your nose. I'm pretty sure women who think hockey players are sexy have never smelled one before he hits the showers."

"I'll keep that in mind. So what are *you* doing here?"

"I was playing some hockey with Aidan and Rick, and this street is a shortcut between the rink and home. I've been walking this way since I was so young my mom would hold my hand on the way to youth league practice."

She smiled. "I bet you were a cute kid."

"I was." He loved the sound of her laugh.

Then she sighed, and he realized they'd run out of standing-on-the-sidewalk small talk and were heading toward awkward silence.

He tried desperately to think of something to talk about—anything that would keep her there and give him an excuse to spend a few more minutes with her. But he'd already had this conversation with himself and he needed to do the right thing and say good-night.

SCREW IT, JAMIE THOUGHT. She was done torturing herself, and the chocolate pudding in her hand was good, but it was no substitute for the man standing in front of her. She wanted him. She knew he wanted her. They were adults and they were both fully capable of showing up when scheduled and doing their jobs. Spending some time together off the clock wasn't going to change that.

So, before he could end the silence by telling her he'd see her around, she demolished the weak, teetering wall of professionalism she'd tried to build between them. "You want to come up? Maybe share my pudding?"

Something flickered in his expression, and then he gave her a wry smile. "Is this an offer you make to all of your coworkers?"

She assumed he was trying to feel out what kind of invitation she was offering. The "ran into a friend and why not share her pudding" kind? Or the "using the pudding as an excuse to get him alone" kind? "No. Sharing my chocolate pudding is a very exclusive offer, just for you."

He shoved his hands into his pockets, rocking back a little on his heels. "I've spent a lot of time this week trying *not* to imagine you inviting me up to your apartment because I don't want to be a problem for you."

"I appreciate that." And she really did. It meant a lot to her that he'd taken what she'd said to heart. "But having all this…tension between us is a problem for me, too. You and I have chemistry. It sure as hell isn't burning itself out, and it seems like everybody can see it and there's going to be speculation no matter what. If my sex life is going to be the subject of gossip for the next month and a half to two months, I'm going to damn well *have* a sex life."

She must have said it louder than she meant to, because a guy passing by paused to look at her. He looked like he was going to say something, but one look from Scott sent him on his way.

"Oops," she muttered.

"I'd love to come up and share your chocolate pudding," Scott said. "I've worked up an appetite."

As she unlocked the side door that gave residents access to the interior stairwell, Jamie decided that was the problem with innuendo. She didn't know if he'd worked up a sexual appetite for her, or if he'd literally worked up an appetite playing hockey with the guys and was going to try to eat all of her pudding.

They wound their way up the narrow staircases to the fourth floor, while she told him about the building. "Obviously you know there's a barber shop on the first floor, since you walk by here all the time and there's a sign. Then there's a two-bedroom apartment on the second floor and two one-bedroom apartments on the third. I've got the studio they managed to fit on the fourth floor."

"This explains why you haven't spent any time in the workout room," he said.

"I could afford the rent because they have a hard time finding people willing to climb this many stairs multiple times a day. There's no elevator, so this is it."

"Do you have decks off the back?"

"No, just a bare-minimum fire escape." At the top of the stairs, she unlocked her door and let Scott into her apartment.

Once inside, he set his hockey bag off to the side and made a relieved sound. "I need to get wheels for that thing."

"Or you could drive."

He shrugged, then unzipped his sweatshirt and

tossed it on top of the bag. "The problem with driving is finding a place to park."

When she toed off her shoes, he did the same, but he didn't follow her when she walked to the counter to put down the bag from the market. She turned to face him, leaning the small of her back against the edge of the fake granite.

"Are you really sure about this?" he asked, his eyes serious as he looked at her from across the room.

"I wouldn't have invited you up if I wasn't. Are *you* sure about this?"

"I've been sure I want you since you first walked into the station. But you were right before, when you said it would be worse for you because you're a woman. I'd like to deny it because it sucks, but I've been around long enough to know it's the truth."

"My record speaks for itself. And if that's not enough… I don't care. I'm not going to spend the next six weeks being miserable because of other people's hang-ups." He didn't move, and she chuckled. "I swear. I'm very sure."

He moved then, crossing the room to her in long strides. When he reached her, he grabbed her hips and tugged so she was standing straight, almost pressed against him. "I swear I haven't been able to think about anything but you for days."

"I've been thinking about you, too, and I don't know why." When he arched an eyebrow, she laughed. "That didn't sound right. I just mean that I've never been this distracted by a guy before. Also, you smell delicious."

"I'm glad I took the time to shower after I left the ice or you'd be opening the windows right now. Or throwing me out."

"You're not going anywhere for a while."

He grinned and slipped his hands under the hem of her sweatshirt, pushing it up until his hands were at her waist. "I love these legging things. They make your legs look wicked long, and the elastic waist is nice, too."

As he said it, he dipped a finger under the waistband and she shuddered as his knuckle tickled her skin. But then she grasped his jaw with her fingers, tilting his face up until he met her gaze. "There's no home run if you skip first base."

He frowned. "I…don't know what that means."

"That's what I get for trying to use a sports analogy, because I'm not sure, either. It's supposed to mean you haven't kissed me since that night in your bar's storage room, and I like a little romance before a guy gets his hands down my pants."

His hands left her waist and he looked at her so intently, she was afraid for a minute that she'd turned him off and he might change his mind. But then his hands cupped her face and he smiled before his mouth claimed hers.

It wasn't a gentle kiss. It was hot and hungry, and she moaned as she buried her hands in his hair. His tongue danced over hers and she ran her heel up the back of his calf. When he nipped her bottom lip, she smiled against his mouth. His hands went underneath her sweatshirt again, but he didn't touch her waistband. His palms slid up her sides, stopping just below the bra she'd thrown on before running to the store.

He kissed her until her knees were weak and she wanted him inside of her so badly her entire body ached. Grasping the bottom of his T-shirt, she yanked it free of his jeans and slid it up over his abs.

"How much romance are you holding out for?" he murmured against her mouth.

"Being naked is romantic," she said, a little breathlessly.

He stepped back and lifted his arms, but before she could get his shirt off, he dropped them again. "This is kind of awkward, but before we start taking any clothes off, I should tell you I don't have any protection with me."

"Really? The grapevine would be so disappointed to hear you don't walk around fully prepared to have sex at any given moment with no advanced planning."

"In my defense, I went out tonight to play hockey with the guys. You're not supposed to keep condoms in your wallet and they'd probably disintegrate in five minutes if closed up in a hockey bag, so…yeah."

"I've got you covered." She paused, and then laughed. "No pun intended."

He groaned. "Really? That was pretty bad."

"Maybe. Why don't we move a few feet to the left, into the bedroom?"

"I kind of like the kitchen and the bedroom being

all one like this," he said when they reached the bed. "And you can see the TV from both."

She sat on the edge of the bed and grinned up at him. "Yeah, so I can lie in bed and watch you make me a sandwich. Naked."

He pulled his T-shirt off and tossed it aside. "That's incredibly hot. You naked. Sandwiches. Maybe a hockey game on the TV, all at the same time. This is basically a perfect apartment."

Once she'd had her fill of looking at his chest and abs, which were impressive, she reached into the nightstand drawer for a condom and set it on the edge of the bed. Then she caught his hand and tugged as she lay back, so he fell over her on the mattress. She was done looking and wanted to touch. "Sex with a hockey game in the background?"

"Hey, a crowd cheering's good for a man's ego." He reached down for her sweatshirt and started working it up over her stomach. "You know, I've heard some women who work in male-dominated fields like to wear lacy lingerie under their clothes to remind them of their femininity."

She laughed and slapped his hand away. "I don't need to be reminded I'm a woman. And I'm not into climbing multiple flights of stairs in sixty-plus pounds of gear with a lace thong wedged up my ass, so if that's what you're hoping to find, you're going to be disappointed."

"You just smiling at me can make my whole fucking day." He pushed her hair away from her face, his gaze suddenly serious and intense. "There is *no* chance anything about you will disappoint me."

Emotion swelled in her chest and she lifted her head to kiss him so they would close their eyes and he wouldn't see it on her face. His kiss was as fierce as the look he'd given her and she ran her hands over his back, his muscles rippling under her palms.

Then he pulled back and hauled her to her feet. "I need to feel you against me."

She pulled the sweatshirt over her head and dropped it on the floor. His hands cupped the white cotton bra, his thumbs brushing over her nipples. Reaching behind her back, she unclasped the bra and let him slip it over her arms.

Scott made a low, growling sound of appreciation before unbuttoning his jeans. After kicking them off, he pulled off his socks and the white boxer briefs followed. Hooking the waistband of her underwear with her yoga pants, she pulled them off and then wrapped her hand around the back of his neck to pull him in for another kiss.

Without taking his mouth off of hers, Scott picked her up and set her on the bed. Jamie ran her hands down his back and over his ass, scraping lightly with her fingernails. He cupped one breast, rubbing his thumb over the nipple, and she moaned against his lips.

But when she rocked her hips up against his, he drew back to grin at her. "Pushy, aren't you?"

"I've been thinking about this for days. I don't want to wait anymore."

"Maybe just another minute," he said, his voice rough as his palm skimmed over her stomach and between her legs.

She sucked in a breath as he pressed against her clit. His fingers stroked her slick flesh and she buried her hands in his hair, not wanting him to stop.

"God, you feel so good."

"I want you inside me now."

"You got somewhere to be?"

She growled, scraping her fingernails down his arm. "You're killing me."

Finally, she heard him rip the condom wrapper open. After a few seconds, he knelt between her thighs and ran his hands down her calves. Smiling at him, she spread her knees wider and lifted her hips.

He took his sweet time about it. Slowly, he entered her, one hand gripping the back of her thigh while the other supported his weight. Each time he pulled back, he went a little bit deeper until he filled her completely.

"Damn," he whispered, a light sheen of sweat gleaming at his hairline. "This has been building for days, and I don't want it to be over."

"That's not the only condom," she said, rocking against him.

He groaned and started moving, meeting each lift of her hips. She wrapped her arms around his waist, digging her fingertips into the middle of his back. Stroke after stroke brought her closer to orgasm, and she closed her eyes, savoring the sensations. He thrust deeper and faster until her back arched and she bit down on her lips to keep from crying out as the orgasm hit.

Only a moment later Scott groaned, his body jerking as he came, and she held him until his orgasm passed. He lowered himself on top of her and kissed her neck as his body relaxed, and she sighed contentedly.

If there were consequences for tonight, she'd gladly accept them. It had been worth it.

Once they'd caught their breath, he kissed her again and then rolled away. "Since you only have one door, I guess that must be the bathroom."

"Mmm-hmm. But there's also a box of tissues on the nightstand and a wastebasket under it if you need it."

She closed her eyes as he disposed of the condom, and then smiled when he rolled back to her, his body spooning hers. "You're so warm. I might never move again."

"I guess I'll let you rest for a few minutes."

Laughing, she snuggled deeper against him. "A few minutes, huh? You sound pretty sure of yourself."

He lifted his head and kissed her neck before putting his mouth next to her ear. "I bet you think I forgot you offered to share that chocolate pudding with me, don't you?"

SEVEN

EATING CHOCOLATE PUDDING naked in bed with Jamie Rutherford. Today was definitely ending a lot better than it had begun, Scott thought. And she'd been right about the pudding. It was damn good, and would have been worth climbing the stairs for even if she hadn't gotten him into her bed.

"What did you think?" she asked.

He looked over at her, smiling at the smudge of pudding at the corner of her mouth before she wiped it away with the tip of her finger. They were sitting up against her headboard, each with an empty bowl of pudding and, even though she'd pulled the sheet up over her breasts when she sat up, everything was pretty damn perfect.

"It was as good as you said it was. I don't know if I should start stopping at that market to get my own, or if I should find a new way to the rink so I'm not tempted by it."

"Tell me about it. It's just around the corner from me, so I have to depend on willpower." She took his bowl and set them on her nightstand before wiggling back down so her head was on her pillow. "I think you being naked in my bed says everything about how strong my willpower game is."

"You're the first woman who's ever given me chocolate pudding after sex. You do realize you might not get rid of me now."

She laughed. "That pudding was supposed be my reward for making it an entire week without having sex with you."

"You almost made it." He moved down on the bed and then rolled onto his side, propping his head on his hand so he could see her face. "What was your two-week reward going to be?"

"A Ferrari? I don't know, and I think the fact I can't think of anything says a lot about my faith in my ability to resist you."

"And that was with me deliberately trying to leave you alone."

"Which just made you even more attractive to me, by the way."

"So tell me something," he said, running his fingertip over her collarbone. "What made you want to be a firefighter?"

"You would think with all the times I've been asked that over the years, that I would have an easy answer for that question."

"Do you have family in the fire service?"

"Nobody. My dad sells insurance and my mom owns a hair salon. One of my sisters works with her and will probably take over when my mom retires. My other sister teaches fourth grade. Both married with kids and all that. Then, when I was in middle school, we had a career day."

"Ah, yes. I've gotten sucked into doing a few of

those. They're usually pretty fun, though, because let's face it, we have the coolest job. Maybe I'll do a few more of them if they actually work on kids."

"Actually, the guy who did it pissed me off."

"Really? You became a firefighter because the guy who did career day when you were a kid pissed you off?"

"Basically, yeah. He had this exciting presentation and he made it sound awesome, but he only talked to the boys. He talked about how real men took care of their communities with no thought to their own safety and—"

She paused when Scott snorted in derision. "Sorry, but sometimes it seems like *all* we think about is our own safety."

"Yeah, but preteen boys wouldn't find endless training classes and inspections exciting. So anyway, once he was done with his grandstanding, he was like, 'Oh, yeah, there's stuff for girls, too, like working in dispatch,' and his entire tone changed when he said it. I raised my hand and told him women can be firefighters, too."

"Of course you did." He tried to imagine a much younger version of her, and didn't doubt that even then, she wouldn't hesitate to set him straight. "I'm almost afraid to ask what he said."

"He said, 'But not good ones.'"

"Oh, ouch. So you've worked your ass off your entire life just to prove some sexist douche bag wrong?" When she blushed, he laughed. "That's one hell of a stubborn streak. I'm impressed."

Jamie slapped his shoulder. "It started out that way, yes. But the first time I went on a real call, I knew I was on the right road for me."

"Were you ever assigned to that guy's company? You said it was a small town."

"No. I would have been, but he was fired and sued for sexual harassment the year before I signed on." She smiled up at him. "Why did you become a firefighter? Because of Tommy?"

"Yeah, there's Tommy. And my grandfather. His father. I'm the sixth generation of Boston Fire in my family, so I'm not sure I even paid attention at career day. I remember back when my mom was alive and my dad was talking about his day, he'd think of some cautionary tale and say 'Someday when you're on the job, son…' and tell me what went wrong so it wouldn't happen to me. Nobody ever questioned that I'd follow in his footsteps."

"How old were you when your mom died? If you don't mind me asking."

"I was nine. Lydia was thirteen and Ashley was fourteen. They alternated between overmothering me to compensate and writing me off as too much like my dad to bother with. He threw himself into the job and, as soon as I was old enough, I did the same."

"Do you ever resent it?"

"Resent what?"

"That your life's path was some kind of foregone conclusion. It seems like you were destined from birth to be a firefighter. What if you wanted to build houses or work with computers or be a chef or something?"

He had to think about it for a minute because he couldn't remember anybody ever asking him that before. "Well, I didn't resent it before, but now that you mention it..."

She laughed, which made her breasts jiggle a little under the thin sheet. "I'm being serious."

"There have been times I resented my dad's job. It made my mom unhappy a lot and I don't think they would have stayed married much longer if she hadn't been diagnosed with breast cancer. But I never wanted to be anything but a firefighter. Even when I was little, I'd see a fire truck go by and feel a rush of pride. That was going to be me. They'd be my brothers and I'd take care of my neighbors just like my dad did. Like Fitz and my gramps. I guess being a firefighter isn't what I am. It's *who* I am."

"I get that," she said, and he knew it was the truth. Nobody would put in the amount of dedication and hard work it took to go from some small-town volunteer gig to being a Boston Fire lieutenant as young as she was unless it was a calling.

"Hey, how old are you?" he asked before his brain's filter could stop him and come up with a better way to phrase the question.

She arched an eyebrow at him. "Really?"

"Yeah, that wasn't very smooth. If it helps, I was thinking about how hard you must have worked to make lieutenant at a young age, and that made me realize I don't know how old you actually are."

"That does make me feel better, I have to admit. And I'm thirty-four." She winced. "Of course I already know you're only twenty-seven since I'm privy to more info about you than you are about me."

"That's not fair." He hooked his finger on the sheet and gave it a little tug. "Thirty-four is an incredibly sexy age."

"Lighting must be good," she said.

"The lighting isn't what's good." He lowered his mouth to her breast, nipping at her nipple before running his tongue over it.

She laughed and slid her arms around his waist, pulling him on top of her. They made love again, and he savored every minute of it. He loved the way she felt and tasted, and the way she unabashedly enjoyed his touch. Jamie was eye contact and naughty smiles and soft moans. With her sex was more than a primal urge to reach orgasm. It was something fun and yet intense they were doing together, exploring each other's bodies and finding those spots that amped up the pleasure, and he never wanted it to end.

When they finally collapsed on the pillows, panting and flushed and totally wrung out, he landed flat on his back and tried to catch his breath. He wanted to say something to her—something that let her know she was exceptional and how much she blew him away—but everything that ran through his mind sounded incredibly corny so he kept his mouth shut. He wrapped the condom in a tissue before dropping it in the basket under her nightstand, and then he rolled to face her.

Jamie's eyes were closed, but she must have felt the motion because she moved closer to him, so her arm and the length of her leg pressed against him. He kissed her, and then dropped his head back to the pillow. It didn't take long, though, for his body to relax to the point he knew he'd be nodding off. Already, Jamie's eyes were closed and her breathing was slowing as she drifted in and out.

"I really should go," he said, without much enthusiasm.

She opened her eyes and shifted her head so she could see him. "Or you could stay."

"I want to." She had no idea how much he wanted to. "But don't forget we're having dinner with my entire family tomorrow."

"Oh, yeah. I guess that just got a lot more complicated."

"And if I don't go home, my dad's the kind of tone-deaf guy who won't think anything of asking me where I spent the night while we're all sitting at the table."

"We really don't want that," she said, though she didn't do a good job of hiding how amusing she found the visual as she leaned over the side of the bed and snagged her sweatshirt off the floor.

While he got dressed, she carried the pudding bowls to the sink and rinsed them, and he watched her as she tossed the empty container in the trash. He kind of liked this all-one-room thing, although watching sports while somebody was trying to sleep wouldn't work out very well.

He took his time, but he only wore so many clothes, so the time to leave came too soon. She looked so inviting, wearing nothing but the long sweatshirt, with her hair free and tousled. When she slid her hands up over his abs to his chest and kissed him, he sighed.

She sighed and reached up to smooth the hair over his ear. "Just so we're on the same page, doing what they speculate we're doing doesn't mean I want to confirm the rumors. Gossip is one thing, but I'm *really* not supposed to be sleeping with you."

"It's nobody's business but ours." Before he left, though, he needed to know where her head was, as far as the whole sleeping-together thing. "So do you think we'll be breaking that rule again, or is there a chance you're going to wake up tomorrow and decide you made a mistake and we should pretend this never happened?"

"Oh, there's no way in hell I can pretend this never happened," she said. "And I intend to break rules with you whenever we have an opportunity. Since my time here has an expiration date, we can keep each other company until I move on and you go back to looking for your television wife."

"Oh, for the love of…" Sometimes the guys could be real pains in the ass. "You heard about that?"

"Of course I did."

"They're exaggerating for their own amusement." He winked at her. "Even I know you don't wear pearls with aprons anymore."

She laughed as they walked to the door, and he tried not to think about how much he *didn't* want to leave. In the past, sometimes he'd stay over and sometimes he'd leave, but it was always about convenience or whatever vibe the woman was giving off. It hadn't mattered to him one way or the other.

But he didn't want to leave Jamie. Over her shoulder he could see the bed with its messed-up covers, and he wanted to take her by the hand and lead her back there. He could wrap his body around hers and fall asleep with his face buried in her hair, and then kiss her awake in the morning.

"Aidan gave me directions to your dad's house. Well, your house, too, I guess. So I'll be there at five."

"I'll see you then. The door at the bottom of the stairs will lock behind me, right?"

"Yeah."

He kissed her, breaking it off before it could tempt either of them into going back to bed, and then put on his sweatshirt and picked up his hockey bag. "I'll see you tomorrow."

"Good night, Scott."

He was halfway down the stairs when it hit him how much he liked hearing her say his name. *Scott.* He wasn't sure if it was a Boston thing or a guy thing, but everybody loved to tack the *ee* sound on the end of any name they could, and he'd been called Scotty by almost everybody for his entire life.

The guys at the station did, but she hadn't fallen into using it, and he liked that. Maybe it was because he was trying to leave his old ways behind him—the merry-go-round of girlfriends and his temper—or maybe it was because it made her different, but he hoped she didn't stop.

Once he'd reached his apartment, he spent almost an hour picking up clutter. It was late and he should already be in bed. And there was almost no chance he'd come up with a plausible excuse for getting Jamie upstairs alone for even a few minutes, but he wanted the place to look decent just in case.

When he did finally lie down, he didn't sleep right away. Instead he stared at the ceiling, wishing Jamie was next to him instead of empty bed.

JAMIE HAD NEVER felt less ready for anything in her life than she did for having supper at the Kincaid house. Sitting down at a table, so soon after they had sex she'd rather everybody not know about, with the five people who could probably read Scott better than anybody else, probably wasn't the best timing ever.

But at two minutes before five, she walked up the steps of the deep front porch and knocked on Tommy's door. She was carrying a plastic container of store-bought assorted fruit pastries because she'd been raised to not show up as a dinner guest empty-handed. Unfortunately, she had no idea what they were having for dinner, so she wasn't sure what to bring to complement it. Bringing wine to the home of a guy who owned a bar didn't make a lot of sense to her. And her mother had once told her that bringing a fancy dessert was rude because it presumed there would actually be a dessert course.

Running short on time and patience, she'd finally

grabbed the pastries. Pastries were flexible. They could be dessert, but they could also be an appetizer. Hell, Tommy could eat them all for breakfast the next morning for all she cared. She needed to bring something and they were handy. Now that she was standing on the porch, though, they seemed woefully inadequate.

Lydia answered the door, a smile on her face. "Hi, Jamie. Come on in. Did you have any trouble finding the house?"

"Not at all. Aidan's directions were perfect. And I suspect I could have knocked on any door and said I was looking for your dad and I would have been pointed in the right direction."

She laughed. "You're totally right."

Jamie held up the container from the market. "I brought some fruit pastries. They're store-bought, but trust me when I tell you it's better than if I'd made them myself."

"Those look delicious." Lydia took the box. "And I'm glad they're store-bought. If the guys start getting a taste for real homemade stuff…well, let's just say I don't want the bar set too high."

They were laughing together when they walked inside, and Jamie realized the front door led straight into the living room. The entire family stopped talking and looked when they entered. Of course her gaze went immediately to Scott and she returned the smile he gave her.

"Hey, Jamie."

"Hi," she replied, and then she tore her gaze away

from him even though she could have happily looked at him for hours. Then she said hi to Aidan, who emerged from the kitchen long enough to wave to her.

"I'd stay and visit, but I've been assigned to lettuce shredding duty for the salad," he said before disappearing back into the kitchen.

A man who was obviously Scott's dad stood and walked toward her. "I'm Tommy Kincaid. Welcome to my home."

He was a big man and Jamie guessed that, even though he was going soft around the middle, he was probably still as strong as an ox. Most of Scott's looks had come from his dad, she saw, though Tommy's hair was mostly gray. "Thank you for inviting me."

"I've heard a lot about you."

She smiled. "Probably almost as much as I've heard about you."

"This is Ashley," Lydia said, and Jamie shook Scott's oldest sister's hand. Ashley had the same dark hair, though slightly lighter than Scott and Lydia's, and she was shorter, too. Probably took more after their mom. "And you've met Danny."

"Nice to see you again, Jamie. How's it going?"

"Pretty well, I think."

He smiled. "That's what I've heard."

She had no doubt he got daily updates. Not so much through any official channels, but from the other guys at the station and particularly from Scott and Aidan.

"We're going to eat in a few minutes," Ashley

said. "I made a lasagna, but if you don't like that, I can whip up something else on the side."

"Who doesn't love lasagna?" Jamie replied.

"I knew I was going to like you," Tommy said.

The entire time, Jamie was keenly aware of Scott's presence in the room, so she actually jumped a little when she heard his voice. "How come you'll whip her up something on the side, but if I don't like something, I have to make a bologna sandwich?"

"Because you're a pain in the ass."

Tommy waved a hand at the couch. "Sit down, Jamie. Do you watch sports?"

"I'm not a big sports fan," she admitted, and she wasn't surprised when he frowned at her. "The guys have been trying to explain hockey to me, though, and I do own a Boston Bruins sweatshirt."

"Good enough. How long have you been in Boston?"

She had to think about it. "Almost two years, I guess. It doesn't feel like that long."

"Hell, you must be about ready to drive the truck."

"No," she and Scott said at the same time, and he chuckled.

"Oh, come on," Tommy said. "Boston's a fun place to drive."

"She finally stopped screaming when I make left turns," Scott said, winking at her.

She laughed, shaking her head. "I shouldn't be able to hear the tires squealing over the sound of the sirens."

"You going to sit down, son, or are you going to

keep hovering?" Tommy demanded, craning his neck to look at Scott.

Since Tommy was in an old recliner and Danny was in an armchair with his leg up on an ottoman, the only place left to sit was on the couch with her. She shifted to one end, leaving plenty of room, and he really didn't have a choice but to sit at the other end.

Part of her wanted to laugh at the stupid situation they'd put themselves in. Less than twenty-four hours ago, they'd been naked in her bed. Now they were sitting on opposite ends of a couch, barely looking at each other.

The other part of her, of course, wanted to crawl across the couch and curl up on his lap.

"So tell me, what made you want to be a firefighter, Jamie? Family business?"

She shook her head. "I'm the first firefighter to shake out of the family tree. It was a career day presentation when I was in middle school, sir. A firefighter came in to talk to us about it and…the rest is history."

She glanced at Scott and he raised an eyebrow as if to ask if she was going to share the rest of the story. No, she wasn't about to go into how offensive men could be about female firefighters when talking to somebody of Tommy's generation. On the surface, he seemed perfectly happy to make her feel welcome, but in her experience, if given the chance they usually had a laundry list of concerns. And they quite often didn't realize those concerns—women weren't brave enough or strong enough or the guys would get in fights over her or they'd be bossy and make them clean too much—were offensive to the women they were talking about. The guys she served with didn't have a problem with her, so she didn't feel a need to open the door to Tommy wanting to justify that old-timer's attitude.

"You're not only the first woman in Engine Company 59," Tommy said, "but you're probably the first person who's ever told me those career day things were worth a damn. I remember the first time Ashley dragged me in for one of those."

Jamie listened to him tell the story, laughing in the right places, but she was conscious of Scott sitting only a few feet from her. He chuckled a couple of times, but mostly he was very quiet and still. It wasn't normal for Scott to be that still, so she assumed he was having as much trouble figuring what "act naturally" should be as she was.

And it was probably why Danny kept looking at Scott as though he was trying to figure out if something was wrong with him. Luckily, none of them knew Jamie well enough to know she probably looked a little off, too.

"Food's ready," Ashley called from the kitchen a few minutes later.

Scott and Tommy both stood and together hauled Danny to his feet. Once his crutches were tucked under his arms, he smiled at Jamie and rolled his eyes. "I can get up by myself, but they think it's funny to move me around like a doll."

They let Danny go first, and he thumped his way

to the dining room with Tommy on his heels. Scott gestured for Jamie to go next, and as she passed by, he put his hand on the small of her back. She paused, very briefly, savoring the warm pressure for a few seconds.

"Thought about that pudding all day," he said in a voice barely above a whisper.

Before she could tell him he was welcome to stop by for chocolate pudding anytime, his hand fell away. Rather than risk a lull in the conversation in front of them coinciding with her saying something mildly suggestive to Scott, she kept her mouth shut and followed Tommy into the dining room.

Ashley was directing traffic around Tommy, who was already seated at the head of the table. The dining room wasn't very big, so there wasn't a lot of room to play with. "Danny, you sit on the end on that back side so your leg's out of the way. I'll put your crutches in the corner. Lydia and I will be getting up to serve, so we should be on this side."

"I'll sit in the middle on the far side, next to Danny, so I'm out of the way," Jamie said.

"I'll be the third," Scott said. "Aidan can sit next to Lydia."

Jamie walked behind Tommy's chair and pulled out the middle chair. As she sat, Scott pushed it in for her before sitting next to her. It was sweet, and she wondered if the others would notice the gesture, but then she saw Aidan doing the same for Lydia. Apparently it was how they did things.

There was a salad at every place setting and everybody dug in, so Jamie did the same. They all talked as much as they ate, and they made sure she was pulled into the conversations. Maybe because she was there, most of the talk was about the fire department, with Tommy occasionally breaking in to tell them how he did things back in the day.

The salad bowls were replaced by plates of the most amazing lasagna, and she looked across the table at Lydia and Ashley. “If you guys always eat like this, you’re going to have to tell me your secret for still fitting in your jeans.”

“We only eat like this when Ashley cooks for us,” Lydia said. “Or, trust me, I wouldn’t be able to.”

“Ash won’t be fitting in her jeans much longer,” Danny said, and his wife blushed.

“Funny.” She looked at Jamie, her cheeks faintly pink. “I don’t know if anybody told you, but I’m pregnant.”

“Congratulations! No, nobody told me. That’s really wonderful news.”

“It is. I originally didn’t want anybody but Danny to know because I’m a little superstitious.”

Lydia laughed. “Jamie’s already noticed that about us.”

“It’s hard to keep secrets in a firehouse,” Jamie said, hoping her cheeks didn’t turn the same shade as Ashley’s had.

“Well, I’m still not sure who knows and who doesn’t.”

“Rick knows,” Scott said, and Jamie looked sideways at him when she heard the tension in his voice. “I don’t know who else heard.”

"It doesn't matter, anyway," Ashley said, her voice high with a too-chipper, false note. "Superstitions don't trump science."

Jamie wasn't sure what was going on, but there was a low-level buzz of tension around the table that hadn't been there before. She put a forkful of lasagna in her mouth and chewed slowly so she couldn't unknowingly say something that made it worse.

Danny leaned closer to her. "We'd just found out when I got hurt. Tommy, Lydia and Scott were the only ones we told, partly because we didn't feel right not telling them and partly because she was having random any-time-of-day sickness and her shifts at the bar were becoming a problem."

She wasn't sure how that tied in with Scott sharing the news. "That must have been scary for everybody."

"It was," Scott said in a flat voice. "When Danny didn't come out, I tried to go back in and Rick wouldn't let me. I told him Ash was pregnant and I couldn't go home without Danny. He still didn't let me go back in."

"Enough," Tommy barked. "We're all here and we're having a nice meal. Put some in your mouths."

"Dad," Lydia said.

Scott turned slightly toward Jamie and she could see the anger in his expression. "We only talk about the good days."

The silence as everybody went back to the lasagna was deafening, and Jamie wished she could think of something to say that would restore the easy banter they'd started with. She shifted her right leg, though, moving it sideways until it pressed against the length of Scott's. He didn't pull away and, through the corner of her eye, she saw the muscles in his jaw relax.

"Hey, did you two pick a wedding date yet?" Ashley asked, and everybody instantly picked up. Jamie knew she was the oldest of the three kids, so maybe she'd had to learn young how to keep the peace between two temperamental siblings and their dad.

"Not yet," Lydia said.

"You have to pick a date. People keep asking me and I have to tell them I don't know."

"I guess anybody who needs to know the date will know it when we do."

"Do you want a big wedding or a small one?" Jamie asked, because weddings were a fun thing to talk about.

"Small," Lydia and Aidan said at the same time Ashley said "Big," and they all laughed.

"So, Jamie, when are you going to come in the bar again?" Tommy asked, and Jamie felt as if she were under a spotlight when everybody looked at her. "I hear you've only been in once."

"I've actually been in three times, but the first two were quite a while ago and I didn't know anybody."

"And did the third time scare you off?"

"No, sir. I just haven't had a chance to come back."

He pushed back his empty plate and rested his hand on his stomach. "You'll have to come in more often."

"I might. I haven't had a burger yet and I've heard yours are good."

They sat around the table and talked while Ashley and Lydia cleared the plates and loaded up the dishwasher, refusing any help from Jamie. Tommy told them of the E59-L37 station's history, which she found interesting, even though it was obvious the others had heard the stories before.

After decaf coffees and pastries, Jamie cursed herself for eating so much lasagna. It was a good thing she'd decided to brave the roads and drive because it would have been a long, agonizing walk home. She didn't even want to think about the stairs.

When it was time to go, she thanked Tommy for the invitation and Ashley for making the lasagna. "It's a good thing we don't work tomorrow because I'll probably still be full."

"You're not walking, are you?" Tommy asked. "Scotty can walk you home. Make sure you get home safe."

Dammit. That would have been a great excuse to sneak some alone time with him. "I drove, but thanks."

Lydia walked to the door with her, so all she could get from Scott was a casual wave. "See you Tuesday."

"Thanks for coming," Lydia said when they were out on the porch. "The family can get a little hard to take at times, but we all mean well."

"I had a great time," Jamie said honestly. "I miss my family, so hanging out with yours was nice."

"You really should stop by the bar," she said. "It's pretty low-key when Scotty's not punching people, which he hardly ever does anymore."

Unless somebody insulted her, Jamie thought. "I will."

About fifteen minutes after she managed to drag herself up all the flights of stairs to her apartment, her cell phone chimed. She thought instantly of her friend Steph, and felt a pang of guilt. She needed to touch base with her, but usually Steph was the one to initiate the conversations because of her work hours and the customer traffic at the pizza shop.

But it wasn't from Steph. It was from Scott. I hope that wasn't too bad.

She wasn't sure if he meant being around all the Kincaids, or the strain of keeping up the appearance they hadn't recently had sex. I enjoyed tonight.

I wish I hadn't promised Rick I'd help him with a few things around his place tomorrow. I want to see you again.

She smiled, though she wished the same thing. You'll see me Tuesday.

It only took a few seconds for him to respond. You won't be naked.

Not on Tuesday.

Wednesday?

Some of her anxiety about how their tour on Tuesday would go had been eased by their success at getting through a family dinner without anybody seeming suspicious, so she didn't hesitate. Yes.

Good. The guys have the game paused for me, so I have to go. Good night.

Sweet dreams.

After setting a reminder on her phone to text Steph at a time the pizza shop was typically slow, she stretched out on her couch and hit the TV's power button on the remote control. There was no way she could go to bed after eating all that food, so she flipped through the channels, looking for something to catch her eye.

When she landed on a hockey game and some of the guys were wearing black and gold, she stopped channel surfing. It must be the game Scott was watching, which made her smile. Over the years she'd survived a lot of sports games on station televisions. Being a fan seemed to mean a lot of yelling and hand waving and cursing, so she'd usually used game time for catching up on paperwork or doing anything she could find to do in a room farthest from the TV. The E-59 guys, though, were taking it as a personal challenge to make her a hockey fan and they spent a lot of free time trying to tutor her.

After watching it for a few minutes, she laughed at herself and starting hitting the channel-up button again. It was hard enough to keep track of the guys flying around on the ice. She had no hope of figuring out where the puck was and the words the announcers were using still meant nothing to her.

After settling on a disaster movie she'd seen enough times that the fact she'd missed the first twenty minutes didn't matter, she pulled the knit throw off the back of the couch and got comfortable.

Her eyelids got heavy fast, though, and as she drifted off, her last thought was that she had to remember to ask Scott what kind of movies he liked.

EIGHT

SCOTT FROWNED AT the puzzle piece in his hand, then looked back at the picture on the box lid. "I think some dipshit mixed up the pieces of this puzzle with another one."

Jeff leaned over on the couch to look at the piece. "That looks like part of a Santa hat."

"We're doing a fall foliage puzzle."

Jeff shrugged. "Maybe it's like one of those *Where's Waldo* things and there's a Santa hat hiding in the leaves."

"Or maybe some dipshit mixed up the puzzles," Scott repeated under his breath.

"I've done that foliage puzzle about nineteen times," Chris said from across the room, where he'd been pretending to nap in a chair. "There's no Santa hat. It's probably the pointy part of a red leaf."

Scott tossed the piece back into the pile and picked up another one. It was a blur of red and orange, like 80 percent of the other pieces. He really hated jigsaw puzzles that were mostly scenery. "We need to put a puzzle fund jar on the table and buy some new ones."

Some tours, they busted their asses for hours

without any rest beyond the short breaks necessary to keep them going. Most varied, with some medical emergencies and accidents and people smelling smoke, but plenty of downtime for meals, rest and getting stuff done around the station. And then there were days like today, when it seemed everybody in their neighborhood was feeling good, obeying traffic laws and not setting stuff on fire. They were good days for everybody but, holy crap, did the hours drag on when the chores were all checked off and the alarm didn't sound.

"Hey, Scotty, Ellen wants to set you up on a date," Jeff said.

"I'm not interested. Tell your wife I said thanks, though."

"She says this new girl at work would be perfect for you. Her dad's a firefighter in Philly, so she knows how it goes. Came up here for college and plans to stay. She's really pretty, smart, makes good money, and wants to get married and have kids in a few years."

"She sounds great, but I'm not into dating right now. Which you know."

"Yeah, but she's not the women you were dating when you decided to take a break. She's the kind of woman you're looking for."

Scott was glad Jamie had gone down to the second floor to do paperwork because he'd have a hard time not looking her way to see her reaction to this conversation. "I'm not looking for any women right now."

"I like pretty and smart women who make good money," Grant said from the kitchen doorway.

"Yeah, but my wife thinks you're a shithead because you flaked out on the charity breakfast last summer and you were supposed to be in charge of the bacon."

Grant sighed. "I was sick."

"You were hungover. And you can fudge a lot when it comes to breakfast, but you can't fake your way out of a bacon issue. It's bacon." Jeff pressed a yellow leaf into place in the puzzle. "Besides, her friend wants a guy who's ready to settle down. Rings. Strollers."

With a grimace, Grant disappeared back into the kitchen, which Scott hoped would end the issue. He didn't want to date Ellen's friend and Ellen wouldn't want her friend to date Grant or Gavin, who wasn't any more ready to settle down. Everybody else was taken, so both companies were a dead end on the road to finding Ellen's friend a husband.

"It's been a while since you talked about going out, Scotty," Jeff said. "You have to go on first dates to know who you want to go on a second date with, you know what I mean?"

He already knew he wanted to go on a second date with the woman who was one floor beneath them, either doing paperwork or asleep at her desk, but he couldn't say that. It was awkward because, if he hadn't met Jamie, it would have been in his nature to at least take Ellen's smart, pretty friend who made good money to dinner and they all knew it.

"Or maybe he's already found somebody to date and he's not telling us," Chris said, and Scott looked up from the puzzle to frown at him. Was he just messing with him, or was he fishing for information?

"Why wouldn't I tell you?" he asked, neither confirming or denying he actually *had* found a woman to date and wasn't telling them.

"I don't know. Maybe she's ninety-seven and you think she'll leave you her fortune."

Scott laughed. "If you don't tell anybody, I'll buy you a pony. And on that note, I'm sick of this puzzle. I'm going to go find Aidan. He said he was going to check the tanks and never came back."

"He's probably hiding in the cage, talking to Lydia," Gavin said as he walked out of the weight room with a towel draped around his neck. At least, unlike the rest of them, he'd worked up a sweat today.

Scott went down one flight of stairs and paused in the narrow hallway of the second floor. The door to the office Jamie and Rick shared was closed, but he could knock. He'd have to come up with a reason to want to talk to her if Rick was in there, but if she was alone, Scott could visit for a few minutes.

But showing up in her office their first tour after sleeping together might make her change her mind about their relationship. If there was any time besides on a run she would be most conscious of the fact they worked together, it would be when they were on opposite sides of her desk.

He continued down the other flight and checked the cage where they kept the air tanks, but it was locked. Then he heard a swishing sound and walked around the back of Engine 59 to see Aidan sweeping the floor with a wide push broom.

"Busywork?"

Aidan looked up and shrugged. "I just don't feel like sitting around today."

"Yeah, I know what you mean. I can only do the same jigsaw puzzle so many times." He went to the bench and grabbed a rag. Even though both trucks were clean, he went around theirs, rubbing the bits of chrome trim until they gleamed. The younger guys tended to do the bumpers and ignore the rest.

"Jeff was telling me Ellen wants to set me up with a new friend of hers from work."

"You going?"

He snorted. "No."

"I didn't think so. Seems like you've got your eye on a woman already and you might hold the record for the number of girlfriends for the company, but I've gotta hand it to you—they were never at the same time."

"I'm not dating anybody," he said, feeling as if he was walking a tightrope of semantics. Technically, he wasn't lying to his best friend. He and Jamie hadn't actually gone on a real date yet. "I'm on a break, remember?"

Aidan hung the big broom on its hook and pulled down the smaller broom and dustpan to pick up the piles he'd made. "Here's the thing. I'm not going to ask you any questions about a certain person that require an outright answer one way or the other because I don't want to force you into a situation where you have to lie to me to protect somebody else. But don't bullshit me."

Scott looked at Aidan for a minute, remembering how much anger and betrayal he'd felt when he found out his best friend had been seeing his sister without telling him. It had almost ended their friendship, but the bond between them was too strong. Even with that blowup only about six months behind them, Scott knew there was nobody in the world he could trust like he could this guy. But there was Jamie's trust to consider, too, so he was going to have to accept the compromise Aidan offered.

"Grant jumped at the chance to be set up with Ellen's friend, of course," he said, evading the issue of Jamie.

Aidan snorted. "Has she forgiven him for the bacon debacle yet?"

"Nope."

"Can't say as I blame her. It was the bacon."

Scott did a final walk around the engine, eyeballing not only the chrome, but every inch of her. She was probably his first love and he never told anybody, but he was secretly relieved when their house was passed over for new trucks every year.

"So Lydia and I set a date for the wedding so Ashley will stop bugging us about it. Fourteenth of May. It's a Saturday."

"No shit." Content now that there wasn't a water spot to be found on E-59's chrome, Scott tossed the cloth onto the workbench. "She's really going to go through with it, huh?"

"Have I told you lately how funny you are?" Aidan folded his arms and leaned against the engine. "No? I wonder why."

"That's pretty quick. What, a little over a month away?"

"Ashley's the matron of honor, of course, and she wants a killer dress for the pictures, I guess. So we either do it now or we wait until after the baby's born."

"And then, because she wants a killer dress, she'll want to lose the baby weight."

Aidan winced. "Yeah, I mentioned that during the discussion with Lydia and you shouldn't ever say that out loud again. It's probably safest to not even think it."

"I love my sisters, but I also know them really well and yeah, if the dress is an issue, you're going to want to get married sooner rather than later. Can you get a place that fast?"

"I know the guy who owns Kincaid's Pub."

"Seriously? You're going to get married at our bar?" It was all well and good to not want to drop a crap load of cash on a fancy wedding, but his sister was basically going to get married at work? "Wait. Does that mean we can wear jeans and T-shirts?"

"Nice try, but no. Suits for us. The aforementioned killer dresses for the bride and her matron of honor. The bar will be closed, obviously, and done up really nice."

"That doesn't sound too bad, really."

Aidan nodded. "Think about it. There's no place else in the world that means more to either of us. When we think about home and family, Lydia and I both think of the bar. All we want is a justice of the peace and a small party with our closest friends and family, so why not? And we're going to delay the honeymoon until fall when it's peak foliage, and then we're going to get a cabin in northern New Hampshire and hide out for a week."

"That's what you want?"

"Yeah, it's what we both want."

"Then I'm happy for you. And I'll try hard not to schedule anything else that day."

Aidan snorted. "I'll kick your ass if you do because I really want you to be my best man."

The punch of emotion in his gut surprised the hell out of Scott. It wasn't as if it was a surprise. They'd been best friends for so long, who else would they ask but each other? Aidan had a brother, but they weren't the *best man* kind of close. Over the years Scott and Aidan had even made passing references to future bachelor parties. Things like "when I get married, you better have smoking hot strippers at my bachelor party" or "you should probably leave that out of your speech when I get married."

But hearing it now, when they were adults and Aidan actually needed a best man, was different. Holy shit, Aidan Hunt was getting married.

"So you gonna be around that day?" Aidan asked when Scott didn't say anything.

"Yeah, I'll be around." He reached out to shake his friend's hand, and then pulled him in for a black-slapping hug. "I'm honored, and there's nowhere else I'd be."

"Your first act as my best man can be informing Tommy we'll need to use the pool table for the buffet."

"You rotten bastard."

THERE WAS A knock on the office door and Jamie looked up from her paperwork, her pulse ticking like an overwound clock. "Come in."

When Cobb poked his head in, she felt a rush of disappointment. Yes, it would be inappropriate for Scott to come lock himself in her office with her. Yes, it would be disastrous for her plan to keep their personal relationship and their work relationship separate. But she still thought it might be him.

"Hey, Chief."

"Where's Gullotti?"

"In his bunk. I guess his fiancée had some evening business meetings so they talked late. With the three-hour time difference between here and San Diego, it ended up being a little *too* late for him."

"That's gotta be tough on a relationship. But I know her grandparents. The Broussards are good people, and I'm happy for the kids."

It amused her to hear Rick called a kid, since he was older than all of them except Chris and Cobb himself. When she'd looked through their files prior to reporting the first day, she'd seen that Rick had been promoted over Chris because the latter hated paperwork and bureaucracy. He preferred being left alone to do his job.

"Do you want me to get Rick?" she asked.

"No, you can fill him in. I just wanted to let you guys know Danny had another appointment today and his leg's looking real good. He's still on track for another five to seven weeks."

"That's good news. I'll let Rick know, definitely."

"Thanks." Cobb started to leave, but then paused. "It *is* good news. Danny's a damn good firefighter and a great officer, but so are you. I'm bummed we only have you for a bit over a month left, and I wish E-59 could keep you both."

She recognized it as high praise from an old-school guy like Cobb, and gave him a warm smile. "Thanks, Chief. This is a great group of guys to work with."

"They're inspecting the equipment right now. The lines and couplers mostly, just because they were starting to bicker like a bunch of kids with cabin fever. It's a nice day so I told them to open the garage doors and find something to do."

"You sent them outside to play, sir?"

He laughed. "Yeah, I guess I did. I would have told them to clean their rooms, but they already did that. I called them in as out of commission for an hour so they could check the line and another house can cover for us."

They definitely couldn't respond to an alarm when the water hoses were spread out on the ground. "I could use some fresh air myself, actually. Maybe I'll go down and join in."

Cobb was right, she realized as soon as she stepped into the engine bay. It was a gorgeous spring day and there was just enough of a breeze so it brought fresh air into the building. Her guys had lines laid out along the floor while the ladder company had their own equipment strewn all over their half of the garage.

"Hey, Jamie," Grant said when he spotted her.

Through the corner of her eye, she saw Scott look up from the coupler he was checking for any defects, but she kept her gaze on the younger guy. "I heard you were all getting some fresh air, so I decided to break out of my office."

"You're just in time to help recoil the lines," Grant told her. "Aidan was telling us about his wedding. He and Lydia finally set a date."

"They did?" Ashley's prodding had paid off, then. She looked at Aidan. "Congratulations. When's the big day?"

"May fourteenth."

"*This* May fourteenth?"

"Yeah. Just a friends and family get-together at Kincaid's Pub with a JP."

"That sounds perfect."

"Hey, Scotty, are you going to bring a date to the wedding?" Grant asked.

Jamie didn't even flinch. She kept her focus on the line she was reeling in, but through the corner of her eye, she could see Scott glance over at her before shaking his head.

"No, I'm not."

"You know there won't be any single bridesmaids, right? Aidan said just a best man and a maid of honor. Or matron of honor or whatever, because Ashley's married."

"I'm going to watch my sister marry my best friend, not pick up women."

"Aw, that's sweet," Gavin chimed in. "But everybody knows women don't like going home alone after a wedding."

It was tempting for Jamie to interrupt and give the guy a verbal slap upside the head, but she'd learned long ago to pick her battles wisely when it came to being the only woman listening to men talk. Gavin was actually a good guy, and talking about hitting on single bridesmaids was how men got ready for weddings, in her experience.

"You should bring a date so you have somebody to dance with, though," Grant said. "You're the best man so you have to dance, but you can't dance with Rick's wife all night. I can hook you up if you want."

"Really, I'm all set," Scott insisted.

"Well, don't ask me to dance when you get sick of standing against the wall watching everybody else have fun," Grant said, and they all laughed.

"Maybe Jamie will take pity on Scotty the wall-flower and dance with him," Gavin added.

She was worried enough about spending an evening in front of all of his family and their friends without touching. She didn't need the other guys setting them up for a dance. "I'm not really much for dancing."

She realized Aidan was looking at her, and he held her gaze for a second before turning back to the guys. "We're not doing the whole plus-one thing. I think Lydia's mailing the invitations this week, but basically we won't have room. I mean wives can come. And a girlfriend if she's like…serious. Somebody we know, like Jess. But we don't have the space for random dates. And we want to be surrounded by people who are special to us, you know? Otherwise we'd do the big wedding thing."

For a few seconds, Jamie wondered if Aidan's strange look had been because she hadn't made the invitation list, but that couldn't be it. Even though she'd be handing the reins back to Danny about the time of the wedding, she was part of the Engine 59 family and he wouldn't leave her out. Plus Lydia seemed to like her, so she was fairly confident she'd be getting an invitation in the mail.

She couldn't help but wonder for a moment, though, how much it would suck to be at a party with Scott—a party with romance in the air and dancing—and pretend they were just coworkers.

But that was weeks away. For all she knew, the sparks between them would burn out by then and that's all that would be. Right now, the sparks were still sizzling, so she'd take each day as it came and enjoy the here and now.

When she turned to look at Grant's line, Scott caught her eye and gave her a look that made her shiver. Oh, yeah, she was definitely going to enjoy the hell out of the here and now.

AFTER AN ENTIRE day of doing nothing, it wasn't an hour after Cobb reported them back in service that the alarm sounded. A car had barreled into a deli and there were multiple casualties.

Scott sounded the horn in addition to the sirens as they pulled out onto the busy street. It was a shitty time of day to navigate the area, but he didn't yield and people got out of his way.

"They've got two employees unaccounted for," Jamie said. "A forty-year-old man and a seventeen-year-old girl."

"I know that deli," he said loud enough for everybody to hear. "It's an old building, so structural integrity's a concern."

He didn't need to say more. They knew that even going inside would be a risk, and it was the kind of risk they couldn't do a damn thing to mitigate. Fire was a fickle bitch and could turn on you in unexpected ways, but water, training and experience with its movements were weapons a good firefighter could use to knock the risk down. An unstable building could stand for years or it could collapse one minute after they went in. Short of waiting for engineers to go in, there was no way to know. But there were casualties and he knew they wouldn't hesitate.

They beat the EMS to the scene and hit the ground running. There were three injured people on the sidewalk, two of whom had been inside but got out after the accident. None looked critical. He watched Rick send Gavin to check them over while the rest of them went in.

Jamie reached the driver of the car first and pulled her glove off before reaching through the smashed window. After a minute, she pulled her hand back and shoved it into the glove, shaking her head. "Elderly male, deceased."

A medical crisis behind the wheel, Scott thought as he lifted a broken table off of a crying woman. The driver probably had a heart attack or a stroke and his body stiffened, jamming the accelerator to the floor. It would explain why the car was so deep in the building.

The woman wasn't hurt badly, so he helped her to the opening as sirens announced the arrival of EMS.

Sweeping the area, they found six more people and, miraculously, none of them were injured so badly they couldn't walk out with some assistance.

When Scott handed a badly shaken elderly woman over to the paramedics, he heard a man shouting at Rick. "They were in the back. Why didn't they come out?"

"We'll find them, sir."

They met up in front of the car, and Rick looked angry. "They haven't cut the power or the gas yet, and this building's creaking like an old bed frame, but there are two still unaccounted for. There may be a blockage somewhere, or they might have been knocked out if the impact knocked things off shelves. We don't know."

"With the gas on, I'd feel better if we at least have a line charged and ready to go," Aidan said.

"We have backup coming, but I don't want to wait," Jamie said. "You stay with the apparatus, Aidan, and we'll go in."

"We'll go around the back and try to come in from the other direction," Rick said. "Masks. We don't know what's going on with the gas piping, and if there's been any structural damage, who knows what shit's floating around in there."

Scott went in first, climbing over the smashed deli counter. He had the Halligan tool, essentially a huge crowbar with an adze head, so he could use it to pry or smash or prop things up, if necessary.

They found the man first, lying on the floor of

a storage room with a shelving unit on his leg. He was overweight and sweating profusely, which was cause for concern.

"Do you have any injuries besides your leg, sir?" Jamie asked after looking him over. He shook his head. "Okay, we're going to get this off you and get you out of here."

"Mandy," he said in a hoarse voice. "She went to the bathroom, which is down the hall, and I heard her scream."

Scott and Grant looked over the metal shelving unit, as well as the boxes strewn around. To Scott, it looked as if the shelving had caught the victim's leg just right, breaking it with the weight of the boxes and momentum, but it wasn't heavy.

Jamie had obviously come to the same conclusion. "Sir, this is going to hurt a little, but they're going to lift the shelves and I'm going to slide your legs out to this side. If you can use your arms to move your butt at the same time, that would help."

"What if I can't? I don't feel very good."

"Then it'll take longer and might hurt more, but I'll move you because we're not leaving you here."

"Okay."

"Hold on just a second."

Scott listened as Jamie turned up her radio. The impact had shifted the building on its ancient foundation and the back of the structure had partially collapsed into the basement. Rick and the others could maybe get through, but it would be slow going.

"Let us see if we can get to her from this direction. She's possibly in the restroom, so have Aidan talk to the owner and see if he can give us a precise location relative to the collapse in the back."

She turned her attention back to the man and signaled to them. Scott and Grant lifted the shelving, and he watched as Jamie helped the man get out from under it. The effort of moving himself caused his face to darken to a scary shade of red, and Scott hoped like hell they could get him to the paramedics before he got any worse.

"Grant, go on his other side and let's see if we can get him up."

"I don't know if I can," the man said. "It hurts."

"Sir," Jamie said, "your leg is probably broken, though it's not a compound fracture. But this building isn't stable and we don't want you in here any longer than necessary. It'll take time to get a stretcher in here and guys to carry it out, and to be honest, it won't be a lot less painful for you."

"We'll support you," Scott said. "You won't have to put much weight on that leg, if any. We'll get you out to the paramedics and they'll take care of you."

"Okay." The man took a deep breath. "I really want to get out of here."

As they got him to his feet and he looped one arm around Scott's shoulders and the other around Grant's, they all felt the subtle shift beneath their feet. *Shit*, Scott thought.

"Let's go."

It only took a few steps for them to find a rhythm, but Jamie stopped them. "You guys get him out. I'm going to look for Mandy."

"Let's get him outside and then we'll come back together."

"There might not be enough time." She pointed toward the front. "You go. If it looks hairy, I'll wait for you guys."

She turned and ducked down the hallway before Scott could come up with a good excuse why she shouldn't. Every muscle in his body tensed as his instincts screamed for him to go after her. He wanted to throw her over his shoulder and carry her out to the street.

Grant looked at him, his eyes wide behind the SCBA mask. Scott pointed him in the direction Jamie had told them to go. Grant shook his head.

"Your lieutenant gave you an order," Scott shouted.

"But she's alone."

God, he knew that. "Move your ass, Cutter. Let's get this gentleman some help."

By the time they got him to the sidewalk, Scott's back was screaming in protest, but all he could think about was Jamie. Once he was free of the guy with the broken leg, he took off his mask and drained half the water bottle Aidan handed him.

"The other guys are coming back around now," Aidan said. "They weren't getting anywhere and it won't be long before the building's in the basement."

"I'm going back in."

He got as far as the smashed car when Jamie came out of the back section with an unconscious teenager draped over her shoulders. Scott climbed the deli counter and put out his arms so Jamie could drop her head and kind of roll the girl to him. Once he had her, he backed up so Jamie could climb over.

"The floor was wet and there's blood on her head and the edge of the sink. I think she slipped and knocked herself out, but her vitals seem strong."

Once everybody was accounted for and in the care of EMS, the guys gathered around the trucks and waited to be cleared to return to quarters. The city inspector was on-site now and there were probably engineers on the way. They'd moved on to *not my job*, as far as Scott was concerned.

Jamie's phone rang and she moved away from them to a quiet spot in order to take the call. He watched her, hating all over again the memory of her going down the hallway. She shouldn't have gone alone and they all knew that, but it was her decision. Any one of them probably would have done the same.

But he still didn't like it and when she ended her call, he also couldn't help joining her away from the others.

"You shouldn't have gone alone," he said.

She looked at him, and he was surprised to see amusement in her eyes. "Which I know, since I've actually been a firefighter longer than you have."

"Funny." He exhaled and ran his hand over his

hair. “I hated that. I wanted to dump that guy on Grant and go with you.”

“Which is why firefighters from the same company shouldn’t sleep together. It can screw up priorities.” She shrugged and took the bottle of water he’d been drinking out of his hand. “But it didn’t because you let me do my job and you did yours.”

He watched her drink his water, some of the tension easing from his body. “I really want to kiss you right now.”

“Tomorrow,” she said, screwing the cap back on his bottle and handing it back to him.

He watched her walk back to the others, shaking his head. This definitely wasn’t going to be easy. But she was worth it.

NINE

"I SAW YOU on the news last night." Steph's face looked out at Jamie from her laptop screen. "They had a story about the car that ran into the deli."

"Did they at least get my good side?" Jamie joked. Steph always looked for her on the news but was usually disappointed, so she would at least text if she got a glimpse of her on the screen. Today they were video chatting because she'd been going on break just as Jamie sent her a text message, so she got her friend's excitement complete with facial expressions.

"They were getting a statement from some older guy, but you were in the background talking to some wicked cute guy. Dark hair. You took his water bottle away from him and drank it."

Of course they'd gotten that on film. "I was thirsty."

"Is there a reason you felt comfortable drinking out of his water bottle, or do you get to drink out of everybody's because you're an officer?"

Jamie grinned at the monitor. "It's a perk. Came with the promotion."

And now she really hoped that not only was Steph one of the few people who'd noticed what was going on in the background of the interview, but that she would be the only one who asked about it. Her mouth had been dry and it had been pure reflex to take the water bottle, but no, she probably wouldn't have done it if it had been any of the other guys in the company.

"I only have a few minutes," Steph said, "but I'm taking Monday off. *Please* tell me you don't have any plans that day."

"Nothing I can think of. Do you want to meet somewhere?"

"No, I want to see your apartment. Plus it's far enough away so if somebody from the pizza shop calls me about a problem or because somebody didn't show up or a tour bus just dumped a shitload of people out front, I can be too far away to do anything."

"I'm so glad I don't work for my family. It must be twice as hard to say no when your parents are the boss."

"It does make it a lot harder to get fired." There was a noise offscreen and Steph turned toward a voice. Then she looked back at Jamie and rolled her eyes. "So I'll see you Monday, right?"

"Sounds great. Text me when you leave your place and give me an estimate on what time you think you'll get here."

"I can't wait. I really want to hear more about the cute guy with the water bottle."

"Nothing to tell."

Stephanie's eyes narrowed. "You're lying, but I don't have time to nag you right now. Monday."

Once Jamie closed out the chat window, she glanced at the clock and decided she had time for a quick run-through of Facebook. Scott had said he'd be over about one, which gave them both time to grab a few hours of sleep if they needed it. She'd taken a short nap, more out of habit than anything, since it had been slow after the deli situation and they hadn't been shorted much rest.

By the time she skimmed past political rants, funny or dramatic memes and everybody's game scores, there was a picture of her niece to like and a status update from her mom about cooking to read. Then she popped onto a few pages related to the fire department and caught up on the news there. Instead of following the pages, she liked to visit them independently of her feed just to keep her personal life more personal.

Her phone chimed and her pulse quickened as she reached for it. I'm here.

Another reason her rent was so cheap, relatively speaking, was the lack of a way to buzz in a guest. Whether it was company, food delivery or a package, she had to go all the way down the stairs and open the door herself. The place definitely didn't have much in the way of amenities, but she'd rather climb the stairs and have more money in her pocket at the end of the month.

When she got to the bottom of the last flight, she paused to watch him through the glass door. He was looking off down the street at something, and he had a shopping bag in his hand. He was so incredibly handsome, she thought, smiling to herself. His profile made her want to run her fingertip over his nose, down to his lips and over his slightly scruffy jawline.

Then, as if he felt her staring, he turned and their eyes met through the door. His mouth turned up in a smile and he held up the bag. “Food,” he mouthed.

She pushed open the heavy door and let him in. “Are you trying to bribe your way into my building?”

“That’s only phase one. Phase two we can’t do here in the hallway.”

They made the trek back up the stairs and Jamie unlocked the door. “What’s in the bag?”

“I’m going to make you dinner.”

She closed the door behind them and kicked off the slippers she’d shoved her feet into. “You get sexier by the minute. What are you making for us?”

“It’s my sister’s turkey tetrazzini recipe. You’ll love it.”

Jamie eyeballed the bag in his hand and shook her head. “Recipe? That bag doesn’t look heavy enough to have a box of macaroni and cheese in it, never mind the ingredients for homemade turkey tetrazzini.”

He gave her a sheepish grin. “Okay, fine. I was hanging out at Aidan and Lydia’s earlier and she was making a double batch of it because she freezes individual servings for him to eat when she’s at work. I made the sad puppy dog eyes at her and she gave me a couple of containers to take home.”

“Microwaveable *and* no pots and pans to wash? Some magazine needs to make you sexiest man alive now.” She took a step toward him, but he backed away.

"I need to put this in the fridge before I kiss you hello, because once I start kissing you, I might not stop."

Jamie followed him to the refrigerator, unwilling to wait any longer than she had to. The second he closed the fridge door and turned, she was there, sliding her arms around his neck. "I missed you."

His mouth came down hard on hers, and she knew they were both releasing the frustration of going through their workdays pretending they felt nothing for each other. They were hungry for each other and she moaned as he buried his hands in her hair.

When she grabbed the hem of his T-shirt and lifted it, he broke off the kiss long enough for her to pull the shirt over his head and toss it aside. Then his lips were on hers again, demanding and hungry, as she ran her hands over the warm, bare flesh of his back.

"I haven't been able to think about anything but doing this since the last time we did this," he said against her mouth. "And that was too long ago."

They stopped again so he could pull her shirt over her head, but he didn't seem to have the patience for her bra. Instead of waiting for her to unclasp it, he pulled down the cups to expose her breasts. Bending his head, he ran his tongue over her nipple before dragging his teeth lightly over the taut skin. The fridge door was cold against her back and she had nowhere to go as he sucked hard enough to make her squirm.

Then she squealed so loudly she was thankful hers

was the only apartment on her floor as he crouched and bent her over his shoulder. Before she could really register what he was doing, he straightened and carried her toward the bed.

"Put me down," she said, trying not to laugh. "What the hell are you doing?"

"I can't wait," he said, slapping her ass with the hand not braced around the backs of her knees.

She'd barely bounced off the mattress before he was peeling her pants down her legs. His urgency inflamed her, and she caught her lip between her teeth as he tossed her clothes to the floor and then stripped himself down to nothing just as quickly. He tossed a condom from the back pocket on the bed before tossing his jeans away.

Then he joined her on the bed, his naked body covering hers. She wrapped her arms around him and pulled him down for a kiss. His tongue dipped between hers and she raked her fingernails up his back.

"I haven't thought about anything but this all day," he said against her mouth.

"And it was a very long day. So long."

His hand slipped between her legs and she hissed when his thumb danced over her clit. "Do you like that?"

She moaned, parting her legs as he slipped two fingers inside of her. "I don't hate it."

He had just moved his mouth to her breast and his chuckle vibrated against the sensitive flesh. His erection was full and hard against her thigh, and his fingers weren't enough. But he bit down on her nipple, just enough to hurt slightly, and she arched her back.

"Are you going to come for me?" He ran his tongue from her nipple up her throat.

"I want you inside me."

He kissed her, almost savagely, before drawing back so he could stand up. He pulled her to her feet and kissed her again before turning her to face the bed.

Splaying his fingers across the small of her back, he slowly pushed his hand up her spine with enough pressure to bend her over. She was aware of him grabbing the condom packet he'd tossed on the bed, and then his hand fisted in her hair and she moaned.

"Don't move," he said, his voice low and raspy.

Only a few seconds later, he ran his hands over her ass and she pushed back against them. She was running out of patience. Finally she felt the head of his cock against her, and she closed her eyes as he slowly filled her.

He scraped his fingernails down her back and she rocked slowly, taking him deeper each time. Then he braced one hand on her hip and bent down to kiss her spine. His other hand skimmed so lightly up her back it tickled, and she shivered. Then his fingers tightened in her hair again.

"Yes," she whispered. He drew back, almost fully, and then drove into her. She cried out, lowering her head. His hand was still clenching her hair, and it pulled with delicious pleasure. "Please, Scott."

He released her hair and straightened, bringing

his hands back to her hips. She moved, meeting him stroke for stroke, and she breathed in small, ragged breaths as the orgasm built up inside of her.

The intensity of it made her gasp and her hands balled into fists, clutching the comforter. Scott's fingers dug into her hips as he thrust into her, and then his body jerked. He groaned and then said her name in a low, ragged voice as his orgasm shook him. His hands slid up her back to her shoulders for one last hard thrust before he collapsed on top of her.

Bent over her bed, with his weight on top of her, Jamie was content to catch her breath and bask in the pleasure for a few minutes. Eventually, though, she started to feel the strain on her legs. "We're going to fall on the floor any second. Which is totally okay with me, but I figured I'd give you a heads-up."

"Tuck and roll," he said, and then he chuckled. After kissing the middle of her back, he stood and disposed of the condom while she dragged herself onto the bed.

The mattress dipped under his weight and then he was next to her, hauling her into his embrace. Sighing, she closed her eyes and soaked in the heat of his body. He was just taller enough than her so their bodies fit perfectly together, and she loved being so close to him.

His hand skimmed down her side and came to rest on her hip as he pressed a kiss to her hair. "I don't really have words for how much I enjoyed that. My thoughts are like comic book bubbles right now. Wow! Bam!"

"Kapow!" she said, and they laughed together.

He was so fun, she thought. Scott liked to laugh, and it was just one more thing on the list of things she liked about him. The list that seemed to get longer every time she was with him. She was going to have to start keeping a mental list of things she *didn't* like about him just to balance things out. Later, though. Right now, she couldn't think of a single thing to put on it.

SCOTT COULDN'T REMEMBER a time he'd felt so content. One of his favorite movies on the television, his sister's turkey tetrazzini in his stomach and Jamie stretched out against him on the couch. Spooning was the only way they both fit, and he didn't mind a bit.

It wasn't originally how he'd pictured things between him and Jamie going, since he was pretty sure they'd both gone into it planning to orgasm and run, so to speak. But, as much as he enjoyed the sex—and he *really* enjoyed it—he also enjoyed talking to her and watching television with her and, yes, even cuddling.

When she was silent through a particularly funny part of the movie, though, he craned his head over hers to see if she'd fallen asleep. Her eyes were open, but she didn't look amused. "Oh, come on. That was funny."

She reached back and slapped her hand on his hip. "I'm sorry, but this is one of the worst movies I've ever seen."

"Oh, come on." Scott waved his hand at the television screen. "This is a classic. How can you not love *Spaceballs*?"

"Up to this point, probably because I hadn't seen it."

He chuckled. "I couldn't believe it when I heard you tell Aidan you'd never seen it."

"I hate to disappoint you, but I don't really get it."

"It's a spoof." He and Aidan had watched the movie so many times when they were younger, they could practically act out the entire thing in a two-man show.

"A spoof of what?"

"Star Wars."

"I've never seen that, either."

"Okay, now you're just messing with me." He didn't think he'd ever met anybody who hadn't seen *Star Wars*. Maybe not all of them, and with varying opinions, but everybody had at least seen the original.

"I don't watch a lot of movies set in space, I guess. Although my dad loved that *Star Trek* series with the captain who always slept with the alien women even though it got him in trouble every single time."

"It's almost over, I promise." Which meant it was almost time for him to leave and he really didn't want to go.

"What time are you supposed to meet Aidan?" she asked, as if reading his mind.

"About nine." He tightened his arm around her waist and kissed her neck. "You should go with me."

"Yeah, right."

"Okay, not *with* me, but either a certain amount of time before or after me. We could have a beer. Shoot some pool."

She was quiet for a long moment. "I don't think we'd have a lot of luck hiding the afterglow from your family and your best friend right now."

Jamie was right, but he hated admitting it. And he wondered if this was how Aidan had felt when he first started seeing Lydia—having to hide out in his apartment because they didn't want anybody to see them and guess they'd been sleeping together. The difference, though, was that Aidan and Lydia had fallen in love and were going to be married in a few weeks. Maybe a casual fling was easier to hide.

"You sure you don't want to go?" he asked again forty minutes later, when he was standing at her door to kiss her goodbye.

"I'm sure."

"What are you doing tomorrow?" He was having a hard time making himself leave until he knew when he'd see her again.

"I have some errands to do. And I might go see some friends."

He tucked a strand of hair behind her ear. "So you're busy, then?"

"Yeah." She sighed and then gave him a tiny smile. "I like having some time between you leaving my bed and me seeing you at work, you know? And before we know it, I'll be moving on and you'll be back on the search for your television wife. I don't want to get too used to having you around."

That, he understood. He could already feel himself getting used to being around her and it felt good. "Again with the television wife thing. The guys are idiots, I swear."

She laughed. "It's pretty funny, though, imagining you married to a June Cleaver type."

Rather than explain again that the guys had taken what he'd said and exaggerated it to a ridiculous degree, Scott just shrugged. "I should buy some button-down sweaters or whatever those things are called."

Smiling, she leaned forward and kissed him. He put his hands on her waist and held her for a moment, deepening the kiss and making it last until she pulled away. "You should go. Aidan's going to be wondering if you stood him up."

"I'll see you at work, then."

Scott walked to Kincaid's Pub, since he'd walked from home to Aidan's place, and then to Jamie's. It was definitely a lot more walking than he was used to, but he chalked it up as good exercise and it meant there was no chance of somebody seeing his car parked outside of her building. Several times, he thought about sending a text telling Aidan something had come up so he wouldn't make it and circling back to Jamie's. But then he'd have to come up with a lie when Aidan asked him what had come up, and Jamie might not welcome his return.

He paused with his hand on the door of the bar,

taking a second to get his head straight. *I don't want to get too used to having you around.*

Her words echoing through his mind, along with remembering the look in her eyes when she said them, didn't help him sort out his own thoughts. It seemed as if she might be feeling the same thing he was—wanting to keep their relationship in a nice little box separate from the rest of their lives, but not finding the box so easy to seal and shove under the bed. He spent way too much time wishing he was with her for that to happen, and he wasn't sure if he hoped she felt the same, or if he needed her to have willpower for both of them.

The door opened and an exiting customer almost walked into him, putting an end to his sidewalk introspection. He stepped out of the way as three guys left, and then walked inside. Lydia was at the bar, and she lifted her hand in greeting when she saw him. He headed toward the bar, giving a wave to his dad and Fitz in the corner. They were deep in a conversation with some other old-timer, so they barely acknowledged him.

And Aidan was sitting at the end of the bar, as far from the old guys as he could get without turning the corner to the side with no stools. Scott sat next to him, smiling at his sister when she set a frosted mug of beer on a coaster in front of him.

"Thanks. Slow night?"

She shrugged. "Not busy, but we've had enough customers to make the time go by. Not that it matters since my guy's here with me."

He watched his sister give Aidan the kind of smile and eye contact that most men would have killed to be on the receiving end of, and then took a few gulps of his beer. The Celtics were playing, so he turned his attention to the basketball game on the big TV.

"They're not having a good night," Aidan said after Lydia walked away.

Scott snorted. "Yeah, because they're not playing hockey."

"You get all your stuff done this evening?"

For a few seconds, Scott was confused. But then he remembered he told them he had things to do when he left their apartment earlier, only saying he'd meet Aidan later at the bar. "Yeah."

His friend nodded, drumming his fingers on the bar. Scott knew it meant Aidan had something on his mind he was reluctant to talk about, and he knew it had to do with Jamie. And Aidan wouldn't ask and Scott wouldn't tell, so that conversational train had reached the end of the rails.

"I talked to my dad about the pool table," Scott said, hoping to change the subject.

Aidan chuckled and stopped drumming. "I heard all about it. We have to put some kind of insulation down to protect the felt from hot dishes, and then plastic to protect it from any spills. Then a tablecloth so it looks nice."

"He'll probably be the one spilling stuff because he keeps lifting the tablecloth to check on the felt."

They both laughed, and Aidan started telling him about some of the wedding plans. They'd decided on an open bar for beer, soft drinks and coffee, but a cash bar for anybody wanting liquor. And they were leaning toward a potluck situation rather than having the cook trying to keep the guests fed.

While Aidan talked, Scott thought about the day he'd figured out his best friend and his sister had been lying to him. Lying by omission, maybe, but he'd been hurt and pissed and felt stupid and betrayed. He'd gotten over it. He loved both of them too much not to, especially when he'd thought about how much Aidan had stood to lose. It was Lydia on one side, and the guy's best friend, his father figure and mentor, and possibly his ability to stay with his engine company on the other. It was hard to hold a grudge against a guy who loved a woman so much he'd risk everything important to him to be with her.

But it had hurt at the time, and he didn't want Aidan to be in that position. It wouldn't be as personal, because Aidan and Jamie didn't have a relationship other than at work, but hiding things from him didn't sit well with Scott.

"Hey, where'd you go?" Aidan asked, bumping his arm.

"Sorry, my mind wandered."

"I can't believe you have anything more important to think about than Lydia's concern that if we just put *potluck* on the invitation that we'll get fifteen slow cookers of chili and one pan of brownies." He rolled his eyes, but then threw an affectionate smile at his fiancée, who was pulling a pint of Guinness for a customer at the other end of the bar.

"That happened at Mrs. Eames's funeral, remember? Except it was like ten pots of baked beans and a vegetable platter." Scott grimaced. "That was a function hall that could have used better ventilation."

"We're open to suggestions."

He shrugged. "I'm the best man, not the wedding planner. But maybe if you add a note there aren't any outlets for Crock-Pots, you can avoid getting too much chili. Nobody's going to start stringing extension cords together at Tommy's bar."

The wedding talk went on for the rest of the night, with a few digressions into basketball, and Lydia joined in when she wasn't busy. They laughed a lot, and Scott found himself relaxing into the familiar rhythm of his life.

The only thing that would have made the night more enjoyable would be Jamie sitting next to him.

TEN

JAMIE SKIRTED THE edge of the scene, keeping an eye on the action around them as they worked on repacking their equipment. It hadn't been a particularly bad motor vehicle accident, but there were four cars involved and the intersection was a mess.

Police officers were managing to squeak one lane at a time around the two cars still waiting for tow trucks, and the ambulances had already departed. Jeff, Grant and Gavin were helping a couple of guys from the city who'd been nearby to sweep up broken glass, and she estimated they were only about twenty minutes from being able to return to quarters.

Usually she paid little attention to the clock other than taking note of the time for paperwork when necessary. Today, though, she was counting the hours until the tour was over. For the last two weeks, she and Scott had fallen into a comfortable rhythm of keeping their distance at work, and then hanging out in her apartment. Sex, talking, movies, food, books, music, card games, more sex.

But tomorrow they were going out on a date. A real date, not in her apartment, and she couldn't wait.

They were going on a nice, long drive to a South Shore restaurant Scott liked, right on the water. As much as she enjoyed curling up with him in sweatpants to watch television, getting to dress up a little and go out in public with him would be a welcome and long-overdue change.

She'd told him the night they'd watched that stupid space movie that she didn't want to get too used to having him around. She'd meant it at the time, but it hadn't worked. She'd not only gotten used to having him around, but she was happier when he was with her.

Only being with him in her apartment was growing old, though, so she hadn't even hesitated when he invited her to take a ride out of the city with him so they could go to a real restaurant.

Laughter drew her attention from what she was doing, and she looked over her shoulder to see Scott and Aidan laughing as they knelt next to the truck, repacking their first aid supplies. She wasn't close enough to hear what they were talking about, but it was obviously amusing.

She loved watching Scott with Aidan and the other guys. Mostly with Aidan, though. So many facets of his personality came through during his interactions with them, maybe because they worked together in a professional capacity, but the nature of their jobs made them almost family. He often played mentor to the younger guys, and he respected the older ones.

But it was seeing him with Aidan that always made her smile, even if she had to stifle it for work. They were a lot alike, though Scott was more intense while Aidan more laid-back. She wondered sometimes if Scott's reputation for being a hothead came mostly from being contrasted to his best friend.

Of course, there had been that fight the first night she went to Kincaid's Pub, but overall he'd either mellowed a lot lately or his temper hadn't been as bad as people said it was.

"Hey, LT," Aidan called, and she wasn't sure if he was talking to her or to Rick. Technically, she was their lieutenant and not him, but nobody had used the nickname for her yet.

Both of them were looking straight at her, though, so she walked over to them. "What's up?"

"What's your opinion on cake?" Aidan asked.

"I'm in favor of cake."

He laughed and stood, swinging one of the first aid bags over his shoulder while Scott did the same. "I mean wedding cake. Ashley wants to make a carrot cake because she says it's traditional."

She wrinkled her nose. "Chocolate coming from cocoa beans is as close as I like to come to vegetables in my desserts."

"See?" Scott nudged Aidan with his elbow. "I told you she had good taste in cake."

They both gave her approving looks and, even though it was stupid, it made her feel good. "Don't some couples do two cakes now? Like a big wedding cake and then a groom's cake?"

"I suggested that," Scott said. "And I got an earful about how all the men have to do is show up in suits and…there was more, but I tuned it out, to be honest."

"Every time I say that everybody would rather have chocolate cake than carrot cake," Aidan said, "Lydia shakes her head and mutters *men* under her breath."

The lightbulb went off in Jamie's head. "Ah. And because I'm a woman, you think if I suggest the chocolate cake, she might listen to me."

"At this point, I'm willing to do anything I have to do to keep my wedding cake from having shredded carrots in it."

"I'll do what I can."

"You're the best," Aidan said, grinning.

And Scott winked at her. "Definitely the best."

She rolled her eyes at them and went back to what she was doing, ready to get out of there and back to quarters. It was time for some food and some rest, in that order.

Later, she lay in her bunk, almost wishing the alarm would sound just to give her some way to pass the time other than staring at the ceiling. But if the alarm sounded, that meant somebody was having a bad night, so she stopped short of hoping it actually happened.

Eventually, it was time to go home. After a long, hot soak in the tub, she forced herself to stretch out on her bed. It had been a slow night, but she'd been restless, so she actually slept for a while. Then she packed a bag and waited for Scott to show up.

"I thought it would never be time," he said once she'd let him in and he'd kissed her senseless.

"I was beginning to wonder if all the clocks were broken because they didn't seem to be moving." When they reached the top of the stairs and stepped inside, she grabbed the front of the blue button-down shirt he was wearing and hauled him close to kiss him again.

"I want you so much, but we have reservations. And it's a really cool restaurant." He stepped back to look at her. She'd thrown on a simple plum maxi dress for the occasion, but it had a scooped neckline and a deep slit on one side. "There are other restaurants, though. Or takeout. Hell, you must have something in the fridge."

Laughing, she stepped out of his reach. "Oh, no you don't. I've been looking forward to this date too much to stay home tonight, even if it means staying here with you."

"Then let's go, because my resistance gets a little weaker with every minute I can see that bed over your shoulder."

They took her car, though Scott drove. He said it was just as easy to walk to her place and there was the better gas mileage to consider, but she knew he went out of his way to make it so his truck was never parked in front of her building for very long. There were enough businesses around so he could explain away being parked there for an hour or so, if anybody asked, but not after hours.

When she wasn't gasping and clutching the door

handle as he worked through the city traffic, they spent the time talking, mostly about the television shows they both watched. A lot of couples probably would have talked about work, she thought, but they rarely did. She wasn't sure what was in his head, but for her it wasn't only the fact they worked together. Talking about work was a reminder to Jamie that they weren't supposed to be seeing each other, and the more time they spent together, the more that bothered her.

"I know it doesn't look like much," Scott said when he finally turned into the restaurant parking lot. "But trust me, the food is amazing. I don't get down here often, but it's my favorite place to eat."

It was one of the things she'd come to really like about Scott. He could have made a reservation at some fancy restaurant to impress her, but instead he was choosing to bring her to his favorite place, even if it looked a little sketchy from the outside.

Scott was that way about almost everything. He didn't pretend to like movies because he thought they were what she'd want to watch. The same with TV shows and magazines and food. He was willing to try almost anything, but his favorites were what they were and he didn't care what anybody thought of them.

Inside, the restaurant had a nice ambience, especially with the lights dimmed to help conceal the slightly shabby decor. But they were led to a private table at the back, in front of a bank of windows that overlooked the water, and she felt herself falling in love with the place.

"It's gorgeous," she said as the hostess put menus in front of them.

Scott grinned and looked out at the water. "I was young the first time we came here. My mom talked my dad into taking us all to the Cape for a weekend, because she was from there originally, and we stopped here on the way down. It was so good, we stopped on the way back, too. When I got my license, I couldn't remember the name to look up directions, but I came down and drove around until I found it."

"Seriously?" She leaned back in the booth, watching his face as he looked out the window. "Because the food was that good or because of your mom?"

He shrugged, turning back to her. "Both? I don't know. It was a happy memory. My parents got along for the whole weekend and it was the only family vacation I remember us ever taking. And the food was that good."

Jamie tried to imagine a teenage Scott, driving around looking for this place. His mom had died when he was nine and he would have been at least sixteen to have his license, so enough years had passed that she was surprised he'd found it. And it could have gone out of business or changed ownership and names. He must have really wanted to reconnect with the place.

"How often do you come here?"

"I try to get here a couple of times a year. It's been a while, though. The last time I was here I brought

Ashley not long after she and Danny split up, just to get her out of the neighborhood for a day. The time before that I think it was me and Aidan and Rick."

"Family, huh? I thought maybe this was your hot date spot," she said, half-jokingly.

"Nope."

That was all he said, but the way he looked directly into her eyes when he said it seemed to give her the answer she'd been fishing for. He wasn't in the habit of bringing girlfriends here, then. So was this simply a two-birds-with-one-stone situation—take her on a date out of the city while revisiting a favorite restaurant?

Or did bringing her to this place that was so important to him he'd gone looking for it as a teenager mean something?

SCOTT LOOKED ACROSS the table at Jamie and, maybe for the first time in his life except for his mom, wished everything could be different.

He wished he and Jamie didn't work together. That their relationship didn't have to be a secret. That he was the kind of guy she would want to have a real relationship with, and that she didn't think he was on the hunt for some kind of television wife who'd stay home and bake cookies while raising their children. When he looked into Jamie's eyes, he could almost see his future…if only their present wasn't so screwed up.

When she gave him a questioning look, he realized his thoughts might be showing on his face and smiled. All that mattered right now was the fact he was sitting in his favorite restaurant with a woman who could set his blood on fire with just a look or a single word.

"What's good here?" she asked, picking up one of the menus.

"Not to be unoriginal or anything, but definitely the seafood."

He already knew he was having that, so he watched Jamie as she read over the menu. Her face was expressive, and he could tell when something sounded appealing to her and when something didn't.

Their server arrived to introduce herself and take their drink orders. Jamie ordered a glass of white wine from their limited list, and Scott asked for an orange soda. While they waited for the drinks, they decided to split the seafood platter and a big basket of fries.

Once they'd placed their order, Jamie sipped her wine and looked out the window, her face relaxed and happy. "I can see why you like to come here. I'm surprised it's not overrun by tourists, though."

"It's just far enough off the beaten path, I guess. And it's a word-of-mouth kind of place. It's been busier since people started using those restaurant review apps, though. There's no hiding from the internet."

"I'm glad you were able to get a reservation for this table. It has the best view."

"It's too bad I have to go with Aidan tomorrow to pick out suits. Otherwise I would also have reserved us a nice hotel room down the street with a deck facing the ocean." He looked at her over the rim of his glass, wanting her so much his body ached. "Maybe I could tell him I'm sick."

"You can't call in sick to best-man duties for your best friend," she said, laughing. "Besides, I'm going shopping with your sisters tomorrow and I suspect I'm going to need a good night's sleep to get through that."

"Shopping? Didn't you just go shopping?"

"Yeah, but for groceries. We're going shopping for dresses."

He laughed and held up a hand. "Okay, I should have guessed that. How the hell did you get roped into dress shopping with my sisters?"

"I didn't get roped into anything. *My friend* invited me to help her and her sister pick out dresses for her wedding."

"That's weird."

She frowned at him. "Taking friends wedding dress shopping with you is weird? For a guy who grew up with two older sisters, sometimes you don't seem to know a lot about women."

"No, not the shopping. Women shop in packs. It's just a little weird that Lydia's my sister. And Lydia's your friend. But there's no three of us together. Does that make sense?"

She nodded. "Yeah, it does. It's weird for me, too. It's like living two separate lives, but the lives intersect in multiple places."

"Yeah." He paused and then smiled at her. "Don't forget to mention the cake thing, okay?"

"I'll do my best to save us all from cake with vegetables in it. But in return I want you to tell me something. What made you decide to take a break from dating?"

The question seemed to come out of left field and he mentally flailed for a few seconds, trying to come up with an answer that might make sense. "It was a lot of things, I guess. Part of it's probably just a natural progression of life. I'm almost thirty, so there's that. It's time to starting thinking about the future and all that. But the last woman I had what I'd consider a real relationship with started asking a lot of questions about my benefits and whether they'd cover plastic surgery. And she said if she got pregnant, I'd have to marry her and put her on my bennies plan."

When Jamie's eyebrows shot up and her lips tightened, he almost laughed. She was angry on his behalf, and he liked knowing that. "Are you serious? Did she have absolutely no self-respect at all?"

"I don't know, but I do know she didn't respect *me*. And I do have some self-respect, so that was the end of that relationship. And I realized I didn't have a great track record when it came to asking out women who I'd want to spend more than a few weeks with. If that long."

"So you thought the best way to find the right woman was to stop dating?"

He laughed, feeling more than a little stupid. "I needed to take a step back and rethink how I went about dating, I guess. Stop hanging out in clubs and stuff like that. When spending the rest of your life with a woman is the objective instead of having sex with her that night, you have to break the behavior patterns and start over."

Jamie leaned forward and propped her chin on her hands, the candlelight reflecting in her eyes. "What made you break your temporary vow of abstinence for me?"

He froze, terrified by what might come out of his mouth. The seconds ticked by as he sorted words in his head, trying to separate what he wanted to say from what he didn't. What he didn't want to say was that, if their circumstances had been different, she might have been the woman he'd broken the cycle to find. That was a lot of depth to throw at a casual friends-with-benefits situation.

"Probably the same thing that made you break your rules about having sex with a guy in your company," he said finally. "We have insane chemistry and I wanted you so much I couldn't resist you."

The blush across her cheeks was faint, but he didn't miss it. "We certainly do have chemistry."

"Okay, fair's fair," he said, wanting to change the subject away from his feelings and more toward hers. "Lydia told me you moved here with a guy—and for the record, I didn't ask her and it just came up in conversation one day—so what made you stay in Boston when he left? Why wasn't he the one?"

She sighed and leaned back in her chair. "We

started talking about the future and hypothetical kids. I said I thought eighteen months between having hypothetical number one and getting pregnant with hypothetical number two would be ideal. I'd have time to get back in shape and get back on the job for a while before having the second."

"And he disagreed?"

"He assumed I'd give up my career and stay home with the little hypotheticals."

"Was his expectation that you would have given up *any* career to be a stay-at-home mom, or was it because you're a firefighter?"

"It was mostly about me being a firefighter." She swirled the liquid in her glass, watching it with an expression he couldn't quite read. It wasn't sadness, really, or annoyance. Maybe both. "If I'd been a teacher or a lawyer or something, I think he might not have been so adamant about it."

"And you wouldn't quit if you had a baby?" He almost recoiled from the look she gave him. "I'm not saying I think you should. But you know I lost my mom when I was a kid. I know how shitty that is, so my kids having a mother in a high-risk job is something that would make me nervous."

She met his gaze across the table, her eyebrows furrowed. "I've heard it's pretty shitty for kids to have their dads die, too, but nobody thinks twice about guys running into a burning building."

"Is there any way for me to say I think it's different without sounding like a sexist asshole?"

"No, not really." After a few seconds, she leaned back and her expression softened. "I get it, though. I know you're not a sexist asshole and I know most people have a harder time with moms having dangerous jobs. But I know how well I do my job and how safely I do it so, when I meet the right guy, I'm going to get married and have children without sacrificing my career."

When I meet the right guy. Because she hadn't yet, of course. If she had, she wouldn't be killing time with him. Ignoring the sharp jab of regret because this was what he'd signed up for, he looked at her across the table. She was staring at him, her gaze boring into him as if willing him to say something.

"He'll be a lucky guy," he said, lifting his glass in a mock toast.

She frowned slightly and her lips parted as if she was going to speak. Then she took a deep breath and lifted her own glass to take a sip of her wine.

The server arriving with their food put an end to their conversation and Scott wasn't sorry. It hadn't been going anywhere good, and he didn't want this night ruined by him being envious of a guy Jamie hadn't even met yet.

"There's no way we can eat all this," Jamie said.

He looked at the paper-lined baskets of all sorts of fried seafood and fries, and grinned. "Maybe not, but we can put one hell of a dent in it."

They talked while they ate. Not about anything serious, since they seemed to have both had their fill of that, but about the other guys in the company. The upcoming wedding. And, of course, about Ashley and Danny's pregnancy.

"I can't wait," he confessed. "They said they're not going to find out if the baby's a boy or a girl, which is killing me."

"Are you hoping for a boy?" she asked. "The next generation of kick-ass, sports-loving, hot-tempered Kincaids?"

He grinned. "You think if I have a niece, she won't be a kick-ass, sports-loving, hot-tempered Kincaid?"

"True." She shook her head, laughing. "Maybe she'll be like her aunt Lydia."

"Danny's a pretty levelheaded guy, unless he's pushed too far. And Ashley's a lot more like Mom than Lydia and I are. We definitely got Tommy's genes in a higher concentration. But, boy or girl, I can't wait."

They lingered a lot longer over dinner than he'd anticipated, and by the time they were in her car and headed back into the city, it was late. Throw in traffic due to drivers rubbernecking a minor accident, and it was very late by the time they got off the highway.

"Your sisters want me ready at a ridiculously early hour," she said, and he could hear the regret in her voice. "I think Lydia has to work in the afternoon, which means morning shopping."

"We're not hitting the suit place early, but I told Aidan I'd meet him for breakfast."

"I hate the idea of you walking this late. Maybe we should head to your place and I'll drop you off there and drive myself home."

He wanted to make love to her in the worst way, but he knew she was right. If he went home with her, it was going to be at least a couple of hours before they were done for the night. And then he'd either have a late walk home or he'd have to get up very early in the morning to do it.

"I guess since it's our first date, I'll let you kiss me good-night," he said, turning his head to smile at her in the lights of the streetlamps.

He pulled up on the street behind his house. Not only would he have quick access to the stairs in the back, but she'd be pointed in the right direction to head home. After undoing his seat belt, he leaned across the center console to kiss her.

Ending the kiss was almost painful, but they'd both be sorry if they didn't go straight to bed and go to sleep. "Thanks for going down there with me."

"Thanks for inviting me." She smiled, running her thumb across his bottom lip. "It's a special place."

"Yeah." He put his hand on the door pull, since sitting on the side of the street wasn't any better a plan than going to her place. "Text me when you get home so I know you made it. And let me know how the shopping trip goes."

"I will." She got out of the car and walked around to the driver's side. After another kiss good-night, she slid into the seat.

"And, Jamie, don't forget the cake."

She was laughing when he closed the door, and he waited to duck between the buildings until she'd turned the corner. After a final wave, he walked to his dad's backyard and climbed the stairs to his apartment.

He should have left a light on for himself, he thought. Maybe then the place wouldn't feel so lonely.

ELEVEN

Since Lydia and Ashley both planned to make breakfast for their guys before hitting the mall, Jamie made herself a breakfast sandwich on an English muffin in the morning. She wasn't much of a breakfast eater and preferred to wait a few hours before a meal, but she'd learned on the job to eat when she had the chance.

After throwing on jeans and a T-shirt with a light hoodie, along with her comfortable walking sneakers, she steeled her nerves for the drive to the mall. She'd been tempted to ask them to swing by and pick her up, but then they would have had to backtrack. And she was trying to learn the neighborhood while sharpening her Boston driving skills. She couldn't do that while riding around as a passenger in somebody else's car, and even that was scary sometimes.

After parking in front of the store entrance they'd told her to meet them at, she locked her car and headed across the parking lot. It was already more crowded than she'd expected, considering the mall had just opened. Lydia and Ashley were sitting on a bench, drinking out of paper cups, and they waved when they saw her.

"We weren't sure you were coming," Lydia said.

"Sorry I'm late," she said, thankful it was only by fifteen minutes. "I still don't have the hang of driving here. I swear, I can drive to the same place six times and it will take me a different amount of time to get there each time I go. Is there a bridal shop here?"

"Oh, I'm not doing a gown. I just want something nice, like a cocktail dress, maybe. Fancy, but not too formal. There are some high-end stores in this mall that might have something."

"We're trying *not* to do all the small boutique stores," Ashley said. "We don't have time for that and I don't want to walk that much."

In the second store, they found Ashley's dress. It was a fit-and-flare style in a dark emerald that suited her figure and coloring as though it had been designed just for her. They were about to give up on the mall when Lydia pulled a dress off a rack and they all sighed. A cream-colored sheath with a cream lace overlay, it was elegant and simple, but not plain. It was very Lydia and when she tried it on, Jamie wasn't surprised when Ashley got teary-eyed.

Jamie watched the sisters bond over the dress, remembering going through this moment with each of her sisters. They'd both had big weddings, so the process had been a lot more grueling for her, but the emotional payoff was the same.

"What are you wearing?" Ashley asked, looking at Jamie while they waited for the dress to be put into a garment bag.

Her eyes widened. "Me? I don't know yet. And nobody cares what I'm wearing."

"When's the last time you dressed up?" Lydia asked.

"I don't know. I went to a promotion ceremony not too long ago. And there was a plaque dedication."

"No," Lydia said. "I'm not talking about dressing up for work. I'm talking about dressing up for fun. My wedding's going to be fun."

"You know, I went to a firefighter's wedding once where they wore their Class A uniform," Jamie said. "Everybody matched. It was great, and I'm sure the pictures were stunning."

Lydia snorted. "Nobody's wearing their dress uniforms to my wedding. Even if the chief gave permission for the guys—and you, of course—to wear them, which even as a favor for my dad would be questionable because we're getting married in a bar and there will be drinking, we all live and breathe the fire department enough without it being the theme of my wedding."

"So what you're saying is that I need to start thinking about what I'm going to wear."

"Yes, you do." Lydia pointed a finger at her, which made her laugh. "You all have it easy every day. Your T-shirts and uniform pants and boots. Turnout gear. Even when you guys dress up, there are rules and a specific uniform. When you're off duty, you still wear the T-shirts and all you have to decide is sweatpants or jeans. Maybe cargo shorts in the summer. You're dressing up, Jamie."

“You should get a dress today,” Ashley said.

“Yes,” Lydia agreed. “And if I have to wear heels, you have to wear heels.”

Half an hour later, Jamie stood in front of a mirror and frowned at the dark navy dress. It fit well and it was comfortable. It was made from some kind of jersey material that had a mock wrap waist and deep V-neck, with three-quarter sleeves she liked. Logically she knew it looked good on her and it certainly suited her more than the floral number Ashley made her try on or the red strapless number she’d vetoed while it was still on the hanger.

There was cleavage, though. And leg. A *lot* of leg.

She took a picture of her reflection with her phone and, after looking at it for a few seconds, texted it to her older sister, Carrie. Her younger sister, Tori, was probably the most fashionable of them, but Carrie was the most honest. Plus Tori and her family would probably be at church.

Yes or no?

Yes. The response was almost immediate. Definitely yes, but what’s the occasion?

A wedding. It’s not too fitted?

Enough time passed so she assumed Carrie gave the dress a second look. It looks perfect on you. Do you have a date for the wedding? If you don't, you will once you get there.

I'm shopping with friends, so can't talk now. I'll call soon.

I see that you dodged the question. Have fun and talk later.

"I can see under the door and your feet aren't moving, so I know you've got the dress on," Lydia said. "Stop looking in the mirror and come out here so we can tell you if you should like it."

Barely managing to keep from rolling her eyes, Jamie stepped out into the hall of the dressing room area. "Have I mentioned how much I hate dress shopping?"

"Oh, that's totally the one," Ashley said, and Lydia nodded. "You have the perfect body for that dress. You're in great shape, but not too thin. And you've got the boobs for it."

Jamie looked down at herself. "And everybody will know I have the boobs for it, too."

"That's the point. And I'm pretty sure everybody already knows you have breasts."

"I don't generally put them on display, though."

"Of course not, but you won't be at work," Lydia said. "And they're not really on display, since you only see a little bit of cleavage. I think it's just that the cut is really flattering on you and you're not used to that fit."

"You have great legs, too," Ashley added. "Scott would like that one on you."

Jamie froze, not sure what to say to that. Almost any denial of Scott's opinion being relevant would skirt too close to lying to them for her comfort. But as far she knew, Scott hadn't told his sisters anything about their relationship and, if they were fishing, she didn't want to take the bait.

"Stop, Ash," Lydia said. "We're all supposed to pretend we don't know she and Scott have been sleeping together for three weeks."

"Oh, that's right." Ashley looked at her, tilting her head as if giving the dress serious consideration. "That neckline means jewelry, though."

"Are you wearing your hair up or down?" Lydia asked.

"Down," Jamie said. She was confused, but she let them change the subject because it bought her time to figure out how she felt about Scott's sisters knowing what they were up to.

It was probably stupid or naive for them to think Lydia and Ashley hadn't caught on to their relationship. Even though they were rarely all together, they saw Scott often enough to guess he had somebody in his life he wasn't talking about. And she was pretty sure Aidan knew—or at least had strong suspicions—but based on Lydia's silence on the issue, Jamie had assumed he hadn't shared them with her.

"Do you know what the mother of the groom is wearing?" she asked Lydia. "I know you're not really doing colors, but I don't want to step on anybody's look."

There was an awkward pause, and then Lydia waved off the question. "Aidan didn't invite his family. We're going to tell them we eloped and do a wedding brunch or something with them later."

"Oh." Jamie wasn't sure what she was supposed to say to that. He was always so solid and laid-back that she'd never guessed Aidan might have family issues. "Sorry about that."

"It's nothing bad. They're very…*very* white-collar and don't understand why Aidan took the career path he did and they're not shy about voicing their feelings. We don't think they'd enjoy themselves."

"They're really snotty and treat him like crap," Ashley said. "And his whole family would just sit in the corner of the bar all night and judge everybody Aidan loves."

"That's it in a nutshell," Lydia said. "He gave it a lot of thought and decided it would be easier on everybody and better for their relationship in the long run if we fudge the truth just a little."

Jamie couldn't imagine getting married without her family, but they didn't treat her like crap over a job, either. "And you'll get a free brunch out of it, since it would be poor form of them not to pay the bill."

Lydia laughed. "That's what Scotty said, too. Free food."

"I want free food. I'm starving," Ashley said, putting an end to the conversation. "After you pay for that dress, because you're totally buying it, we should have an early lunch before Lydia has to go back to work."

"You're always starving," Lydia replied. "And don't even tell me you're eating for two. The only way that excuse works for your current appetite is if you're having septuplets."

They decided on a burger place in the food court for convenience's sake, all of them laughing when Lydia pointed out they couldn't do it often or they wouldn't fit in the new dresses they'd run out to the cars.

"I'm not very hungry, anyway," Jamie said, once they'd carried their trays to a nearby table. "I had the best seafood ever last night and I ate so much, I swear I'm still full."

They both paused in the act of putting condiments on their burgers to stare at her. Jamie replayed the words in her head, but she didn't think she'd said anything remotely stareworthy. She'd had seafood for dinner. So what?

Ashley replaced her top bun, but didn't pick up her burger. "Nice little place? South Shore? On the water?"

She should have known spending half the day with Scott's sisters wasn't going to end well. But she'd hoped they'd be so wrapped up in dresses and wedding plans that they'd barely pay attention to her. "I… Crap. Please don't make this a thing."

"It could be a thing," Lydia said. "In fact, we can't figure out why it's *not* a thing."

"Because sometimes there's chemistry between two people who, number one, shouldn't have a relationship for professional reasons and, number two, have different ideas of what their futures will hold."

"You don't want a family?" Ashley asked. "Not that there's anything wrong with that. I guess we just make assumptions, you know."

"I do want a family. But I don't intend to give up my career when I have kids." She shrugged and dipped a French fry in the small paper cup of ketchup on her tray. "Other people think mothers shouldn't risk themselves in dangerous jobs, even though it's okay for fathers to do it."

"You already know he mostly grew up without our mother," Lydia said. "That's probably a big part of it. But it's kind of a pervasive way of thinking in the neighborhood, too, you know? It's old-fashioned and tightly knit. He was raised in a community of alpha guys, really, where the wives and children kept the home fires burning."

"That's not a great metaphor," Ashley said, and they all laughed. "I do agree with it, though. He probably has certain expectations of his future wife, but expectations change. He respects the hell out of you, Jamie. All the guys do."

"We can be a stubborn family," Lydia said, "but we come around."

"Danny getting hurt hit all the guys pretty hard, but Scott was the worst. It's all tangled up, you know? The brotherhood, the friendship and the family ties." Ashley paused, running her finger around the rim of her water glass. "You wouldn't believe how happy and excited he was when we told him I was pregnant. Seriously, it's like being an uncle is going to be the best thing that ever happened to him."

Jamie smiled, not having any trouble imagining his joy. He lit up whenever he talked about his sisters, and whenever he mentioned his future niece or nephew, he practically beamed. She'd seen it last night at the restaurant, and she would have loved to have seen his reaction when he first heard the news.

"I think that's why he had such a hard time," Ashley continued. "Because the fire was so soon after we told him. When he realized Danny hadn't come out of the structure with the rest of the company, I guess it was pretty bad and it stuck with him for a while. I mean, he's Scotty, so he tried to hide it and crack jokes and stuff, but it was there. He didn't want my baby coming into the world without a dad, I guess."

"It weighed on his mind a lot," Lydia agreed. "Losing Mom and the possibility of that little peanut losing its daddy before he or she's even born shook him up. Hell, it shook all of us up, but Scotty's a smart guy. When push comes to shove, he's not going to walk away from something he wants because of the risk. If that was in his nature, he wouldn't be a firefighter."

"We haven't seen you guys together as a couple, obviously," Ashley said. "But we like you. And we like how Scotty is right now. As his oldest sister, it's a big deal when I say I'd really like to see you guys be a thing."

But how hard was Jamie willing to push? And did he want a future with her enough to compromise, or was she simply a spill he'd taken off the no-dating bandwagon?

Her phone chimed, saving her from having to respond to Ashley. But she sighed when she saw the message from Scott. The guy had seriously bad timing. Are you done shopping yet?

God, she hoped so. If she didn't get out of here soon, she was going to end up spilling her guts to his sisters and then things would get messy. We found dresses. Refueling now. You?

We didn't have to shop because Lydia picked our suits. But we've been measured in uncomfortable places and won't look like ragamuffins at the wedding.

She laughed, belatedly realizing Scott's sisters were both watching her. "Sorry."

"If that's my brother, ask him if they're done with the suits," Lydia said.

"Uh." Jamie hesitated before the realization sunk in that it would be nothing short of stupid to even try to pretend at this point. With them, anyway. "He said they won't look like ragamuffins, so I assume they're all set."

"Tell him they need ties, too. They're going to try to sneak parts of their uniform past me because they're lazy."

Your sister said to get a tie. No uniform ties.

There was a long pause before the response came through. She knows I'm texting you?

Please. Have you met your sisters? She appreciated that the two women had obviously gone out of their way to play along and give them space, but the gig was up.

Fine. We'll get ties. Call me later. Oh, and don't forget the cake.

Smiling, she tucked her phone away. "So, Lydia, have you done any cake tastings?"

"Oh, for God's sake, carrot cake is not a vegetable." She pointed a French fry at Jamie. "You might be part of the whole firefighter brotherhood thing, but don't let those two yahoos drag you onto their side."

"Can I ask why you just don't have a chocolate groom's cake?"

She blew out an exasperated breath. "Because that will be the groom's cake, not my wedding cake. I want my husband to share our wedding cake with me, but he's not going to if there's a chocolate cake sitting next to it."

"Okay." Jamie nodded slowly. "So this is one of those stubborn Kincaid things and Aidan's going to eat his vegetables and like it."

"Yes." Lydia shrugged. "He knew what he was getting into."

Ashley laughed, and then waved her hand at them. "I love this. This dynamic, I guess you could say. Jamie's our perfect third."

Below the warm feeling that came from being so openly accepted was a cold jangle of nerves. The genie was out of the bottle now, and she wasn't going to be able to shove him back in. Her and Scott's time of quietly, privately enjoying each other's company with no expectations was over.

She had no doubt his sisters were going to try to make it a *thing*.

MY DAD'S OFF with Fitz somewhere until late. Want to come to my place for a change?

Scott sent the text and tried not to hold his breath as he waited for Jamie's answer. He knew she'd had an exhausting morning with his sisters, and they'd just seen each other the night before, but he really wanted to see her again. And he wanted to see her in his apartment for some reason he didn't care to analyze too closely.

Sounds good. It'll be about an hour, though, if that works.

Perfect. See you then.

He exhaled and then looked around. Luckily, the place didn't look too bad since he didn't have a lot of clutter and he'd learned over the years of sharing a small space with a lot of guys to pick up after himself. But he did change the sheets because it seemed like the gentlemanly thing to do.

Then he dropped onto the couch and started flipping through channels so when she did show up, she wouldn't catch him with his face pressed to the glass sliding door, waiting for her. Even when he heard her footsteps on the wooden deck, he kept his eyes on the screen until she knocked on the glass.

He wasn't sure what he trying to prove to himself by acting casual, because on the inside he was jumping up and down like a black Lab whose human had finally come home.

"Hey, come on in," he said, pulling open the slider for her. Before closing it, he peeked down into the driveway. "You didn't walk, did you?"

"You walk all the time. But no, I drove. Unlike your jacked-up truck with the fancy chrome and firefighter plate, my car's just another gray compact job parked on the street. It blends in with the crowd."

After he closed the slider, he took her hand and pulled her close. "My truck is not jacked up."

"It came that way?"

"It's a stock three-quarter-ton pickup and the chrome came with the package that included the heated seats and remote start."

"Okay, so you're not one of those macho truck guys. Just spoiled a little bit."

He laughed. "Macho truck guys? No, I'm not. And as for being spoiled, I spend enough time freezing my ass off on the job. When I get in my truck, my ass is warm."

She ran her hands down his back and then tucked her fingers into the back pockets of his jeans. "It's definitely an ass worth pampering a little."

He kissed her, feeling the curve of her smile against his lips. Her hair was up in a ponytail, but without taking his mouth off hers, he pulled the fabric-covered elastic free so he could bury his hand in the soft strands. He loved her hair and it would probably have been the hardest part of her to resist touching at work if she didn't keep it braided whenever they were on duty.

When the kiss was over, she sidestepped him and looked around the apartment. "You don't really have a lot of knickknack-type stuff, do you?"

"No, but neither do you."

She ran her hand over the granite bar, looking at the kitchen. "I've moved so many times, I've learned to travel light. But you've lived in this house for your entire life. Maybe not on this floor, but still."

"Trust me, there are boxes and boxes with my name written on them down in the cellar. You want a drink?"

"I'll have a soda. Whatever you've got."

He took out a couple of cans and popped the top on hers before holding it out to her. "How was dress shopping?"

"It was more fun than I thought it would be, actually. I'm not big on shopping, but Lydia and Ashley are a lot of fun."

He winced. "I guess they're also more intuitive than I gave them credit for."

"There wasn't much point in denying anything, although I did manage to avoid being pinned down too much, conversationally."

Scott really wanted to know what they'd said, but then again a part of him didn't. If they'd done a full-court press on her and wanted to talk love and marriage, pushing her for details might get awkward. He didn't want her first time in his apartment to go sideways on him.

"I honestly don't know if I've ever successfully kept a secret from those two," he said.

"So everybody must know, then, if they do. At the station, I mean."

"I don't think so. Aidan and Danny, probably." He paused. "Okay, Aidan almost definitely, though he's never asked and I've never confirmed or denied. But if you're worried they're all talking about us, don't. Family loyalty still comes first."

"Do you think Tommy knows? He's family."

"I doubt it. He'd have to figure it out on his own because he's the last person my sisters would talk to about my personal life. He can be a bit of a bull in a china shop when it comes to shit like that, and Lydia and Ashley don't usually throw me under the bus with him."

She sighed, and then gave a little shrug. "It doesn't matter. People can say what they want."

Wanting to bring the mood back to where it had started, Scott set his soda on the counter and moved closer to her. She took a long sip of hers, and after she put down the can, he pulled her hard up against his body.

"You gonna dance with me at the wedding?"

She smiled at him, and he felt the familiar rush of pleasure he got every time she looked at him like that. "I don't know. What do you think the chances are you can keep your hands where they're supposed to be?"

He cupped her ass, squeezing a little. "I can behave."

"That's probably the one thing I *haven't* heard about you, Scott Kincaid."

"I should give you the grand tour."

She looked around his shoulder. "I can see most of the apartment from right here."

Since her head was cocked sideways, he took advantage of the opportunity to kiss her neck. "You can't see the best part, though."

"You mean the gigantic television?"

He grinned and, with his hands still on her ass, pulled her close enough so she could feel his erection press against her. "I have a gigantic bed, too."

"I'd hate to miss the main attraction."

Letting go of her with some reluctance, he took her hand and led her into the bedroom. The bed was big, though hardly gigantic, but it dominated the room. He didn't have a TV in here because he tried to be strict about his sleep schedule and the bed meant sleep.

Today, though, the bed meant Jamie. She looked

around the room, which wasn't any more cluttered than the rest of the place, and then at the bed. He wondered if she noticed the condom packet on the nightstand, kind of tucked beside the lamp. "Nice bed. Definitely bigger than mine."

Laughing, he stepped close enough to kiss her. "We don't need a lot of space for what I have in mind."

He slid his hands under her shirt, cupping her breasts and rolling her nipples between his thumbs and forefingers. Even through the fabric of her bra, his touch made her squirm. They stripped quickly and he admired the view as she climbed onto his bed. Then she held out her hand to him and he knew he should be reciting box scores or algebra problems or something in his head. But the only thing in his head right now was the sight of her, naked and beckoning to him.

Once he was on the bed, she shoved him backward and laughed when he splayed out on his back. He opened his mouth to make a smart-ass comment, but Jamie threw one leg over his hips and nothing came out of his mouth but a guttural sound.

She bent low so she could kiss him, her hands holding his wrists over his head. The position pressed her breasts against his chest and he groaned, fighting the temptation to prove which of them was stronger by flipping her onto her back and driving into her.

Then she kissed his chin. His Adam's apple. First one nipple and then the other, sucking just hard enough to make him hiss. Then she started making her way down his abdomen, punctuating her kisses with flicks of her tongue, and he held his breath.

When she wrapped her fingers around his dick, Scott thought he might never breathe again. She stroked him, lightly at first, but then her grip tightened as she flicked her tongue over her lips.

He couldn't look away from her mouth, but he still jumped when she closed her lips around the head of his cock. She lowered her head until her mouth bumped into her fingers, and then kept going. Her hand slid down the length of his shaft, along with her mouth, and his hips arched up off the bed.

Then she took away her hand and took him only with her mouth. The wet heat scrambled his senses and he fisted his hand in her hair. Not resisting or forcing. Just clenching the strands as he struggled to think of anything but how much he wanted to come in her mouth.

Only a few more strokes and he pulled her hair slightly, holding her head still. "You have to stop, honey. I can't..."

Jamie kissed her way back up his body to his mouth, and then he had to release her hair so she could reach for the condom to hand to him. She kissed him hungrily while he put it on, and then gave him a saucy smile as she straddled him. Taking him in hand, she lowered herself onto his erection with excruciating slowness.

His breathing turned ragged as she rocked her hips, taking him deeper inside of her with each stroke.

She arched her back and he reached up, cupping her breasts. Her neck was exposed and he wanted to kiss that hollow at the base, but he couldn't reach it with his mouth. He settled for stroking her neck with one hand, sliding his fingers over her jaw until she turned her head and sucked lightly on the end of his finger.

When he groaned, her rhythm changed. Each rise and fall of her body was faster and harder, and he knew she was close. Since he was on the ragged edge himself, he lifted his hips to meet each stroke, driving up into her. Reaching down, he rubbed his thumb over her clit and watched her body jerk.

He felt her muscles clench as she came with a small cry that seemed to set his blood on fire. Grabbing her hips, he rocked her body, harder and faster until his orgasm hit like a wrecking ball knocking him senseless. Losing himself in the intense sensation, he rode it out and was glad he was lying down because it seemed like his entire body was boneless.

Jamie collapsed on top of him, turning her head so it was on his shoulder. He kissed her hair and wrapped his arms around her back to hold her tight.

After a few minutes, when they'd caught their breath, he reached between them and held the condom as he pulled out of her. She shifted slightly to one side, but didn't get up, so he was content to stay right where he was for a little bit longer.

"I almost didn't send you a text because I thought you'd be tired out from shopping," he said. "I'm glad I did."

"Me, too. Very glad."

"I did a little shopping today, too. Guess what I bought?"

She lifted her head to look at him and he took the opportunity to grab a quick kiss. He could never get enough of kissing her.

"I'm almost afraid to ask," she said, amusement shining in her eyes.

"I stopped at the market over by your place and bought some chocolate pudding."

"Ooh." She made a sound he'd previously only heard during sex. "You didn't mention that in your text."

He gave a mock sigh. "Then I would have wondered if you were only here for my pudding. I needed to know if I was enough."

She laughed and pushed away from him. "Trust me, you're enough. Sometimes I wonder if you're *too* much."

He wasn't sure what that meant, exactly, but she hadn't said it in a particularly negative way, so he shrugged it off. She was here. That was exactly enough.

TWELVE

"WHY DO I have five gloves?" Scott tossed them into the growing pile of locker debris on the floor behind him. "Did I have four and lose one, or did I have two and stole one of somebody else's?"

"If anybody's missing one," Aidan said, "they'll know who to go after."

"I have five gloves," Grant said. "But I don't know if I started with four or six."

Scott heard Jamie's laughter behind them. "Maybe you should just have a big basket of gloves and share them all."

He didn't turn and face her, but he felt the familiar warmth at the sound of her voice. They hadn't been able to spend a lot of time together in the three days since he took her out to dinner, but at least he was guaranteed forty-eight hours per week with her.

Unfortunately, he couldn't touch her or kiss her or check out how amazing her ass looked during those forty-eight hours. But he could hear her voice and listen to her laugh and talk about all the inane things people talked about at work. And every once in a while, there would be an opportunity for his hand to brush hers, or even for him to press his palm to the small of her back. But never more than that.

It was a warm and dry day, so they had the engine bay doors open and were cleaning out all the cold-weather things they'd collected over the course of a winter. There was a lot of foot traffic on the street as people embraced spring, and their work was constantly interrupted as they waved to little kids and even let a few of them look at the apparatuses. They didn't mind, though. There wasn't a single one of them who didn't remember feeling the wonder of the fire station as a child.

But part of his attention was on the stairs in the back, waiting to hear Danny Walsh come thumping back down on his crutches. The cast was gone and he was doing physical therapy, but they still wanted him to use the crutches if there would be strain on the leg for a little while longer.

He'd shown up about half an hour ago and, after spending some time catching up with the guys, had gone upstairs to see Cobb. Scott guessed he was probably giving an update on his progress and he might even have a tentative date for his return.

And that screwed with Scott's head in a way he didn't like. He liked Walsh and always had. The guy was a damn good LT who took good care of Engine 59. He was also Ashley's husband and the father of Scott's future niece or nephew. Scott wanted nothing but a full recovery for his brother-in-law, as soon as possible.

But his return meant there was no room for Jamie and she would leave. It had been inevitable from the first, and maybe even for the best considering they didn't see eye to eye when it came to two firefighters having a family together. But he couldn't imagine not having her in his life, and his mind shied away from even trying.

With his locker emptied out for the most part, he turned to start sorting through the pile of gloves, intending to at least see if the colors or sizes would help identify them. He doubted it, since they were all black wool and the only one of them who didn't wear a standard men's size was Jeff, but it was worth a shot.

But when he turned, he got distracted by Jamie. She'd been at the workbench, doing an inventory of the miscellaneous small supplies lying around, but now she was staring in the direction of the staircase, as if her mind had wandered.

So she was waiting, too, he thought. They both knew Danny coming to the station marked the beginning of the end of her time there, and she didn't look any happier about it than he felt.

He scooped up the gloves and carried them to the bench, dumping them beside her clipboard. "The light's better over here."

She looked at the gloves and then at him, one eyebrow arched. "You need light to see that you have five black gloves?"

"To read the tags, maybe." It was a thin excuse, to be sure, but he wanted to be near her.

"Are you aware you have five gloves, but four of them are for the left hand?"

He scowled at the pile, then cursed under his breath. "I guess it's time for a glove swap because somebody has too many right hands. Remember when we were kids and they had those mittens with the long string between them so you couldn't lose one?"

"Yeah, I do. But I don't think they make those in adult male sizes."

He didn't miss the amusement in her voice, and it made him want to lean closer to her, but he forced himself to keep a normal amount of distance between them. "Maybe I'll get lucky and Grant's mommy wrote his initials inside his gloves."

"Hey, I heard that," Grant said, and most of the guys laughed.

He took his time checking the gloves over for any identifying marks. The fact there weren't any wasn't a surprise, but it gave him an excuse to be near Jamie.

"You okay?" he asked in a low voice.

"I keep wondering if I should go upstairs and be nosy, but if there's something I need to know, I guess they'll tell me." She shrugged. "I guess they're probably talking about when Danny's coming back, though."

He was going to ask her how she felt about leaving—if she would be sorry to leave them or if she was looking forward to landing someplace on a more permanent basis—when Ashley walked through the open bay door.

He grinned at his sister. She wasn't showing yet, but if you knew to look for it, she was already starting to waddle a little bit when she walked. "Hey, Ash."

"Hi, guys," she said, giving a wave that encompassed all of them. She didn't stop by the station very often, but between being Tommy's daughter, Scott's sister and Danny's wife while running the bar, there was almost nobody in the firefighting community she didn't know. "Is Danny still upstairs?"

"Yeah," Scott responded. "I was thinking about texting him to see if he was still with Cobb or if he was stuck at the top of the stairs and can't get down."

"I'll text him." She pulled out her phone and typed as she spoke. "He has an appointment and we're not running late, but we will be if he doesn't get his ass down here. He was supposed to come back to the market and meet me ten minutes ago."

Because of the appointment, Danny didn't waste any time talking to them when he finally made his way down the stairs. While everybody was focused on saying goodbye to him, Scott looked at Jamie and saw the tension in her face. It mirrored the tension he felt.

She met his gaze and forced a smile before giving a little shrug. Whatever was going to happen would happen, and it wouldn't be a surprise. They'd known all along there was an expiration date on her presence in his life.

But now that it was imminent, Scott dreaded knowing what that date was. He didn't want to know when his time with Jamie was coming to an end.

AN HOUR LATER, Jamie was surprised when the intercom system in the engine bay crackled to life. It wasn't something they used often, since most of them just used text messaging if they had something to say to somebody not in the room.

"Rutherford, I'd like to see you in my office for a minute."

Jamie tensed at the use of her last name. It was something they all did with each other, switching between first names and surnames and nicknames, but Cobb had always called her by her first. But she pushed the button on the wall and spoke into the speaker. "Right away, sir."

Several of the guys were in the bay and looked at her as she went toward the stairs, but it was Grant who spoke. "What did you do now?"

She gave him a grin that belied the nerves dancing around in her stomach. Even though it was probably an update on Danny's return, she couldn't deny she was nervous about the way she was being summoned. "Probably a meeting about all the complaints we've received about your socks smelling."

Once she'd stepped inside Cobb's office, he gestured for her to close the door and sit down. Judging by his expression, she would have preferred to stand. It was less awkward to take an ass chewing for something standing at attention and staring at something over and behind the boss's head. Sitting was more intimate and involved eye contact.

But he had rank, so she sat. He sighed, staring at the pen he was fiddling with and shifting his weight in his chair, so she remained silent. Clearly he was uncomfortable and trying to figure out how to start, and she got a bad feeling in the pit of her stomach. This wasn't going anywhere good.

Finally he straightened up and looked at her. "Are you involved in a personal way with Scott Kincaid?"

Her gut was rarely wrong. "Respectfully, sir, that's none of your business."

"It really is my business, actually."

"Have I performed any of my duties in a less than satisfactory manner?"

He sighed and rubbed the bridge of his nose. "Hell, no. You know I think highly of you."

"Then, again with all due respect, I don't believe we need to have this conversation."

"Stop with the—" he waved his hand, as if trying to summon the right word out of thin air "—formality or whatever. This isn't an inquisition, it's a conversation."

"And are you having this conversation with Scott?"

"The standard's different for you."

She narrowed her eyes. "Because I'm a woman?"

"Because you're a goddamned officer," he snapped. Then he blew out a long breath and leaned back in his chair. "This is going all kinds of wrong on me."

"As it will when a male superior asks a woman under his authority about her sex life."

"Is there a threat buried in there, Rutherford?"

She looked him in the eye, and then shook her head. "No. I'm just on the defensive, I guess."

"Okay." He leaned forward and slapped his palms on the desk. "Let's start this over so I can come at it from a different direction because you and I like and respect each other and that wasn't the conversation I was trying to have."

"Thank you, sir. Can I ask if the timing of this conversation and the fact Danny Walsh just left are connected?"

He looked startled by the question. "What? Oh, no. He interrupted what I was doing and then I figured I should get this out of the way before I went back to it. Just a coincidence."

That made her feel a little better, at least. She hadn't been burned by his family. "I'd like to know where this accusation came from."

"It's not an accusation. It's just scuttlebutt. I went to a memorial ceremony yesterday and afterward went to a diner with some guys I've known for decades. Shit, we were probably putting out fires before you were born."

She laughed. "Not quite, sir."

"A long time, anyway. They know Tommy, of course, and he came up in a story one of the guys was telling. That was the opening for the gossip about Tommy's kid and the female lieutenant in my company. I guess there was a fight at Tommy's bar?"

"It's not the first time I've been subject to that kind of speculation, sir. People talk."

"I'm not going to ask you if what they're saying is true. Quite frankly, as long as nobody's job suffers and there's no hanky-panky under this roof, I *don't* consider it any of my business. But I called you in here because I wanted you to know there's talk. Whether or not you care is up to you."

"I do care. People talking about me like that can affect my career. Where I'm assigned can be changed because somebody's worried about the dynamic in the house or a sexual harassment suit or jealous wives hanging around. If they perceive me as being a certain way, I might not even get the chance to prove myself. It's not fair, but when you're a woman, your personal life is questioned as well as your ability to do the job."

"Have you had to deal with that?"

"I've been luckier than some women in the fire service. Back in my early days, I had a group of wives petition to have me transferred because they didn't like me spending so much time with their husbands. I was in the process of moving to a new city, anyway, so nothing came of it. And there was an older guy who refused to go out on a call if I was along because he said women couldn't fight fires and he didn't have time to take care of me. In that case, he was transitioned into a desk job, but I believe he had other infractions going on his record about the same time. Overall, men have treated me with varying degrees of acceptance in their companies, but I haven't had many out-and-out jerks."

"I had some concerns in the beginning," he said. "My initial reaction was what if she can't pull her weight? Or what if one of the guys refuses to work with her or she wants her own bathroom all to herself or somebody says something stupid or tells a joke that gets us slapped with a sexual harassment suit. But your record speaks for itself and, like you said, there's a good group of guys here."

"I appreciate you giving me a chance to prove myself."

"Speaking of this being a good group of guys, I'm going to jump the gun and give you a heads-up before you get the official notification. You'll be with Ladder Company 41, effective immediately upon Danny Walsh's return to duty."

Ladder 41. She closed her eyes for a moment, visualizing the map of stations in her head. It was on the western fringe of the city, maybe twenty minutes away on a decent traffic day, in an affluent neighborhood. More single-family homes, office buildings and upscale shopping, which probably meant fewer fires and more medical calls. It would be an adjustment.

Jamie gave herself a few seconds to process the information and her emotional response to it. She thought she'd managed to keep the fact this was temporary in the back of her mind the entire time she'd been with E-59, but the knot of emotion in her throat and gut told her she hadn't done a very good job of it, after all. And it wasn't only Scott. She'd really felt at home not only with the entire engine company, but the ladder company, too.

"You won't be filling in," Cobb said. "Their LT is moving out of state for family reasons and the district chief wants you. The timing's perfect, too. I'm guessing you heard that there's no reason Walsh shouldn't be able to resume his duties on the twentieth," Cobb continued.

"I'm sure everybody will be glad to have him back," she said, her voice sounding a little hoarse to her own ears. Only two more weeks and she'd have to say goodbye.

"They will. But that doesn't mean any of us want to see you go."

"I understand." She was afraid she was going to cry, and she focused on keeping her back straight and her eyes dry. "Thank you for letting me know."

"They're decent guys, too. I think you'll be a good fit there."

"I've met some of them, sir, and I don't anticipate any problems." And if there were any, she'd deal with them. Being the new "guy" was a situation she'd had a lot of experience with.

"I'll leave it to you whether you want to share the news or not," he said.

"I will when it's a little closer to the date. After the wedding, maybe." She wanted some time to come to grips with the transfer before she was presented with the feelings of all of the other guys. And Scott. She couldn't imagine not working with him anymore, and it was going to take a lot of self-control to keep her emotions in check when she told him she had a transfer date.

Cobb stood, so she did the same, and then he extended his hand. "I stayed awake in the training seminars long enough to know I'm not allowed to hug you."

When she walked out of his office, Jamie felt the first stirrings of a headache and decided a cup of coffee was in order. She climbed the stairs to the third floor rather than going back to her office, with its single-cup brewer, because she felt restless. If she went and sat at her desk, she'd probably do more brooding than she did work.

She wasn't surprised when, after the few guys hanging around the television waved at her, Scott got up and followed her into the kitchen. There was nobody else in there, so he stood close while she grabbed her mug and made herself a coffee.

"Is everything okay?" he asked. She nodded, but didn't volunteer any more information. "Was it about me? About us, I mean?"

She didn't really want to talk about it here, but he looked so worried, she didn't have the heart to put it off. Part of it, at least. "Some gossip got back to Cobb from another house."

"Shit." He leaned against the wall and ran his hands over his hair. "How bad is it?"

"Not bad. He's not concerned about us doing our jobs, but he wanted me to know it was out there."

"Does it bother you?"

"Of course it bothers me." She took a sip of her coffee and wished she'd grabbed some ibuprofen from her desk before coming up. "But we already talked about that. I knew it might happen and I'm okay with it."

"Was that it? He just wanted you to know there's talk?"

She didn't want to lie to him, but she also didn't want to tell him her transfer was in place yet. Not until she'd settled her own feelings about it, and not until they were alone and there wasn't a chance one of the other guys could walk in at any second.

"Mostly. And some administrative stuff," she hedged.

He snorted. "Bureaucracy is one of the reasons I'm not in any hurry to take the lieutenant exam. I might be like Eriksson. Show up, do my job and go home until it's time to retire."

"I've seen your paperwork, so I'll thank you on behalf of everybody who won't have to deal with extra piles of it in the future."

He leaned close, chuckling, and she knew from his body language that if they were anywhere else, he'd grab her and they'd tussle until they ended up kissing. "You're a pretty funny lady, ma'am. We should talk more about my paperwork inadequacies later, when we have more privacy."

She should admonish him for not only the suggestive words, but the way his voice dropped into that low, sexy range that made her toes curl. Instead, she just gave him a stern look and then took her coffee into the TV room before he could say anything else that might tempt her into doing something stupid.

Especially when she was feeling vulnerable because, unless Scott's vision of his future had drastically changed, the clock was now undeniably ticking on the time they had left together.

"HOW ARE THINGS going with that woman of yours?"

Scott set the clipboard bearing Lydia and Ashley's lists on a shelf and pulled the wheeled cart closer. "What woman of mine?"

Tommy gave him a look that let Scott know exactly what he thought of the evasion. "I'm a lot of things, son, and perfect definitely ain't one of them. But stupid or blind, I'm not. And I'm not deaf, either. You know as well as I do that the firefighting community is like a small town unto itself, no matter how big the city is."

"Unless my best friend's seeing my sister. Then everybody has better things to talk about."

"Don't go dragging that shit up the night before their wedding just because you don't want to talk about what's going on with you."

"I'm not dragging anything up. You know I'm happy for them and I wouldn't have agreed to be Aidan's best man if I still had a problem with him. I'm just sick of the way everybody protected him and Lydia but aren't shy about running their mouths about me and… I'm just sick of it."

"Maybe people were afraid that temper of yours would destroy your friendship and maybe even your family."

Scott grabbed a box off the shelf and set it on the cart with a thump. "Maybe they should be that concerned about a woman's career, too."

He could feel his mood going sideways on him, and he tried to rein it in. They were doing the prep work for the wedding tomorrow, which meant he and his old man were going to be stuck in the storage room together for a while. He didn't want to butt heads with him the entire time they were getting ready for a celebration.

When he reached for another box, Tommy reached out a hand to stop him. "We're supposed to check each box off the list."

"Shit." He looked at the end of the box for the label and then picked up the checklist. "These are the coasters."

Once Tommy had accepted the bar would be hosting his daughter's wedding and that his beloved pool table would be used as a buffet, he'd thrown himself into making sure it would be special. And he'd started with special coasters listing Aidan's and Lydia's names, along with the date. There were also napkins and plates for the buffet, along with a variety of other things.

"What exactly are you doing in here?" he asked his dad. "I'm doing the boxes and the checklist."

"I'm supervising."

Scott laughed. "Yeah, my ass you are. You do the checklist."

They were supposed to be consolidating the wedding supplies Tommy had ordered on the cart so the staff could set up the place before the wedding. The bar would be closed, but the staff would work and they'd be getting double time. Karen Shea, an emergency room nurse who filled in now and then on a part-time basis, would be working behind the bar. Scott had wondered how that would work, since she and Rick Gullotti had once dated. But Jessica, Rick's fiancée, had met her and didn't mind at all, according to Lydia.

"Seriously, son, how are things with you? I've spent a lot of time worrying about you over the years, and you've seemed different the last few weeks. More settled. Happy, even."

"Happy maybe, but not more settled."

Especially over the last week. Something had been different since Jamie's meeting with Cobb the week before, but he couldn't put his finger on a reason. He kept telling himself it was simply a matter of the gossip bothering her a little more than she'd anticipated it would, but his gut told him there was more to it.

"Ashley told me Danny's recovery is going well and he shouldn't be out much longer."

"That's what I hear. It's good news."

"Is it?"

He looked at his dad, scowling. "Of course it is. Jesus, he's my brother-in-law. He's my friend. Of course I want him recovered and back on the job."

"Does Jamie know where she's going yet?"

"I don't know. I haven't asked her."

"How come?"

Because he didn't want to know. He didn't want to think about what was going to happen when Danny returned and she left the company. He didn't want to think about her moving away and not being around anymore. "If she wants me to know, she'll tell me."

His father gave him a long look he couldn't quite

decipher, and then slowly shook his head. "That's a good way to go about it, if you want to end up old and alone like me."

There was no way in hell Scott wanted that. If he did, he wouldn't have taken a break from dating in the first place. He would have just kept on having company when he felt like it and being alone when that's what he was in the mood for.

"What if a guy doesn't want to end up alone raising kids because their mother got killed on the job?"

Tommy slid a crate over and sat down on it, gesturing for Scott to do the same. He regretted asking the question, if it was going to lead to a lecture. But the question was one he'd been thinking about a lot lately. Was there any sense in trying to extend his relationship with Jamie past her departure from the company if it was doomed to end in failure, anyway?

"Son, you're talking to a man who was left to raise kids alone. I certainly don't have to tell you I screwed it up nine ways to Sunday, but you all made it to adulthood and you're all doing well in life, if I do say so myself."

"But Mom died from breast cancer. It wasn't a choice she made."

"No, it wasn't." His dad sighed. "I don't know that a well-trained, smart firefighter is that much more at risk on the job than she would be doing anything else, to be honest. It's dangerous, sure, but not enough to miss out on a good life together."

"It's hard," Scott said in a low voice. "Growing up without a mom. Not having her anymore still hurts in so many ways even though it's been almost twenty years."

"I know it's hard. I miss her, too. But look at the bigger picture, son. Lydia's getting married tomorrow. Ashley's having a baby. This life your mother and I made together goes on and it's still a beautiful thing, even though she's not here with us. The thought of missing out on all this because of fear of the what-ifs is sad as hell."

Maybe his old man was right, but Scott knew it was a lot more complicated than him coming to grips with Jamie's job. He knew as well as his dad did that they did everything possible to minimize the risk every time that alarm sounded.

Mostly he was hung up on the fact she hadn't talked about the future with him. If she knew where she was going to be transferred, she hadn't told him. And she hadn't talked about Danny's return or how she felt about that with him. He could only assume it was because she didn't see any of that being particularly relevant to their relationship because it was coming to an end along with her time at Engine Company 59.

The last thing he wanted to do was make things messy by throwing his feelings into the mix. He was still trying to sort through them himself, and he didn't want to ruin the time they had left together by making things awkward.

"Maybe after the wedding's behind us," he told his dad. "I want to enjoy Aidan and Lydia's wedding and then I'll talk to her about her transfer."

"And you'll tell her how you feel about her."

Scott shrugged and got up, picking up the clipboard to give himself something to focus on besides the fear that knotted up in his gut at the thought of telling Jamie he didn't want to give her up when Danny came back, transfer be damned.

"Yeah. After the wedding."

THIRTEEN

JAMIE LOOKED AT herself in the mirror and decided what she saw in the reflection was as good as it was going to get. Even though she didn't have a full-length mirror in the apartment and could only see herself from the waist up in the mirror over the bathroom sink, she thought she looked pretty damn good tonight.

Despite Ashley's declaration that the neckline required jewelry, Jamie wasn't wearing any with the dress. Maybe the neckline demanded it, whatever that meant, but she'd never been a fan of necklaces. She'd put the small diamond studs her dad had bought her when she graduated from high school in her ears and that was as fancy as she got.

Her hair looked good, too. Because she wore it in a French braid to work and often threw it in a ponytail, she wasn't in the habit of styling it, and she didn't really have a knack for it. But she'd gotten lucky today and it was smooth and shiny, hanging slightly past her shoulders. Makeup was another thing she was woefully out of practice with, but she managed to do up her face without getting lipstick on her teeth or poking herself in the eye with the mascara wand. That was a huge win in her book.

The shoes were an issue, and after much deliberation, she'd decided to take a cab to the bar. It wouldn't cost much, and would pay for itself in saving her the hassle of finding a place to park. Walking was out of the question. She'd be lucky if she could walk across the bar without falling on her face, never mind walking *to* the bar.

When the cab pulled up in front of Kincaid's Pub, she was surprised to see a few people waiting on the sidewalk. She paid the driver, watching the line slowly move inside. Hopefully it would move a little faster, she thought as she got out of the cab. It was a little chillier than she'd anticipated and nobody liked to ruin a good look with a hoodie.

The reason for the line became obvious as she stepped into the doorway. Aidan and Scott were greeting people as they entered, and there were a lot of hugs and words being exchanged.

"Hey, Jamie," Aidan said when it was her turn, and she was glad to see he was positively beaming. No nerves or cold feet for this guy. He was unabashedly happy and excited tonight. "Thanks for coming."

She hugged him quickly, finding it a little awkward because her subconscious was always monitoring her interactions with the guys she worked with and hugging didn't usually happen. "Thanks for inviting me."

When she moved on to Scott, her subconscious perked up again, in an entirely different way. Him, she liked touching and she had to remind herself before stepping into his embrace that they were surrounded by people. A quick in and out, and she couldn't let her breasts make contact with his chest.

"It's good to see you," he murmured against her ear, holding her for a few seconds longer than was probably appropriate.

She shivered and made sure a polite smile was fixed on her face before pulling back. "You guys look sharp in your suits."

"My sisters have good taste." He swept her body with a look that was not even in the neighborhood of polite, and while his expression didn't change, she didn't miss the way his jaw clenched for a second or the very slight flush of heat over his face. "That dress is… I like the… Damn, woman, you are going to kill me tonight."

Very aware that Aidan and the guest he was welcoming behind her were wrapping up their chitchat, Jamie just smiled. "Like you said, your sisters have good taste. They made me buy it."

"I'll thank them later."

She would have liked nothing more than to stand there and talk to Scott for the rest of the night, but there were still people arriving and she didn't want to hold up the line. After looking around, she walked to Rick Gullotti, who was standing with Jeff and

Chris, along with two women Jamie assumed were their wives.

"Hey, Jamie." Rick smiled when she stepped into the circle. He introduced the other two women, and then smiled at the pretty blonde woman next to him. "And this is my fiancée, Jessica."

"It's nice to meet you." Jamie shook her hand. "I've heard a lot about you, so it's nice to finally meet you in person. Rick said you were coming back from San Diego for the wedding."

Jessica nodded. "For two weeks, actually. I've decided I want an office space separate from the house so I don't follow in my dad's workaholic footsteps, so I'm going to scout some locations."

"When do you think you'll make the move permanent? If you don't mind my asking."

"At least two more months," she said, wrinkling her nose. "My dad and I have been working on building a client base here, but it's a tight market. Soon, though. And it's worth it."

"Yes, it is," Rick said, and Jamie watched L-37's lieutenant give his future wife such a sappy look she almost laughed.

"Did you see the cake?" Ellen Porter asked. "It's gorgeous!"

"I haven't seen it yet," Jamie said, and before she knew it, Jeff's wife was leading her through the crowd to the pool table room.

She stopped several times to introduce Jamie to different people, though she luckily knew quite a few of them. Jamie didn't mind putting herself in the other woman's hands. Being in a social setting with the guys' wives and having them not regard her with subtle suspicion or, even worse, overt jealously, was a pleasant surprise and she was a lot more relaxed than she'd thought she would be.

"You're right. It's gorgeous," she said when they finally reached the alcove. The pool table had been covered with a protective cloth and had so much food on it, Jamie was surprised the wooden frame wasn't groaning under the weight.

But on a table off to the side, which had been decked out in a white cloth with ribbons, was a three-tiered wedding cake. She wasn't surprised it was a traditional style, with fondant roses around the edges and a porcelain couple on top.

What did surprise her was the second table in the corner. There were at least two dozen chocolate cupcakes on a platter, with two in the middle that had tiny cardboard cutouts of hockey players in Boston Bruins jerseys on top. One had Aidan's name in small script and the other had Scott's.

"Even Kincaids can be reasonable once in a while," Scott said from just behind her, and she turned. He kept about a foot between them, maybe because Ellen and a few others were milling around, looking at the buffet. "It was Ashley's idea, actually. She's always been the family peacemaker—the one who handles negotiations when one of us digs in our heels."

"Technically he's not betraying the actual wedding cake?" When he nodded, Jamie laughed. "Of course not. They're just cupcakes."

"He has to eat the carrot cake, though. That was the deal. He shares the wedding cake with her and does the ceremonial first bite and all that. Then he's free to stuff his face with chocolate cupcakes."

"So it is possible to budge a Kincaid who's being stubborn," she mused. "Good to know."

She heard his phone chime and grinned when he rolled his eyes. "It's a good thing I have unlimited text messages or I'd have to charge a fee for being best man. I thought we'd just take some friends to a bar and have a good time, but there are so many details."

"You had Aidan's bachelor party at a *bar*?"

"Yeah, but it wasn't *this* bar." When she snorted, he looked up from his phone to smile at her. "Okay, when I say bar, I really mean it was a strip club."

"Ah. That explains why I didn't hear anything about it."

"That and the fact it appears men reach an age where shoving money at women just to watch them dance in thongs doesn't seem like all that good a deal anymore, you know?" He shrugged. "Gavin had a good time. The rest of us watched a game on the TV over the bar and occasionally remembered to roast Aidan."

"Sounds like a good time." She'd gone to Lydia's bachelorette party, which had been hosted by Ashley at a bowling alley that had glow bowling, a private room and a bar. They'd had a few drinks, snacked on fried foods and bowled under black lights, and Jamie had a good time, despite not really knowing any of the women besides Lydia and her sister.

"What?" Scott prompted. "No lecture on how barbaric male wedding traditions are?"

She laughed. "Yeah, because I do that so often. And women usually have their traditions, too. Like spending ridiculous amounts of money on raunchy lingerie the bride-to-be is forced to hold up in front of her mother and future mother-in-law, and that she'll never wear because it's all scratching and uncomfortable and she'd rather wear her husband's T-shirts."

"At least bachelor parties usually take place at a venue with some kind of sports on a screen." He leaned a little closer. "And as much as I like you in that dress, I like you in my T-shirts even more."

Her face flamed and she turned back to the tray of cupcakes so nobody would wonder what he'd said that made her blush so badly. "I knew you couldn't behave yourself for an entire night."

"I have to go wrangle wedding things," he said, and then in a lower voice, "but make sure you save me a dance."

She used her cell phone to take a picture of the cupcakes to have an excuse to regain her composure, and then turned back to the pool table. Ellen was taking a photo of it, and something about her demeanor made Jamie think she was going out of her way to look like she hadn't been paying attention, rather than she simply hadn't noticed the exchange between Jamie and Scott.

Great, she thought. At this rate, there wouldn't be anybody left in Boston who didn't know they were a thing before the reception was over.

SCOTT WAS IN the kitchen with Aidan when he got the text from Ashley that they were about five minutes away and would be coming through the back door. There was a follow-up text threatening bodily harm to Scott if he didn't keep Aidan out front where he couldn't see the bride before Tommy walked her up the makeshift aisle.

He reminded himself this was still twice as relaxed as the show the Kincaid family had put on when Ashley married Danny, and kept his return text short. I've got this.

"Is that Ashley?" Aidan asked, craning his neck to see the screen.

"Five-minute warning."

"We should go out front, I guess. Lydia will kick my ass if I screw up and see her before I'm supposed to. I guess it's the kind of bad luck even Bobby Orr's picture can't fix."

"There's a line for taking a beating if we screw this up. I think Ashley has me in front, since I'm the best man."

Aidan laughed, but for the first time, he looked a little shaky. "I can't believe it's finally time. And,

God, I'm so glad she said we didn't have to write our own vows. I don't even remember my own name right now."

"You're not going to pass out on me, like all those guys in the funny videos online, are you?"

Aidan grimaced. "I hope not, but thanks for making sure I worry about that, too."

"Don't lock your knees when you're standing there and you'll be fine." Scott laughed, and reached out to adjust Aidan's tie. "You clean up nice, at least."

"Before we go back out front, I just want to tell you this wouldn't be the happiest day of my life if you weren't standing next to me as my best man."

"You've been like a brother to me since we were kids. Now you'll actually *be* my brother. I'm glad I got my head out of my ass so you didn't have to ask somebody else."

"I don't know if I could have asked anybody else," Aidan said, and then he sighed. "I don't know if I could stand out there and marry Lydia if I didn't have your blessing."

"This is the happiest day of my life, too, so far. I mean that." He hugged Aidan, slapping him on the back. "You haven't been keeping track of how long this little love fest has taken, have you?"

"You're the best man. Throwing yourself in front of the bus is implied if we run out of time."

Scott laughed, but stopped when Tommy turned the corner. His dad looked dapper as hell in his suit, and he grinned when he saw Scott and Aidan. "You boys better hustle. She's coming through that door in about two minutes."

They hustled because the last thing either of them wanted to do was cause Lydia even a second of stress on her wedding day.

The guests quieted for a few seconds when they walked into the bar, and then the excitement level in the room ratcheted up a notch when they realized it was almost time. Scott walked with Aidan to the far end of the bar, where the justice of the peace was waiting.

His phone chimed and he read the text message. "They're inside. Danny's getting the flowers out of the walk-in and then they'll be ready."

As they'd planned in advance, Grant was watching and as soon as Danny emerged from the hall and gave him a thumbs-up, he hit a button on the phone he'd docked in a portable speaker system. Wedding-sounding music filled the bar and everybody quieted.

He couldn't help looking for Jamie in the small crowd, and he found her in the back. She was sitting with Cobb and his wife, and she smiled at him when their gazes met. Since Cobb wasn't looking, he winked at her. Then he cursed silently when a few heads turned toward the back. Since he and Aidan were at the front, people had been watching them and naturally wanted to know who he'd winked at. Luckily, there were a lot of people between him and Jamie.

Scott heard Aidan take a really deep breath before slowly exhaling, and he reached over to squeeze his friend's shoulder as Ashley turned the corner into the bar. She'd definitely gotten her wish as far as wearing a killer dress, he thought, and he struggled not to chuckle at the way Danny looked as he watched his wife walk up the aisle.

When Ashley reached them, she stood on her toes to kiss Aidan's cheek before stepping into her place on the other side of the JP. She gave a quick nod to Grant and a few seconds later the music faded out and then the traditional "Wedding March" began to play.

Seconds later, his sister walked into the bar with her arm tucked under their father's arm. Tommy was standing tall and proud, but Scott could see the emotion in his eyes. The man loved all of his kids, but Scott and Ashley had always known Lydia was his favorite. And they hadn't minded because it diverted his attention away from them.

Lydia looked beautiful. Her dress was amazing and he wasn't surprised to see that she'd worn her hair down. It was thick and wavy and didn't behave very well, so it was usually in a ponytail. But down like it was, the dark curls framed her face perfectly and contrasted the cream-colored dress.

It all paled in comparison to her expression, though. She only had eyes for Aidan and she looked so happy walking toward him, Scott had to clear his throat and blink a couple of times to avoid embarrassing himself. Then she smiled at her almost-husband and Scott almost felt like he was intruding on a private moment by staring, so he let his gaze wander over the crowd.

Jamie's eyes were on the bride, of course. Everybody's were, so he let himself look at her for a few seconds. Her expression was soft, almost dreamy, as she watched his sister walk down the aisle, and she looked beautiful. Then there was the dress, of course. The dress made him think all sorts of indecent thoughts that could get him in trouble when he was standing up in front of his friends and family.

When Lydia reached them, Scott turned and watched his dad kiss her hand before handing it over to Aidan. Then he watched his best friend and his sister exchange an excited, love-filled look that sent envy burning through his veins. He wanted a woman to look at him like that.

The justice of the peace started to talk and Scott had to stifle a snort when he saw Aidan shift his weight so he wasn't locking his knees. He and Ashley handed the rings over when they were called for, and Aidan got through his vows without so much as a hesitation.

"I now pronounce you man and wife. You may kiss the bride."

The cheers and applause could have shaken Bobby Orr's picture right off the wall if the frame wasn't bolted to the brick. He grinned, clapping his hands as Aidan dipped Lydia so deeply for a kiss that she lifted her leg for balance. Behind them, Scott saw Jeff's wife look at her camera's LCD screen and do a small fist pump. She was the best amateur photographer in the community and she'd volunteered to take the photos.

Once he'd set his wife on her feet, Aidan turned to Scott and pulled him in for a hug. Tears burned in Scott's eyes, but he laughed when Lydia wiggled her way into the embrace. He kissed her cheek. "Congratulations, Mr. and Mrs. Hunt."

FOURTEEN

ONCE THE CEREMONY was over, Jamie practically made a beeline for the bar. She knew she couldn't drink enough to blot out the memory of Scott's face when he embraced his best friend as his brother-in-law for the first time, but maybe she could take the edge off the extreme case of warm and fuzzy it had given her.

And maybe a little indigestion, because she knew someday Scott would have that look on his face for his own bride, and Jamie hated that unknown woman with a burning passion.

The woman behind the bar, who was a friend of Rick's, gestured to the lineup of glasses when she approached. "We have beer, champagne and soda. There's a coffee urn over there, with all the fixings, and I can get you water with ice. If you want hard liquor or a cocktail, I can make you one, but Tommy's a cheap bastard so those you have to pay for."

Jamie laughed and took a flute of champagne. "I think I'm in the mood for bubbles tonight."

"Everybody!" Grant stood on a chair and clapped his hands. "Lydia wants Ellen to take some pictures before we eat because some of you eat like toddlers."

The crowd, including Jamie, laughed. There was a lot of milling around as Ellen directed people in front of the bar. With the brick backdrop, and Bobby Orr, along with the old-style lighting, Jamie had to admit it was a good spot. Perfect, really, considering the emotional attachment both the bride and groom felt for the building.

"Hey."

Jamie was surprised to find Lydia at her elbow. She gave her a quick hug. "Congratulations and that was so beautiful and aren't you supposed to be having your picture taken right now?"

"No, *we* are. Come on."

Jamie balked. "What are you talking about?"

"We're starting with the big group pictures because everybody's here. If we start with just me and Aidan, people will get bored and wander off and Ellen will never round them up again. So probably us and the two companies first, like a big old family picture."

"I'll just watch. I can make funny faces if Ellen has trouble getting somebody to smile."

"Shut up. Of course you're going to be in the picture."

"It's not a good idea." She resisted when Lydia tugged at her hand. "I don't belong in a family wedding photo."

"You guys *are* family."

"They are, but I'm moving on. Every time somebody looks at the pictures, I'd just be that woman who filled in for him while he was on medical leave."

Because Lydia and her brother were so much alike, and Jamie knew Scott so well, she didn't have any trouble recognizing the temper rising in the bride. "That's bullshit, Jamie. You think when you peel the name tape off your locker door, we're going to forget who you are? That you've been a part of this family?"

"Do you want me in the picture because I'm part of Engine Company 59 or because of Scott?" When Lydia hesitated, uncertainty flickering in her eyes, Jamie knew she'd hit on the truth. "I *am* moving on and maybe I'll always feel a connection with this fire company, but you don't want to have a family photograph with your brother's ex-girlfriend in it. Or ex-whatever."

Lydia sighed, shaking her head. "Okay, fine. But I want a picture with you and me and Ashley because moving on or not, you won't be my ex-friend."

"Absolutely."

Ellen was starting to get annoyed, judging by the pitch of her voice and the way she was waving her hand, so Lydia gave her a final *I mean it* look and walked away. They started lining up, but when Scott sent a questioning look in Jamie's direction, she shook her head.

Then she sighed when Scott pulled his sister off to one side. She watched him and Lydia talking, their conversation obviously intense, while she sipped her drink. He looked mad, and his sister was obviously trying to calm him down. If Jamie had to guess, she'd say Scott thought Lydia had made a decision to exclude Jamie from the photograph.

She'd just decided to go over and tell him what

was going on—or just be in the damn picture if that's what it took—when the fight went out of Scott. She didn't know what Lydia said but, after a quick look in Jamie's direction, he shrugged and got in line where he was told.

Once the bride and the photographer were content with the shots they had, Grant put on some dance music and the party started. They ate, drank and made merry as hell, and Jamie moved from group to group. There were stories and laughter, and the more drinks that were served, the more people danced.

And maybe because Aidan and Lydia had limited the guest list to friends and family who mostly all knew each other, there was no drama and everybody was having a good time.

She might have had a better time if she wasn't trying to stay one step ahead of Scott, Jamie thought. Or, more accurately, many steps away from him. He wasn't drinking tonight because he'd volunteered to make sure everybody who left the reception had a designated driver or a cab waiting, but he was enjoying himself and she wouldn't put it past him to forget himself if he got within arm's reach of her.

Rick Gullotti stepped over to her, so close their elbows were almost touching. "Hey, Jamie."

"Hey, Rick. You having a good time?"

"Yeah. How about you?"

She nodded, looking around the room. "I am."

"You are, or you could be?"

She frowned, turning slightly to face him. "What do you mean?"

"I'm not sure how to say this without overstepping, but this is…a safe place. Everybody in this bar right now has your back. We have Scotty's back. Dance with the man. Hold his hand. Enjoy your night."

And again she was put in a position of not wanting to either deny or confirm. She sipped her drink and looked at Scott across the room, wondering what the hell she was supposed to do now.

"It's not something you can hide, you know," he continued. "It's the small things. Glances. The way you talk to each other. You're both more relaxed when you're together. Couple shit, you know?"

"Couple shit?" She laughed. "So tell me, if everybody thinks Scott and I are involved, why were Grant and Gavin trying to hook him up with a date for the wedding?"

"Yeah, those two aren't exactly relationship experts. I don't think either of them knew back then. But Gavin came to me a few days ago with some rumors he heard while taking a shift for a guy in another ladder company. Nothing too bad, but bored guys will talk about anything."

"And what did you tell him?"

"I told him you both show up for every tour and do your jobs, and unless it affects the companies, it's not really our business. Of course, when you don't deny something outright, people usually take it as a confirmation. But Gavin told me that his response when asked if it was true Tommy's son was messing around with his lieutenant was basically that you're a great firefighter and he couldn't give a shit less who you sleep with."

She looked him in the eye because he was a man she had a lot of respect for professionally, besides liking him personally. "What's your opinion of the situation?"

"If I thought you and Scotty being involved would cloud your judgment and put a single firefighter at risk, you'd be gone already. And if I thought it would cause friction in the house, we would already have had a discussion." He didn't even blink as he spoke, and she knew he meant every word. "But it hasn't been a problem. Trust me, I had to deal with the fallout when Scotty found out Aidan had been seeing Lydia behind his back, so I can tell you whatever you two are doing isn't even a blip on my potential problem radar."

"And I'll be leaving soon, so it would be a temporary situation anyway," she said, and no matter how many times she verbalized the inevitable, she felt the sharp pang of sadness.

"You'll be transferring to another station. But you'll still be in Boston, so you're not really leaving us." He sighed. "You know, if the situation was different and it wasn't Danny Walsh's chair you've been sitting in, I would push Cobb to keep you here. I really hate seeing you go and I want you to know that no matter where you end up, you have my respect and support. Danny's, too. And Cobb's. Hell, everybody's."

Tears burned Jamie's eyes. "That means a lot to me. Thank you."

"Jesus, go dance with Scotty before he thinks I made you cry and tries to kick my ass."

She laughed and saw Scott's head turn until he located her and their gazes locked across the room. "I think I will."

Scott watched her approach, his gaze sweeping down her body and back up before locking with hers. As she passed a table bearing a tray, she set her empty glass on it and kept walking. His eyebrow arched and she guessed her intent must have shown on her face.

"Hey, gorgeous," he said when she walked up close enough to him to leave no doubt.

"I was told I should dance with you and hold your hand."

"Really?" He scanned the crowd, then looked back at her. "I saw you talking to Rick."

"Yeah. And Rick suggested that everybody in this bar has our backs and we should just enjoy this night."

He laced the fingers of one hand through hers while twisting to set his glass down. "I always did like Rick."

His other hand wrapped around her waist before coming to rest at the small of her back, and she lifted her arms to cup the back of his neck in her hands. Then they were swaying to the music. Maybe they were in time or maybe they weren't. Jamie barely even noticed the song.

She was finally in Scott's arms, and nobody around them cared.

SCOTT TURNED THE lock on the front door and collapsed against it with a sigh. "I thought they'd never leave."

Jamie laughed and then looked around at the debris from what had been one hell of a good party. As wedding receptions went, it had definitely been one of her favorites. "In all of the details they sent you by text, did your sisters happen to tell you how much of this you have to clean up before you go home?"

"We've got this," Karen called from behind the bar. "I actually have some friends arriving in about half an hour who Tommy is going to pay a crap ton of money to play cleaning fairies. A few hours from now, it'll be like it never happened."

"That's my kind of magic," Scott said. "I'm beat."

"But it was fun," Jamie said. She'd definitely never believe this night had never happened. And it had already been magical, as far as she was concerned.

"How many drinks did you have?" he asked, pushing her hair back behind her ear.

"Not enough so I'm drunk, but definitely enough so I'm not sober. But I took a cab here, so I wouldn't be driving anyway."

"I'll bring you home."

"You just said you were beat." She put up the token protest because he did look tired.

"Not *that* beat." He grinned. "Besides, making sure everybody had a designated driver was one of the duties assigned to me, remember?"

"Great. I just need to find my shoes. I think they got kicked under the pool table earlier."

"I'll grab them."

She made herself useful while she waited, dumping plastic glasses into a huge lined garbage can on wheels that somebody from the kitchen had brought out. It hadn't escaped her notice that, after the reception had begun and the formalities and photographs were taken care of, all of the glassware had been swapped out for plastic stemware and cups. Nice ones, but still disposable.

"Okay, I found your shoes." Scott dangled her heels from one hand. But then he held up the other hand, from which a pair of cream pumps hung. "I don't know whose these are, but somebody left here barefoot."

Karen laughed. "This wouldn't be the first wedding venue to have a lost and found. I'll put them here behind the bar and stick a note on the register for Ashley."

"I can't believe she has to work tomorrow," Jamie said. "I know she didn't drink because of the baby, but being in a bridal party is exhausting even if you're not pregnant."

"Yeah, but I worked tonight and won't be leaving for several more hours." Karen shrugged. "And we all thought it would be nice to give Lydia the day off. Now go on, you two. Let us get to work."

"Are you giving me a ride home?" Jamie asked, taking her shoes from him and then groaning as she stepped into them. No wonder one of the other guests chose to leave with bare feet.

"I'm sure as hell not letting you walk. And, no, you're not taking a cab, either, so let's go."

He was parked out in the back lot, so they said good-night to Karen and then stopped in the kitchen to say thank-you and good-night to the staff who'd remained to help. They'd stay until Karen's cleaning fairies showed up because no employees were ever left totally alone at Kincaid's, especially the women.

Then they went out into the brisk night, the chill setting in immediately. Screw the hoodie, she should have ruined the dressy look with a parka. But he'd hit the remote start at some point because the engine was running and the parking lights were on.

He opened her door first, and then laughed when she looked from the ground to the running board and up to the seat. "Here, let me help you up."

His hands slid under her armpits and he lifted just enough so she could get her foot onto the running board without tearing her dress or flashing any surveillance cameras monitoring the parking lot. Then she turned and sank onto the warm leather seat.

She sighed, closing her eyes, and heard him chuckle. "Guess you're glad I'm spoiled right about now."

"I take it all back. Also, I'm buying a truck."

He was laughing as he closed her door, and a moment later, he climbed into the driver's seat and inserted the key. "You can get heated seats in a car, you know."

She opened her eyes and turned her head in his direction, suddenly very tired. "Yeah, I know. I hate spending a lot of money on vehicles, though. I just need to get from point A to point B."

"Yeah, but I'm taking you to point B with a nice, warm backside."

It didn't take long for them to get to that point B, but parking was a bit of an issue. "You can just drive by and push me out if you want."

"You've been drinking. I'm walking you to your door."

"I told you I'm not drunk."

Scott nodded, then suddenly whipped the truck down a side street so fast she almost smacked her head on the window. "Yeah, and you also told me you're not sober."

He pulled into a space she wasn't sure actually *was* a space and killed the engine. She knew that, as long as he wasn't parked in a way that was blatantly illegal or caused complaints, he'd get a little more leeway than other drivers because of his job. Besides the Firefighters Memorial license plate framed by a Boston Fire holder and the sticker in the back window, most of the police officers in the neighborhood knew him and would recognize his truck.

Her door opened and he put his arms up to help her out. She clutched his shoulders and was thankful he held on to her a few extra seconds so she could find her balance on the heels. Maybe she'd had a drink or two more than she thought she had.

He laced his fingers through hers and they walked

down the sidewalk together in silence. The neighborhood was quiet and she might have enjoyed the stroll if she wasn't freezing. And if her feet didn't hurt so much she could feel each impact with the concrete up into her shins.

Once they were inside the front door, she stopped and stepped out of the heels. Walking up barefoot wasn't ideal, but she wasn't going to make it up all those flights of stairs in the shoes.

"Do you want me to carry you?" he asked. She imagined him draping her body over his shoulders and laughed. "I'm serious. I know how to do that, you know."

She laughed harder, until he actually shushed her. "You're going to wake up the whole building. Start climbing, Rutherford."

By the time they reached the top of the stairs and entered her apartment, Jamie was ready to just fall on the floor and sleep there. And Scott didn't look much better, despite the fact he hadn't had anything to drink.

"Are you staying?" she asked, tossing the heels into the shoe pile. She'd put them back in their box under the bed tomorrow and maybe add a sticky note to the lid noting she shouldn't try to wear them for more than two or three hours, and even then only if there were a lot of opportunities for sitting.

"I'd like to." He looked down at himself. "I'll have to do the walk of shame in the morning."

"If you're going to do the walk of shame, you may as well do it in a fine-looking suit."

He pulled her close and kissed her until the chill of the night had been chased away and replaced by heat. "I had a good time tonight."

"It was a beautiful wedding and a great party."

"I had a good time *with you* tonight. It was nice to touch you and hold your hand and laugh with you without worrying about it being a secret."

"It was." She wasn't sure how she'd feel walking into the station for their next tour, but she had no regrets. Even if it turned out to be awkward, she didn't have a lot of time left there.

"What just happened?" He put his finger under her chin and tilted her head back a little so he could see her face. "You looked sad for a minute."

"I'm not sad." She smiled to prove her point. "Just tired."

He hooked his finger into the neckline of her dress and slid it up until he could pull the fabric off her shoulder. "We should get you out of this dress, then, and get you into bed."

They made love slowly—almost tenderly—and afterward Jamie curled into his embrace. It was nice, she thought, that he wasn't going anywhere. She could close her eyes and drift off with his arms wrapped around her.

And in the morning she would tell him about the transfer.

FIFTEEN

Scott slowly opened his eyes, not surprised by his urge to smile into Jamie's hair. He wasn't much of a morning person, but waking up with her curled against him was definitely getting the day off to a good start.

He kissed her hair, pretty sure she was awake since she wasn't snoring. Her bunk might be on the second floor, but she'd nodded off on the couch or in the chair on the third floor often enough for him to know she snored like the rest of them. It just annoyed him less when she did it.

"Good morning," he said when she tried to burrow deeper into her pillow.

"Coffee."

"Are you hungover or is that how you greet every new day?"

"Coffee."

He chuckled and brushed her hair away from her neck so he could kiss her nape. "Five more minutes."

She rolled over so she was facing him, also managing to move a little farther away in the process. Her eyelids were not only very heavy this morning, but still bore some traces of last night's makeup since they'd been so tired they made love and fell asleep almost immediately.

"Good morning," she mumbled.

"Do you have stuff to make breakfast or should we go out?"

She shrugged one shoulder, making the comforter slip a little. "I don't know. I have coffee, though."

He realized that she might not want to go out to a restaurant, despite the fact they'd obviously been a couple last night. Rick had told her everybody in the bar had their backs, but the reception was over. But what could it hurt to be seen sharing a meal at this point? Everybody who really mattered to him had been at the wedding and they already knew there was a good chance they'd spent the night together.

"What are you thinking about?" she asked, her voice more clear as she shook off sleep. "You look very serious all of a sudden."

"I was wondering if we could go out to a restaurant or if we're back to hiding in your apartment."

"We might as well go out." She pulled up on the sheet to cover her mouth while she yawned. "The only people who don't know are people who don't matter much, especially since I already know what's going to happen."

He frowned. "What's going to happen with what?"

Her eyes widened and he realized she hadn't meant to say that. She was probably still groggy and her think-first filter wasn't awake yet. "With my transfer."

"You found out the day Danny stopped in, didn't

you?" It made sense to him now. "It wasn't only the conversation with Cobb that made you seem off. You found out where you're transferring."

"Yeah. I didn't want to say anything until after the wedding."

Because it was bad news. Or at least news that didn't bode well for them, he thought, if she was worried it would be a damper on the celebration. "Where are you going?"

"I'm transferring to Ladder 41, effective immediately upon Danny's return to full duty."

"Ladder 41. They're good guys."

"Yeah, I've met some of them at different events and they seem to be. I know they have a good record."

"They're not close, but I guess they're not that far away, either. Are you going to move?"

She shrugged. "Not right away, if at all. I might see how the commute goes for a while because I like my apartment. Plus L-41 is in a pretty swanky neighborhood, so I'm not sure I can afford to live close enough to work to make it worth moving again, anyway."

He waited a few seconds, wondering if she'd give him some kind of clue that he might factor into her decision, too. Maybe a comment about how staying in her apartment meant they'd be able to continue seeing each other. A joke about her still being on his route to the ice rink, at least.

But the words he wanted to hear from her didn't come. He rolled over to sit on the edge of the bed and scrubbed his hands over his face.

He'd known it would happen. Their relationship was never meant to be anything but temporary. He couldn't have gotten any bigger a clue they were nearing the end than he had last night.

Denying the bride's request to be in a wedding photo was kind of a big deal, so Jamie must have felt pretty strongly about not being in what Lydia considered the family picture. It was awkward when the formal family shot had an ex-girlfriend in it, she had said according to his sister.

Ex-girlfriend. She already thought of herself as his ex and they hadn't even broken off the relationship yet. He'd put it out of his mind, especially when she'd walked across the bar and into his arms, but now the pain of hearing that explanation from Lydia returned with such a vengeance, it made his stomach hurt.

"Danny said he's on track to return to duty next Friday," she said, her voice very quiet.

"Yeah, that's what he told us."

"Scott." He didn't respond right away, and then he jumped when he felt her hand on his back. "Hey."

All he could think about was how glad he was that he'd put off taking his dad's advice to tell Jamie how he felt about her. While he'd been falling in love with her and trying to wrap his mind around how their future would look together, she'd known the details of her departure and hadn't even bothered to tell him.

At least he'd be spared the embarrassment of having his feelings rejected. The pain would be bad enough. He didn't need humiliation piled on top of it.

After making sure his expression wouldn't reveal any of his emotional turmoil, he shifted on the bed so he could see her. "We'll miss you around the station."

He could tell by her eyes that the words had hit their target and she hadn't missed the far less personal *we.* "I'll miss you…all, too."

"It's not time to say goodbye yet," he said, as much for himself as for her. "I'm going to make coffee and then we can figure out what we want to do about breakfast."

She smiled, but it didn't quite reach her eyes. "That sounds like a plan."

Scott was brewing the first cup when he heard her get up and go into the bathroom. Blowing out a long, slow breath, he leaned his hip against the counter and tried to get his head on straight.

He could end it today, he thought. The door was open to a *hey, it's been fun but you need to focus on moving on* talk. Sure, they still had a couple of shifts left to work together, but their relationship hadn't been a factor on the job up to this point, anyway.

But the idea made him almost physically ill and he knew he wouldn't be able to say the words. Not today, anyway. Even after the double whammy of the ex-girlfriend comment last night and learning she hadn't told him about her transfer this morning, he wasn't ready.

He wasn't sure he'd ever be ready, actually. But he knew the moment wasn't now, so he'd keep on going the way they had been and hope she didn't see the truth in his eyes.

JAMIE SAT DOWN at her table, tucking one leg under herself, and opened her laptop. She hated sitting in the kitchen chair when she talked to her mom, but the alternative was standing at the counter. She'd learned the hard way curling up with her laptop on the couch led to some unflattering camera angles.

She poked around Facebook until she got the text from her mom that she was ready whenever Jamie was. After taking a sip of her coffee, she initiated a video chat. And when her mom's face appeared on the screen, she smiled. The Rutherford household had a desktop with a large monitor that her mom had angled so it was flattering, but she was fussing with her hair when it went live.

"You look beautiful, Mom. As always."

"Oh, hi, honey." She leaned forward, peering at her monitor. "You look a little tired."

Jamie smiled because she knew her mom said it out of concern and not criticism. "Restless night, I guess."

"Is everything okay?"

"Yeah. Probably something I ate." She didn't like lying to her mother, but the truth would worry her a lot more than thinking her daughter ate something too rich before going to bed.

She'd screwed up by not telling Scott about the transfer right away. He hadn't said anything, but his mood had changed and she didn't think it was the transfer itself. They'd both known that was going to happen.

After far too much time tossing and turning, alone

in her bed last night, she'd decided it had to be the timing. She'd wanted to wait until after the wedding to start the process of saying goodbye, but because of their relationship, she should have confided in him the day she found out where she was going.

Their relationship. She wished she knew what that meant.

"Jamie?" Her mom's voice broke into her thoughts. "What's wrong?"

"Nothing." She forced herself to sit up and look chipper. "So when do you think I should come home?"

"Is it that young man you've been seeing?"

"We're not really seeing each other." Jamie sighed. She really didn't want to try to explain Scott to her mother.

"You told me you'd gone on a date. But I heard a man laughing once while I was on the phone with you, and assumed he was watching television. And when you sent me a picture of how you organized those baskets in your living room, there was a hockey stick leaned up against the wall. Since you can't ice-skate *or* roller-skate, I assume it wasn't yours."

"And yet you didn't ask."

"You're my private one, sweetie, and you talk when you're ready. I took for granted you'd tell me if it got serious." Jamie looked away, taking a sip of her coffee, and she heard her mom sigh. "Uh-oh."

Looking into her mug, Jamie mimicked the sound. "So I kind of love him, I think."

"Oh, that's wonderful."

She looked at the screen, knowing she was about to disappoint her mom. "Not really. We're not…it's not. Dammit. We work together, so it's awkward."

She wasn't surprised when her mother's eyebrows shot up. She knew how her daughter felt—or *had* felt—about becoming involved with fellow firefighters. "He's in your company?"

"Yeah."

"How does he feel about you?"

She shrugged one shoulder, leaning back in the chair as she untucked her leg before it went to sleep. "We have a good time together, but that's it. And I'm leaving anyway, so it's a moot point."

"Your text said you'd be working in a different part of the city, but that you're not giving up your apartment. Maybe not working together will be a good thing."

"We're not really marriage compatible. We kind of have different views of raising a family, I guess."

"Because of your job?"

Jamie nodded. "Yeah. Plus, it was always kind of meant to be temporary. It wouldn't be fair to spring something more on him at this point."

Her mom pointed a finger at her computer's camera, which made Jamie smile. "It wouldn't be fair to *you* to walk away from a man you *kind of love, you think* just because coming to a compromise might be hard work."

"I know he likes me, Mom. We like being together."

"You should tell him how you feel, Jamie."

She nodded, though the thought made her stomach hurt. "I should. But I should wait until I'm done at that station in case things get awkward. I don't want it to spill over into work."

Her mom narrowed her eyes. "You mean you want to wait until after this casual thing of yours should be over because then if he calls you or stops by, you'll take it as a sign he might want it to continue."

She chuckled, not bothering to deny it. "Maybe. But also because I don't want things to be messy at work. Now, when do you think is a good time for me to visit? I'd like to wait until at least July so I'm settled in at the new station before I take a couple of tours off."

As she hoped, the prospect of nailing down details distracted her mom from Jamie's *kind of* love life. She looked down, frowning, and she knew her mom had her planner open on the desk.

"I think Tori's planning a family vacation the week after July Fourth, so maybe later in July? Let me look."

While her mother looked at the calendar on which she tracked four households in two states, Jamie drank her coffee and thought about what her mother had said. While she was serious about not wanting to take the chance of souring their relationship while they still worked together, her mom knew her better than anybody and she probably wasn't wrong about waiting to see if Scott wanted to keep seeing her once she'd transferred.

Maybe working beside her for weeks had changed

his mind about her job being too risky for a mother. It was one thing to imagine a woman rushing into a burning building when she had kids at home. But he knew her. He knew she was damn good at her job.

"Maybe the third week of July?"

Jamie pulled up the calendar on her phone to see if she had anything scheduled for then, though she was sure she didn't. It was time to give her mom her full attention and put Scott out of her head. They had two more tours together and then they'd see if the end of her time at Engine Company 59 was also the end of their time together.

SIXTEEN

"You look tired, Hunt. Maybe you should go take a nap and catch up on sleep."

Scott laughed at the ribbing Jeff was giving Aidan. They'd been at it most of the day, giving the newlywed a hard time about everything from looking sleep deprived to trying to get him to do an air management test with his SCBA and tank now that he was dragging around a ball and chain.

Jamie laughed, too, and he tried hard not to look at her. She was sitting in one of the chairs, a book in her lap, but he hadn't seen her actually turn a page for at least fifteen minutes.

They hadn't seen each other since he left her place the morning after the wedding, and they'd seemed okay then. Yesterday, he'd gotten sucked into doing errands and chores for his old man, and she'd promised her mom they'd do a video chat to talk about when would be a good time for Jamie to go home for a visit. Other than a few text messages, they hadn't spoken until they arrived for their tour today.

She'd smiled and said good-morning, as she always did, and they'd gone about their usual routine. He also noticed that none of the guys acted any differently toward her or made remarks about her relationship with him, which was good. He knew she'd been worried about that, no matter how much Rick had assured her it wouldn't be an issue.

So everything was the same. And yet everything was different. Because now he knew when she was leaving and where she was going. And he also knew she hadn't cared enough to share the information with him. He was just a guy she was killing time and having a good time with.

Just like he'd offered to be.

Tossing the magazine he'd been flipping through onto the coffee table, he stood and headed for the weight room. He couldn't stand sitting around anymore while his mind ran in circles. He might not be able to stop thinking about Jamie, but he could wear out his body.

He wasn't surprised when Aidan followed him in. Besides the fact the poor guy probably wanted a break from the teasing, they usually spotted each other. Aidan kicked the door closed behind them and hit the button to turn the radio on.

Scott grabbed a pair of gloves from the shelf and walked over to the heavy bag because he felt more like hitting something than lifting weights. Aidan positioned himself on the other side of it, ready to hold it for him.

"You're not going to knock me on my ass, are you?" he asked, peering around the black bag.

"Only if you're weak."

Aidan laughed. "That's it. Make it my fault you're

in a bad mood and want to beat the shit out of something."

"Who says I'm in a bad mood?" He'd gone out of his way to make sure he didn't act any differently today than he did any other day.

"You might be able to bullshit them, but you can't bullshit me."

Scott fidgeted with the closure on the left glove until it was as tight as he liked it, and then shoved his right hand into the glove. Then he held it out to Aidan so he could fasten it for him. "Jamie's going to Ladder 41. The end of this week when Danny comes back."

Aidan nodded, pressing the Velcro down to secure it. "That's pretty quick."

"I guess, although we knew from day one she'd transfer out of here. She's temporary."

Aidan couldn't have looked more serious if he'd been at a funeral. "Is she?"

"Is she what?"

"Temporary."

Scott growled and hit the bag. "I just said she was. She was just filling in for Danny."

"What about you guys? She's not temporary to you, is she?"

He hit with the left, getting into a rhythm of solid jabs to warm up. "Did Lydia tell you why Jamie wasn't in the pictures?"

"Yeah, she did. But how does she know your feelings about the relationship have changed if you don't tell her?"

He threw some hooks, mixing it up a little. The blows were hard enough so Aidan had to brace himself to avoid getting knocked around on the other side. “Who says they have?”

“Seriously, why do you even *try* to bullshit me? I know you, Scotty.”

Scott was winding up to take a swing at the bag that just might knock Aidan back against the wall when the alarm sounded. He ripped off the gloves and tossed them aside as they ran for the door.

“Three-story, multifamily residence. Juveniles reported trapped on third floor.”

Shit. They went for the pole. It was rarely used anymore because it wasn’t the safest way to get to the ground floor, but every second counted.

He barely paused long enough to shove his feet into his boots and pull up the bibs. The coat and helmet he took with him and he ran around the truck to climb into the cab. Firing the engine, he immediately hit the sirens so by the time the rest of the company was on board, he was ready to roll and—hopefully—drivers and pedestrians on the street had ample warning to get the hell out of the way.

The second E-59’s nose cleared the door enough for Jamie to see and tell him he was clear, he hit the gas pedal hard. Usually he noticed her reactions to corners and his aggressive way of getting through intersections, but today he had no attention to spare.

He brushed a car, parked illegally too close to a corner. “Fuck.”

Jamie pulled out her phone, but didn’t make a call

as they approached another intersection. Once she'd let him know the side street was clear, she slipped it back into its pouch. They'd report the damage and drown in the paperwork later.

They pulled up in front of the address, both drivers having to lay on the horns to get the idiot bystanders out of the way. There was plenty of flame and smoke for them to capture on their cell phones, but they needed to do it from well across the street.

The guys were spilling out before the trucks even stopped and he pulled his coat on as he climbed down. The ladder company was busting ass getting their landing pads down so they could raise the ladder, and he joined his guys, who were pulling out the line. Jeff had the spanner wrench to open the hydrant.

"Are there any adults up there with the kids?" he yelled to Jamie.

She shook her head. "They don't think so. Latchkey kids, home alone. Oldest is ten."

"Shit. Any visual confirmation?"

"No. The neighbors are sure they're in there, though."

Probably hiding. Maybe under the beds or maybe in a closet. Best-case scenario, they were all together and as soon as the ladder was up, a shout would have the oldest guiding them to the window.

"Fire started on the first floor. Cigarette and oxygen tank." Jamie cast a quick glance around to make sure they were ready. "All right. We need to keep those flames down until they get those kids out."

As they moved onto the porch, ready to blast the first floor with water, Scott registered movement on the ladder. Gavin was on his way up, scrambling toward the window. He could hear the crowd across the street, shouting pleas for them to find the kids. Sirens blaring as more police officers and fire companies and the EMS arrived. The incident command SUV skidding to a stop.

He was about to step from chaos into hell, and as he always did when it looked like things might get rough, he sent up a quick and silent prayer to his guardian angel.

Okay, Mom. I need you to watch my back. He grabbed on to the line behind Aidan and tapped his shoulder to tell him to go. *And today watch out for Jamie, too, okay?*

JAMIE HIT AIDAN'S shoulder to get his attention because either it was too loud for him to hear her or her radio was cutting in and out. She hadn't taken the time to figure out which. "We need to get up to the second floor. Flames in the back and they don't have the kids yet. Another company's at the rear, but they don't have a good angle."

He nodded, and they moved toward the stairs at the front. She hated moving floors before the fire was contained to at least a minimum degree, but they had guys on the third floor. Since she knew they wouldn't retreat without finding the children, they had to do everything they could to keep the fire from breaching that floor for as long as possible.

She didn't know if the entire building was decorated in cheap synthetic fabrics or if there were chemicals they didn't know about, but the smoke was thick and dark. It played hell on visibility, but they got the line to the second floor and turned the water on the flames. If they could beat it down from this direction while the other companies attacked it from the rear, they might be able to keep it from spreading any further.

Static crackled in her ear and she wanted to shake her head to clear it. Something was definitely wrong with her radio and it was an extremely shitty time to have a malfunction. Gullotti's voice came through in pieces, though.

They had the oldest and middle children. The toddler had been down for a nap and by the time they realized what was happening and went to find her, she'd already hidden. While the flames hadn't reached them yet, smoke had, and they'd gotten disoriented. They were being treated and the L-37 was going to have to do a room-by-room sweep, looking in every nook and cranny until they found the little girl.

"We have to keep this contained," she shouted, and her crew acknowledged.

She lost track of how long they worked, beating back the flames only to have them jump or reflame. It wasn't exactly a hoarding situation, but the apartment was full enough to offer plenty of fuel for the fire while hampering their movements.

It would have been tempting to back down and

get her guys out of harm's way, but she couldn't surrender the third floor to the fire.

"Shit!"

She turned in time to see a beam fall, narrowly missing Grant's helmet. He reacted, jumping to the right, but then went right back to the line. Looking past him, Jamie saw the old furniture surrounded by stacks of magazines and swore under her breath.

"You need to find that kid *now*," she shouted into her radio. Not that they weren't trying their best, but they were losing ground and she needed him to pick up on the sense of urgency.

It was at least five more minutes before they found the toddler hiding in a lower kitchen cabinet and got her out onto the ladder.

"We're pulling back," Gullotti reported. "Ladder 37 is clear of the structure."

"Let's get the hell out of here," Jamie shouted. The fire could have the building and the piles of junk somebody had been collecting since probably before she was even born.

They started their retreat, which wasn't easy since they had to manage the line as they went. And they were halfway back to the stairs when the building shifted and a ceiling joist dropped onto Grant, whose knees buckled.

Shit. Jamie moved to his side, wondering why the hell this house had it out for the young guy. He was already trying to get back on his feet, but he was wobbly and she could see the joist had damaged his tank connections.

They had to get him out of there.

"Go," she yelled, gesturing at the other guys. They could handle the line and make sure she didn't run into a dead end of flame. "Make sure the exit's clear."

She grabbed Grant's coat, pulling him close. But before she could get into position to hoist him up onto her shoulders, Scott was there. "I'll take him."

"I told you to clear the exit." The smoke was seriously hampering visibility now, and she knew the flames were devouring the place almost unchecked at this point.

"Aidan's got it, and there's another company in support. Let me carry him down the stairs."

She was so angry she couldn't even speak for a few seconds. Carrying Grant down the stairs she could do. Physically it was harder for her to backtrack out of the structure while wrestling with the line, and therefore more dangerous for everybody. "I gave you an order."

He ignored her and hauled Grant onto his shoulder. The younger guy struggled, trying to tell them he could walk, but he was so shaky and disoriented, it would be faster to carry him.

The building shifted again with a creaking groan, and she knew they couldn't spare even another second to have a pissing match about who was in charge. She took off toward the stairs, staying just far enough ahead to make sure their path was clear without losing sight of Scott and Grant.

They caught Aidan, and Jamie grabbed the line

behind him as he sprayed what had to be a reignition point. She waved for Scott to take Grant behind them and then pointed at a window. It had already been smashed out, probably by another engine company, and it was only a few seconds before guys appeared on the other side to take Grant.

Scott didn't go out, though. He came back and tapped her on the shoulder. "I've got this. You should get out."

She ignored him and shouted to Aidan. "We're clear, Hunt. Let's get clear."

Once outside, they grabbed waters and protein bars from the volunteers and walked as a group to check on Grant.

He was sitting up on the stretcher in the back of the ambulance with a white collar on, looking annoyed. The paramedic who seemed to be in charge looked at them and, noting the rank on her helmet, addressed her comments to Jamie.

"He says he's fine." She rolled her eyes. "I think he might have a mild concussion. Initial smoke inhalation, but he snapped out of that pretty quickly when we put the oxygen mask on him. We're taking him in to have a look at his neck and spine just to make sure there aren't any hairline fractures in there. It looks like his tank took the brunt of it, but his tank's on his back, so we want to be cautious."

"I'm fine," Grant called, trying to catch Jamie's eye.

She pointed a finger at him, having had her fill of people not doing what they were told. "You're going to the hospital. When they say you can leave, you can leave. Do you understand?"

"Yes, ma'am."

Once the ambulance doors were closed, they walked back to the truck to start getting their equipment together and repacked. They'd hang around for a while in case it took a long time to burn down, but for now they could rest for a few minutes.

"Jamie." She heard Scott's voice and turned to face him, giving him *the look.* It was the look she'd been about to unleash on the guy in the bar before Scott punched him instead. He stopped in his tracks, his eyes widening.

"I gave you an order and you disobeyed it." She didn't want to do this in front of both companies, but if he wasn't going to give her a choice, at least she could steer him toward keeping the conversation about the job.

"For a good reason."

"The only good reason for you to disregard what I say is if you think I'm unfit for duty or command. You didn't indicate to me or to anybody else that you believed that to be so."

"I had personal reasons," he said, not giving up.

Keenly aware of the fact they had an audience, Jamie made sure her voice was low. "Your personal reasons have no place here."

She turned to walk away, which, in hindsight, was probably a mistake. Scott grabbed her arm, spinning her to face him. In her peripheral vision, she saw the other guys stop trying to pretend they couldn't hear as they all turned to look. Aidan even took a step forward, but Rick held out his hand to stop him.

"I couldn't do it," he said in a hoarse voice. "I couldn't stand there and do nothing but listen to the radio, praying to hear your voice. I did that with Danny and I knew I couldn't leave without you. And if you think I was disrespecting your ability to do your job, then I'm sorry. But I love you, Jamie. I fell in love with you and I couldn't stand by and do nothing."

His words fell on her like blows. At any other time, in any other place, those words might have made her the happiest woman on the planet. But not here, on an active scene in front of the guys in her command.

She jerked her arm away. "If you loved me—hell, if you really knew anything about me and paid attention—you would never have done this here."

Without giving him a chance to say anything more, Jamie turned and walked away with her back straight, her eyes dry and her heart splintering into ruin.

SCOTT LOOKED UP when the swinging doors to the emergency room opened, but the nurse walked to a family sitting across the hallway from them. Since it wasn't anybody about Grant, he dropped his head back against the wall and stared at the ceiling tiles some more.

He'd blown it. His temper and lack of impulse

control had gotten him into a lot of trouble over the course of his life, but he'd never sabotaged his own happiness the way he had today.

"Stop beating yourself up."

Scott wanted to ignore Aidan, but right now he was the only person Scott had to talk to. The others were back at the station, since Jamie had volunteered the two of them to go to the hospital and wait for news on Grant. Or to bring him back if he was released.

He knew she'd just wanted him out of her sight.

"Why the hell did I do that? I mean, I know why I disobeyed her. It was wrong and stupid, but I know what happened. But telling her I did it because I love her in front of everybody? I opened my mouth and it came out."

"I have to ask. Is it true?"

"That I love her?" He sighed. "Yeah. I do love her. But I also know that wasn't the time or place to tell her that. And I knew it when I was saying it."

"I have a theory, but it's probably best if you figure it out on your own."

"Really?" Scott swiveled his head so he was looking at his best friend. "What the hell is that supposed to mean?"

"It means just that. I have a theory, but I think you should figure it out on your own because I might be wrong and then I'd just look like an asshole."

"You can't look more like an asshole than I do."

"That's pretty much been my life motto since the

day we met. I can't look like more of an asshole than Scotty Kincaid does."

Scott actually chuckled, which he knew was Aidan's intention with the insults. But his amusement was short-lived. "Even if you're wrong, at least you have a theory. I can't wrap my head around why I would pull a stunt like that. I *knew* she wouldn't forgive that."

"Because you're scared." Aidan's voice was very serious now. "You're scared of taking a chance on Jamie, so you did something you knew would make her walk away and not come back."

Scott swallowed past the lump in his throat and shrugged. *And not come back.*

"Why am I scared?" Deep in his gut, he suspected Aidan's theory might be right. "We're great together. We have a good time and we enjoy each other's company. We laugh and talk. I mean, I love her. I know I do. How can I love her and be scared of being with her?"

"I don't know. I think if you want to dig deeper into that psyche of yours, you'll need a professional. Or Lydia."

"I don't even want to think about telling Lydia what happened. Don't tell her."

"Really?" Aidan shifted in his chair, leaning forward with his elbows propped on his knees. "I knew there would come a time when my loyalty to you would conflict with my loyalty to my wife, but I thought I'd have more than three days."

The swinging doors opened again and this time

Grant walked out. He looked annoyed and slightly chagrined, but whole. “Hey, guys.”

A doctor was with him, and he looked at them over the top of his glasses. “Mr. Cutter here will be fine. He was lucky and escaped with a very minor concussion. He needs to rest for a couple of days, but as long as he remains symptom free and pays attention to any messages his body might send him, there’s no reason he can’t resume his duties on his next shift.”

“Thanks, Doc.” Aidan looked around the waiting room. “Can I take him out in a wheelchair?”

The doctor didn’t even crack a smile. “He can walk. You guys have a good day and be safe.”

They rode back to the station in silence. Grant probably because he had a raging headache. Scott because he was still trying to make sense of his moment of stunning stupidity, and Aidan because nobody else was talking.

Everybody was on the third floor when they got back, except for Cobb and Jamie. He went into the kitchen to make Grant a cup of coffee, which he probably wasn’t supposed to have but really wanted, while the kid shared the diagnosis. Because it was good news, Grant took a ration of shit, which would have made Scott laugh if he wasn’t so focused on Jamie’s absence.

When he saw Rick by himself, Scott walked over to him. “Where’s Jamie? She’ll want to know that Grant’s back.”

Rick gave him a look that could have set a glass of

water on fire. "The lieutenant's in her office, doing paperwork. Not the least of which has to do with the car you hit today. And she already knows Cutter is back."

Temper at being iced out by a guy who'd known him as long as Rick had flared in Scott, but he shoved it back. This wasn't personal. Scott hadn't done what he was told to do. Firefighters doing whatever the hell they wanted put their companies at risk. And anything that put Engine 59 at risk was probably going to put Ladder 37 at risk, too.

"Yes, sir." It killed him to say it and not try to defend himself, but he didn't have anything to say that would make it okay.

But as he turned away, he caught a flicker of something on Rick's face. "Scotty."

He turned, bracing himself for more censure. "If Jamie wasn't leaving this week, we'd have a problem."

"I know. But I'm the root of the problem, not her. What happened today shouldn't reflect poorly on her at all."

"Oh, I'll make sure it doesn't." Rick gave him a humorless smile. "Luckily, I think the only guys paying attention were our own, so that issue's moot. But on a personal level that's none of my business, you need to make this right. Not only for her sake, but for yours. Even if it's over, this isn't the way you want it to end."

"I don't want it to end at all," he said, though his subconscious must have differed for him to so blatantly shoot himself in the foot. "I'll talk to her. Maybe try to make her understand."

"You should. But not here and not today. I've got a couple of guys coming in. I want you to take Grant home and make sure he has whatever he needs to keep him on the couch for a couple of days. And then you can head home, too."

"Am I being suspended?"

Rick shook his head. "Not in an official capacity, that I know of. But she doesn't need you here. And if we have to go on a run, everybody's going to be distracted and less confident. Go home. Or go see your old man. Have a beer with Tommy and see if he can help you figure this out."

Scott snorted, not really able to picture his dad giving him advice. "Okay. I guess space is best for everybody."

"Yeah, but not too much. And not for too long." Rick slapped him in the shoulder. "I'm rooting for you, you know. Even if you are a dumbass."

Once Grant was ready to go, Scott followed him down the stairs, but he paused on the second floor. Maybe he should knock on her door and at least apologize briefly. He could test the waters, so to speak, and see how open she would be to seeing him later, when he could really apologize. Leaving without saying anything at all didn't sit well with him.

But they were still at work. He'd disrespected her once already and there was a good chance she'd see him knocking on her door as more of the same.

She didn't want to talk about their personal lives at work.

With a last glance at Jamie's office door—which remained firmly closed—Scott shoved his hands into his pockets and followed Grant down the last flight of stairs.

SEVENTEEN

Jamie sat with her elbows braced on her desk and the heels of her hands pressed to her eyes, praying like hell the alarm didn't sound. Red, puffy eyes and a stuffy nose from crying wouldn't do much to inspire confidence.

He loved her.

Even now, when everything had gone to crap and she'd shut him down before sending him away, her pulse quickened at the thought. She'd known he cared about her more than he let on. She felt it in the way he touched her and the way he looked at her.

And when a woman was in love with a man, she was sensitive to those kinds of things.

He could have told her he loved her when they were tangled up in her sheets, hot and out of breath. He could have told her while they were curled up on the couch watching one of his stupid movies. But not Scott.

Instead he'd pissed her off by defying her orders and then he'd turned what should have been the sweetest words she'd ever hear into professional embarrassment. He knew what that scene would do to her—that he was pushing one of her biggest hot buttons—and he'd done it anyway.

And that made her doubt that what he had said was actually the truth.

And damn, there were more tears again. She rubbed at her eyes and then pressed the wet washcloth she'd grabbed from the bathroom to her face. It wasn't cold enough to help anymore, but it calmed her a little.

He loved her. He'd told her he loved her and she'd rejected it. Coldly and as publicly as he'd thrown it out there. It was over. Her time at E59-L37 was over and her time with Scott was over.

Rather than give in to more tears, Jamie pushed back from her desk and looked around the office. There were very few personal items in it. Most belonged to Danny, and the stuff that was hers would barely cover the bottom of a box. But she had things in the officer's bunk room to pack. And she'd have to remember to take the box of tampons from under the bathroom sink so nobody was traumatized by it after she left.

That thought made her smile. She probably wouldn't feel like laughing any time soon, but she wasn't going to curl into a ball and weep for hours, either. At least not here.

Too many hours later, she left the awkward silences and too-polite conversations behind her and went home. Her apartment felt emptier than usual. Quieter. And she knew it would feel that way for a while because Scott wouldn't be filling it with his energy and big personality. She was alone again.

After forcing herself to take a shower, she put on

her comfort pajamas—old sweats she'd stolen from a college boyfriend—and crawled into bed. If she slept a few hours, maybe things wouldn't look so depressing when she woke up.

But life didn't look any better when she finally decided to roll out of bed and force herself to eat something. Sleep hadn't been easy, and the nodding off and waking up and trying not to cry had given her a headache.

She was halfway through a bowl of cereal she didn't want when her phone chimed. She really wanted to ignore it, but there was a good chance if it was a well-meaning friend who knew what had happened, that friend would show up at her door.

It wasn't, though. It was Scott. *Can we talk for a few minutes? I'm downstairs, but I can keep walking if you want.*

It was tempting to tell him to keep moving, but she couldn't do it. *I'll be right down.*

She took a few seconds to look in the mirror, and then wished she hadn't. Her hair wasn't awful, but her face had the look of a brokenhearted woman who'd cried too many tears and not slept enough hours.

There was no help for it, though, so she forced herself to go down the stairs to get some closure. She saw him through the glass door and her heart ached so badly she had to resist the urge to raise her hand to her chest to rub the spot.

At least he looked almost as miserable as she did, but without the red eyes.

She pushed open the door and stepped back to let him in. Once the door swung shut, she leaned against the wall and folded her arms. "I'm not going to invite you upstairs."

"I understand." He paused, staring down at the bag in his hands before lifting his gaze to meet hers. "I'm sorry."

The sincerity came through so strongly, she wanted to wrap her arms around him and hold him close. He looked sad and tired, and she couldn't help but contrast it to the fire scene, when his expression had burned with intensity as he told her he loved her.

"I'm not sure what else I can say," he said. "I know that...what I said before wasn't what you wanted to hear, but—"

"You're wrong. I did want to hear you say those words to me. I *really* did."

He was silent for a few seconds, probably realizing what that meant, and then he cleared his throat. "I shouldn't have said them there or then. And I shouldn't have used my feelings for you as an excuse for disrespecting you professionally."

At least he got it. "You had to know I wouldn't want that in front of everybody."

"I did." He shifted his weight, sighing heavily. "I did know that, and I think subconsciously I did it on purpose. Talking about your transfer and everything made me think about the future, but we weren't really supposed to have a future together. We're just not on the same page. But I fell in love with you and I was starting to wonder if we could make it work. In the fire, in the structure after Grant got hit, I just… I panicked. I didn't want you in there and that scared me. And I imagined how that would feel day after day and I guess I sabotaged whatever we had."

Jamie processed his words, letting them sink in. They made sense to her. He'd lost his mom so young and then had to live with a father who was a firefighter and had survived a heart attack. And Ashley had told her how shaken he'd been by Danny's accident.

At least it had come from a place he couldn't quite control, because love and fear weren't always rational, and that was a comfort. It helped to know he hadn't simply been acting with blatant disregard for her feelings.

"You proved that you can't really handle letting me do my job. I'm not the television wife you're looking for, Scott."

She watched the impact the words had on him. He paled slightly and his jaw clenched. "You're the woman I fell in love with."

Curling her hands into fists so tight her fingernails bit into her palms, Jamie absorbed the blow of the words. "I fell in love with you, too. But I won't be happy in the box you want to put me in."

"I don't want to put you in a goddamned box."

"You *did* put me in a goddamned box. You already did it. You decided you knew better than I did what was good for me, and even if I *wasn't* your lieutenant and we weren't on the job, that's not something I'm going to accept in *any* part of my life." She looked up for a few seconds, blinking rapidly to keep the sheen of tears at bay. "Imagine how much stronger that fear would have been if I was also the mother of your children."

He nodded, so much sorrow in his eyes, she couldn't stop her own tears from spilling over onto her cheeks. "I love you, Jamie. I respect you. I really do respect the hell out of you. I want you to know that."

"I know you do. And that makes this so much harder."

"I didn't want this." He blew out a breath and ran a hand over his hair. "I should go. I hope you like being with Ladder 41 and that it all works out for you. I'm sure I'll run into you at events and stuff. And I, uh, brought you something."

When he held out the bag, she took it and peered inside. The little tub of chocolate pudding from the market made her breath catch in her chest and the tears kicked it up a notch.

"I only got a single serving," he said. "So you wouldn't think I was trying anything. But I thought it might help you feel better later."

Jamie couldn't talk, so she just nodded, clutching the bag. After a few seconds, he put his hand on her arm and leaned forward to kiss her cheek. She turned her face into it, the contact lingering for a few seconds.

And then he stepped back. "I'm sorry, Jamie."

He pushed open the door and walked away. She watched him shove his hands into the pockets of his sweatshirt, his shoulders hunched as if to fend off a cold wind. And once he was out of sight, she walked back up the stairs and set the bag on the counter.

It was over. Not just a bump in the road and *maybe we can get through this* over. But a *hey, enjoy your new assignment and I'll see you around* kind of over. She should throw the pudding in the garbage and forget he ever existed.

She didn't have the strength to do either, though. Instead she pulled out a spoon and cried her way through the sweetest, most painful parting gift she'd ever gotten.

SCOTT SLAPPED THE puck and watched it sail between the pipes. Then he slapped the next one. Taking shots on an empty goal wasn't much of a challenge and barely qualified as exercise, but it was somewhat satisfying when he hit them and they shot like bullets into the net.

The ice was the only place he'd ever been able to work out his feelings without getting himself in trouble. Even then, his temper sometimes got the best of him, but it wasn't the same as getting into a fight or kicking the crap out of his truck because he was pissed. Times like this, when it was just him on the ice and a line of pucks, were almost like meditation sessions for him. Usually they cleared his mind.

His mind was refusing to clear today, though.

Jamie loved him, too. That's why he hadn't slept worth a damn. Why he couldn't stand the thought of eating. Why half the pucks he shot were bouncing off the pipes and coming back at him. He'd gone over there to try to apologize and try to end things on a more positive note and hearing her say that had driven home just how badly he'd screwed up. He'd thrown everything away.

The click of a blade on ice broke into his thoughts and he turned toward the bench area, expecting to see one of the other guys or maybe the kid who was working that day. But it was Ashley, wearing jeans and a fleece pullover, along with ice skates she'd obviously gotten at the desk.

"Jesus, Ash. What the hell are you doing?"

"What do you mean?"

"You're pregnant. You can't just go flinging yourself around on ice skates."

She laughed and ignored him, skating toward him. "I don't really intend to fling myself at anything. And I might not be very good at hockey, but I'm the one who taught you to skate, dumbass."

"Slow down, at least."

"I'm barely moving. And the baby is fine. I've got plenty of built-in padding for safety."

He shook his head, knowing it was futile to argue with her. "What are you doing here?"

"I was going by and saw your truck. And I just asked Danny the other day if he'd been on skates yet and he said you guys haven't planned any ice time, so I figured you were in here alone. Probably brooding."

"I think better on skates."

"You always did." Sighing, she looked at the pile

of pucks in and around the net. "Figure out the solution yet?"

"Solution to what?"

"Don't play dumb with me, Scotty."

"There is no solution. Or I guess you could say it already resolved itself. I was an asshole and that's not a quality she's looking for in a man."

"So stop being an asshole."

He clenched his jaw, wishing he could unleash his temper on a puck, but he wasn't taking the chance of it taking a weird turn and hitting his sister. "If it was a switch I could turn on and off, I would have done it years ago. Maybe."

"You can't let her go because you're afraid to love her. It's too late, you know. You *already* love her, so why be miserable?"

"How do I live with that fear every day?" He heard his voice rising, echoing through the rink. "I was so afraid for her that I did something stupid and we're not even… I hadn't even told her I loved her yet. We don't share our lives. There are no kids waiting at home for their mom. How would I handle that?"

She looked at him, her expression slightly sad, but also bemused. "The same way we all do. You've seen this your entire life, Scotty. You're just on the other side of it and you don't know how to handle it. But you deal with the fear the same way I do and the same way Lydia does and that Mom did and that this baby will. You trust your firefighter will be safe and smart and come home to you."

"And what if she doesn't? Come home, I mean."

"Then you keep going. If Danny had died that day—"

"Don't say that."

"No, I *do* get to say that, Scotty, because it's my reality. That possibility is something I live with every time he walks out the door. And if someday he doesn't come home, I won't regret loving him. I won't regret having his child. The baby and I will keep going. Just like we all did when Mom died, except I won't do like Dad and tell my kid to suck it up and get on with life. There would be counseling and support, like we should have had."

"Dad did the best he could," Scott said, defending the old man out of sheer reflex. "It was never the same after, though."

"Of course it wasn't." She sighed, and he couldn't help but feel like he was missing something. "I'm not going to give you the speech about how Jamie could get hit by a car or fall down the stairs or be the first victim of the zombie apocalypse. But you need to ask yourself why you wouldn't think twice about asking a woman to spend the rest of her life taking it on faith you'll come home from work, but you won't do the same for her."

"I don't know how to stop wanting to take care of her."

"That's part of the way you're wired. You keep people safe." Ashley sighed again and took his hand. "And you're supposed to want to take care of her. You take care of each other. But wanting her to be something she's not isn't taking care of her."

"I miss her so much my stomach hurts and it's only been a day."

"I know what that feels like," she said. "After I told Danny we were done, I cried so hard I puked and then cried some more. But we worked through it. And that's your second mistake. You guys hit a wall and instead of looking for a way over or around it, you said *fuck it* and went home."

"I didn't say *fuck it.* I just decided not to hurt her any more than I already had."

"If she does love you, this—the emptiness—hurts more than anything you could say to her." She squeezed his hand. "Pick up your pucks and let's go. You can buy your niece or nephew some ice cream."

Once they were back in sneakers and he'd put everything away, he took her hand and they walked out of the rink together. The sun was warm and being outside with Ashley made him feel better. Less hopeless at least, and he knew he needed to get out of his own head for a while.

"Thanks for coming, Ash. Somehow you always know what to say. Sometimes it doesn't sink into my thick skull for a while, but I don't know what I'd do without you."

"That's what big sisters are for. And you're lucky to have two. Lydia to kick you in the ass and me to give you a hug."

He laughed and put his arm around her shoulders. "Let's get some ice cream."

She grinned. "I want a small scoop of chocolate with a pound of whipped cream and jimmies on it. And half a jar of cherries."

"That baby's got good taste." He squeezed her hand and they started walking toward the ice cream shop. For now, he'd shove his pain and confusion into the dark corners of his mind and enjoy an hour or so with his sister.

IT SEEMED LIKE just Jamie's luck that the guys got called out on a run just before she finished packing the few things left in her office and the bunk room, and emptying out her locker.

Maybe it was for the best, she thought, looking around the empty engine bay. She hated goodbyes and she'd been especially nervous about this one because she was afraid she'd cry again.

She'd spoken to each of the guys at some point during the morning, anyway. They'd all wished her luck and there had been jokes and promises to keep in touch. She could tell they were thrilled to have Danny back, which made it slightly easier for her to move on. This had never been her place, really.

She'd barely seen Scott. He kept himself busy down in the bays, taking inventories and cleaning the trucks and chatting with people who walked by and stopped to talk. Every time she saw him, even from across the room, the pain was so sharp she struggled not to let it show.

It was definitely time to go. There was no way she could hang around, caught up in her own thoughts, and not bawl at having to say goodbye and hug each one of them. And she would either have to say goodbye to Scott again, or she'd have to ignore him.

She put the last box in her car, which she'd managed to get reasonably close to the station, and then took one last look around. All traces of her were gone, so after sending a mental goodbye to Engine 59 and all the guys, she got in her car and drove away from the curb.

Jamie hadn't intended to go to Kincaid's Pub when she pulled away from the station, but she wasn't surprised when she found herself on the sidewalk, staring at the door. Her mind had been totally wrapped up with Scott, and here she was at his family's bar. As if coming here would somehow offer up a clue to what had gone so horribly wrong or how to fix it.

Everything had changed when she told him she was transferring to Ladder Company 41. It hadn't been an easy thing to tell him because she'd hated saying the words out loud. She'd known that things were going to change and that meant their relationship would change.

She'd been right. Except their relationship hadn't just changed. It had crumbled like a dried-out sand castle.

Jerking open the door, she went inside. She was pretty well braced against the memories that threatened to emotionally overwhelm her, but she got a little shaky when Lydia saw her and smiled.

"Hey, you." Lydia looked at the clock hanging on

the wall. "I've never seen you in here at this time of day, but it's five o'clock somewhere, right?"

"It's definitely five o'clock." She climbed up onto a bar stool, thankful the place was practically empty.

Lydia tilted her head, frowning as she looked at her. "You want a beer or do you want me to break out the good stuff?"

"I'd actually love a coffee. I'm not much of a beer drinker and I'm not doing cocktails on an empty stomach."

"Coming right up."

When Lydia set a huge mug of coffee in front of her, along with a small dish of creamer cups, Jamie smiled her thanks. She wasn't sure what, if anything, Scott had told his sister, but she didn't seem to be acting any differently toward her.

"Do you want something to eat?"

Jamie shook her head. She knew she should eat, but she wasn't hungry and was afraid if she forced herself, she'd only make herself sick. "No, thanks. Just the coffee, I guess."

"Okay." But Lydia reached under the counter and dropped a few packages of oyster crackers in front of her. "Do you want to talk about it?"

Tears prickled her eyes and she tried to blink them away. "Not really."

"Neither did he." Lydia sighed and leaned against the counter. "That's probably half the damn problem, you know. If you guys would talk to each other, neither of you would be so miserable."

"Some things just aren't meant to be," Jamie said.

Saying it to Lydia was a good reminder for herself, and she forced herself to sit up straight.

"Things don't just *be*." Lydia paused, then shook her head. "Okay, that made a lot more sense in my head. But some things *are* meant to be, but you have to work for them and not expect all the pieces to magically fall into place."

Jamie fiddled with a package of crackers to give her hands something to do. Part of her resented the lecture, but she knew her subconscious hadn't come here accidentally. She'd pulled up a stool in front of one of the two women who cared about both her and Scott, and one who wasn't shy about telling a person what she thought.

"You know, I didn't want to come back to Boston," Lydia said. "I got out and I intended to stay out. I was done with firefighters. I was done with the entire firefighting community and my dad and this bar. I wanted no part of it."

"Since I was here when you married a firefighter *in* this bar, I guess you changed your mind."

"We talked."

"That's it? You talked?"

Lydia shrugged. "Basically. I mean, he *was* willing to walk away from everything for me, but I guess knowing I meant that much to him was enough for me. But if he hadn't come and talked to me, I would have been gone and I probably wouldn't have come back."

Jamie ripped the end of the package open and popped an oyster cracker into her mouth. Chewing and swallowing gave her time to think about how much she wanted to say, because this was her friend. She was also Scott's sister and Jamie knew that relationship trumped hers.

"We did talk," she said finally. "And this is where we ended up, so there's really nothing more to say."

"At this time of day, to come in here and not want a beer or food, you must have come here for another reason, Jamie. You're not ready to give up on him yet."

"I came to say goodbye." As much as she hated saying the words, she knew they were the right ones to say. "I cleaned out my office and my locker this morning. I'm officially done with Engine Company 59."

Wow, that hurt to say. And it wasn't only because of Scott. She would genuinely miss all of them.

"I know everybody's sad to see you leave the company, but what the hell is this goodbye bullshit? You're going to Ladder 41, not Michigan."

Jamie gave a short laugh, which surprised her. "Why Michigan?"

"I don't know." Lydia shrugged. "I don't know anybody who's ever gone to Michigan, so it seems like you moving there would merit a goodbye."

"You'd never met anybody from Nebraska before me, either. I guess I'm all about broadening your horizons."

"No, you're all about trying to change the subject. I'm a bartender. I can sense these things."

"I know I'm not moving to Michigan. I don't know if or when I'll move at all. But I don't think I'll be coming in here for a good long while. This is pretty undeniably his turf, you know?"

"You're my friend. I'm not letting you disappear on me."

Jamie's throat tightened and she prayed she wouldn't burst into a full-on bout of tears. "And I'll see you when you're not working, like most people see their friends."

"I can't accept that you're not meant to be together."

"I'm having a hard time accepting it myself." Jamie wished Lydia would move on. Unfortunately, if she kept pushing at her about Scott, Jamie knew their friendship would eventually wither and die because she wasn't going to rehash it every time they spoke. "I should probably go home. I've got my stuff in the car and I want to go through it and see what I'm taking with me to L-41."

"The coffee's on the house today. I know you won't stop in, but text me or call me and we can get together, okay? I want to hear about your new assignment."

"I will."

The phone rang and Lydia gave her hand a squeeze before walking to the register end of the bar to answer it. Jamie saw her chance to escape without further drama and slid off the stool, but the picture on the wall caught her eye.

She stared at the photo of Bobby Orr, the light reflecting off the glass highlighting the many—possibly even hundreds—of fingerprints smudging it. There had probably been a lot of broken glasses over the years. Kincaid's Pub had probably seen its share of broken hearts, too.

"I don't know if you do broken hearts," she said to the man in the picture. "But I feel like my heart shattered like glass, so you're worth a shot, right?"

She kissed the tips of her fingers and pressed them to the picture, holding them there until the glass warmed under her touch. And then she laughed at herself and walked out of the bar.

EIGHTEEN

JAMIE STOPPED BY to say goodbye. Are you okay?

Scott read the text from his sister twice, wishing she'd left well enough alone. It was hard enough sitting on the couch feeling as if he'd lost everything while the guys went on with their lives around him.

They'd come back from a call and every trace of Jamie was gone, as if she'd never been there. The others were in good spirits, glad to have Danny back, and he tried. He was genuinely happy to have Danny back, too, but there was a void in Scott's world he couldn't ignore.

He typed in his response to Lydia. Yeah, I'm fine. Busy. Call you later.

Okay.

He wouldn't call her later. Right now, he didn't want sympathy *or* a lecture and he knew she'd give him one or the other.

The couch creaked as Danny sat down next to him and propped his legs up on the coffee table with a sigh.

"How's the leg?" Scott asked.

"It's good. It'll probably ache a little later, but it's better than I'd hoped. Mostly it's just being up and around for so many hours. I had too many weeks of sitting on my ass, watching television."

"Says the guy sitting on his ass in front of the television," Scott said, and they both laughed.

"How are *you* doing?"

"Fine." That was going to be his party line for the foreseeable future. He was fine. Life was fine. Work was fine. Everything was fine.

Maybe if he repeated the lie often enough, it would eventually become the truth.

"You want to talk?"

Scott realized it was quiet and the other guys had all found someplace else to be. "Not really."

Danny leaned his head back against the couch, pinching the bridge of his nose between his fingers. "I'm your lieutenant. I'm your brother-in-law. I'm your friend. I get to worry about you from all different angles."

"You heard what happened, then."

Danny snorted. "Was that in question? If anybody should know you can't keep a secret around here, it's you."

"Yeah. Nothing like embarrassing yourself in front of everybody."

"Embarrassing yourself? Nobody's laughing at you, Scotty."

He snorted. "No, but they're talking."

"Of course they are. Number one, they all consider you a friend and nobody likes seeing you hurting. And nobody wants to say or do the wrong thing and set you off."

"I'm not going to go off." The only person he was mad at was himself.

"And I won't lie to you. Everybody respects the hell out of Jamie Rutherford, so it also made them all a little uncomfortable."

"Sorry to cause them discomfort." He started to get up, but Danny put a hand on his shoulder and shoved him back.

"Scotty, don't be a dick. As your friend, I just want to know if you're okay. And as your LT, I want to know if you're okay to be here or if you want to take some time off."

Time off to what? Wander around his apartment and take stock of how empty his life was? To think about how full it had been for a few weeks before he'd thrown it all away? Maybe he could hit some clubs and hook up with somebody who could never be Jamie just to hate himself a little more.

"I need to work." He said the words quietly, afraid to show just how badly he needed to be anywhere but alone at home. "I might even cover for some other companies. Lots of guys looking for some time off with summer coming."

"If she was the one, you won't be able to work hard enough to forget her," Danny said. "That's not how to fix this."

"I'll never forget her," Scott said, clearing his throat when his voice almost betrayed him. "I just want to work hard enough to sleep at night."

Jamie couldn't handle being in her apartment and she had no idea what to do about it. She'd already escaped the loneliness that seemed to echo through the place by going to Kincaid's to see Lydia. She'd even done a few errands. But with hours stretching ahead of her, she was afraid she'd do nothing but flop on her bed and cry until she made herself sick.

She thought about reaching out to her family but, as much as she loved them, they wouldn't give her what she needed and might even make it worse. There would be sympathy and gentle advice that would feel like empty platitudes. And she would cry, which would wreck her mother. Not being able to hug over the computer would be too hard.

Grabbing her car keys from the kitchen drawer, she put on her shoes and gave herself a pep talk before heading deeper into the city. She took a couple of wrong turns, almost went the wrong way down a one-way street, and got flipped the bird at least twice, but finally managed to land a parking space within walking distance of the pizza place Steph's family owned.

When she walked inside, assaulted by the delicious aroma of food she had no appetite for, she was glad to see it wasn't too busy. She might be able to steal Steph for a few minutes. Walking up to the counter, she smiled at Steph's dad.

"Hi, Mr. Lawson. Is Steph around tonight?"

"She's out back, chopping veggies," he said.

Mrs. Lawson looked up from the pizza she was boxing and, after a look at Jamie, waved her around the counter. "I'll take over for her for a few minutes. You girls go have a break for a little bit."

She could have cried tears of gratitude for Mrs. Lawson's *mom radar*, but she just smiled. "Thanks."

When Steph looked up from the line of tomatoes she was slicing, her expression made Jamie laugh. "Hey, what are you doing here? Did you drive?"

"I drove. And your mom said she'd take over the veggies so we can visit for a few minutes."

"If you'd told me you were coming this way, I would have tried to get somebody to cover for me."

"It was kind of a last-minute, impulse thing."

Steph looked at her, and then waved for her to follow. Winding through the busy kitchen, they dodged the three employees assembling orders and went into the break room. After closing the door behind them, Steph gestured for her to sit at the small table.

"What happened?" she asked. "You look exhausted and sad."

"Scott and I broke up."

"I'm sorry." Steph tilted her head. "I hate to be dense, but wasn't that the plan all along?"

"It was, but the plan fell apart when I fell in love with him."

"Oh, honey." She stood. "Hold on two seconds."

It was more like two minutes, but since Steph came back carrying a big basket of French fries and a dish of cheese sauce, she forgave her. Jamie hadn't thought she'd be able to eat anything tonight, but that was serious comfort food.

"Okay," Steph said, once they'd each had a few

fries dripping with cheese sauce. "Tell me what happened."

Jamie told the story, starting with her chat with her mom, during which she'd decided to wait until they were no longer with the same company before figuring out if they had a future. And then she walked Steph through the fire and Scott disrespecting her authority in an attempt to keep her safe, despite the fact she knew exactly what she was doing.

Steph held up her hand, shaking her head. "He did that to you? What an asshole."

It wasn't until she heard the words come out of Steph's mouth that Jamie realized why she'd come here. It wasn't just visiting a friend so she wasn't alone. She'd wanted somebody to be pissed off with her. Because she *was* pissed. She was hurt and sad and lonely, but she was also mad as hell at Scott.

"And then he told me he did it because he's in love with me."

Steph sat back in her chair, eyes wide. "Are you serious?"

"Yeah. We were still on the scene with both companies right there."

"He's in love with you?"

"That's not really the point."

After dredging a fry in cheese sauce, Steph popped it into her mouth, frowning. Considering how long she chewed, Jamie knew she was just buying herself time to think.

"So you fell in love with him. And then he said he's in love with you… And?"

"He said it in front of everybody," Jamie clarified for her. "Even knowing how important it was to me to keep our personal and professional relationships very separate."

"But he was scared for you."

"And *that* is the point. He got scared for me and interfered with my job and then embarrassed me in front of guys under my command."

"Because he loves you," Steph pointed out. "Did he apologize?"

"Yes. And he brought me chocolate pudding."

"Aw." Jamie must have made a face because Steph straightened up and scowled. "He's still an asshole, though."

That made her laugh, but it was short-lived. "That's the problem. He's really not. He knows he screwed up, but it doesn't change the fact he'd probably do it again. No matter what he says, his actions spoke louder than his words. And I'm not changing how I live my life."

"I'm sorry, honey." Steph slid the dish with the last bit of cheese sauce across the table to her. "What are you going to do now?"

"I'm going to focus on being the best damn fire lieutenant that Ladder 41 has ever had."

She said it hoping to lighten the mood, but Steph didn't laugh. "You don't think you can fix things with Scott? I mean, you love each other. Doesn't that mean you're supposed to be able to get through stuff together?"

"I'm not giving up my career and I can't change

who he is or how he feels about my job, so it's better to recognize it won't work now, rather than down the road."

She said the words without her voice choking off, and she really believed them, but it would take time for her to accept that it was really over. They were done. Tears welled in her eyes and she swiped at them with her sleeve before they could fall.

"I'd get you a beer," Steph said, "but you can't drive for shit sober. I'm not giving you alcohol."

"Hey! I'm a great driver. It's this city. Nobody can drive in Boston."

Steph snorted. "So it's not you. It's *all* of us?"

"Yes." Jamie nodded. "I know you have to get back to work, but thanks for the talk. And the cheesy fries."

"Why don't you hang out and have some real food to eat? Once the late dinner rush is over, we'll head to my place. Watch a movie. Drink some wine. You can crash on my couch."

Jamie thought about how painful it was to think about Scott every time she walked into her apartment and knew she'd have to get over it at some point. But not tonight. "That sounds wicked awesome."

"*Wicked* awesome," Steph said, and then she laughed. "You're starting to sound like us now, Jamie."

"That's okay. As long as I don't start driving like you."

NINETEEN

TWO WEEKS. SCOTT SAT at the bar, nursing a beer and watching the evening news on the big screen with no sound. Two weeks with no Jamie. With no love and no laughter.

And then, suddenly, she appeared on the screen, with her helmet gleaming in the sun and smiling at the reporter who had a microphone in her face. Her name was on the bottom of the screen, along with a caption. *Happy ending for child who climbed a tree to rescue kitten.*

He stared at her face, drinking in the sight of her, as his heart ached in his chest. God, he missed her. He missed her face and her laugh and her touch and every damn thing about her. He missed the sound of her voice.

"Hey, Lydia. Turn up the TV for a second?"

She looked up at the screen as she moved toward the remote control next to the register and then stopped. "No. If you want to hear Jamie's voice, you can grow some balls and go talk to her like a man."

"Jesus, you can really be a bitch."

"Nothing warms a man's heart like the love his children have for one another," Tommy said from the corner.

"I love them." He glared at Lydia. "I just love Ashley more."

She laughed at him. "Because she coddles you and gives you ice cream."

"Hey, the ice cream's for the baby."

"Sure it is. Because every growing baby in the womb needs ice cream three times in a week." She stepped closer, a bar rag dangling from her hand. "Go talk to her."

He pointed at the screen. "She's rescuing children who rescue kittens."

"That was yesterday afternoon. Slow news day, I guess, so they're replaying the feel-good stuff." She sighed and shook her head. "I happen to know she's home and was planning to clean out her refrigerator today. I know this because I tried to talk her into coming in to visit and that's what she told me."

"How often do you talk to her?"

"Almost every day."

That hurt—the reminder that she wasn't really gone. She was only gone from *his* life. And it was his own damn fault. "How is she?"

"She's fine. She's really happy at Ladder 41 and the commute isn't too bad."

"That's not what I mean and you know it."

"I do know what you mean, but this is one of those fuzzy boundary things. I'm her friend."

"You're my sister."

"Yes, I am. And if you weren't such a dumbass, you might have caught on to the fact I've told you *twice* to go talk to her since you walked in."

"Oh." Hope flared to life as he realized if Lydia thought he should go talk to her, that meant Jamie hadn't totally put him in the rearview mirror. There was a chance.

"Yeah, *oh.* I think you should lay off the hockey for a while. You've taken too many hits to the head."

He drained the rest of his beer and then slid off the stool. "I'm leaving now. You can save your abuse for the paying customers."

"Are you going there now?"

"I think so, before I chicken out. If I don't go straight there, I might talk myself out of it."

"Don't." She reached across the bar to take his hand. "Leave your pride at the door and talk to her."

He lifted her hand and kissed the back of it. "Just so you know, I don't really love Ashley more than you. You're both equally pains in my ass."

"You might want to come up with other ways to express your feelings before you get to Jamie's." She smiled. "Call me later."

Hope buoyed him for most of the trip to her apartment building, but he felt himself faltering when he stood on the sidewalk in front. He had no idea what he could say, other than he loved her. He still loved her and that was all he had, but it didn't feel like enough.

But he knew if he walked away right now, he wouldn't come back. Seeing her face on the television and Lydia letting him know he still had a chance had given him the courage he needed, but it was fading.

And he wished the damn downstairs door didn't

lock. It seemed like being able to knock on her door would make it easier. Asking her if she'd come down three flights of stairs to let him in was a lot more awkward.

I'm outside your door. Can I see you for a minute?

The wait for a response was probably only thirty seconds, but it felt like hours. Did you bring pudding?

The last thing he thought he'd do standing outside her door, about to beg for another chance, was laugh. But he did, and he remembered how much he loved that about her—about them. They laughed a lot.

No. He sent that and then typed again. But I'll go get some.

I'll be right down.

The grip he had on his phone made him realize his hands were shaking, and he put the thing in his pocket. Every minute he waited seemed like an eternity but then, finally, he saw her through the door.

His heart pounded and he felt the hair stand up on his arms and neck as he watched her come toward him. God, he'd missed her so much. His hands were still shaking and he didn't want to put them in his pockets, so he curled them into fists so maybe she wouldn't see how nervous he was.

She pushed open the door, and his heart skipped a beat when she smiled at him. "Hey, you. Come on in."

Scott wanted to touch her. He wanted to wrap his arms around her and squeeze her and not let go until they physically couldn't stand there anymore. "Thanks."

"You want to come up for a few minutes?" The smile was still there, but her eyes were sad.

"Even though I didn't bring pudding?"

"Normally I wouldn't offer hospitality to somebody showing up empty-handed like this," she joked. Then her lip quivered and she gave a tiny one-shouldered shrug that almost killed him. "But I've missed you, so I'll make an exception."

He followed her up the stairs, trying to think of the right words to say to her. But he also didn't want to overthink it because the only way he was going to get Jamie back was if he spoke from the heart. She wasn't going to settle for any less.

"I saw you on the news," he said when they reached the last flight, just because he couldn't stand the silence anymore.

"I couldn't believe it when the news crew showed up. A kid climbed a big-ass tree to rescue the neighbor's cat." She unlocked her door and pushed it open. "Needless to say, once the kid got up there, the cat came down. The boy didn't. But there are worse days, so I don't mind those kinds of calls."

Walking into her apartment was like coming home. They'd spent so much time here that everywhere he looked, he was reminded of the weeks he'd had with her—the best weeks of his life.

"I've missed you, and when I saw you on the television, I couldn't… I had to come, you know?"

"How have you been?"

"Shitty." There was no point in sugarcoating it. "I screwed up again by just walking away. I don't know if giving you space was the right thing or if I should have pushed and tried to get you to forgive me. I don't know and I took what I thought was the easy way out."

"It hasn't been easy."

"No. So I'm here and I'm still in love with you and I'm still sorry." He realized they were both standing there in the living room, and he wished they could sit down. His knees felt a little wobbly. He changed his stance so his knees weren't locked because passing out wasn't going to impress her any. "I don't want to put you in a box, Jamie. I want you to be you because you're the person I love. I don't want to change anything about you."

She folded her arms over her chest, her lips pressed together for a few seconds. "I feel like it's easy for you to say that now because I'm not going through the door with you anymore. I'm at Ladder 41 and you're not there when I'm in situations you don't want me to be in. Removing the situation doesn't mean the feelings that trigger the behavior are gone, too."

"Maybe that's part of it. But there's a chance we'll end up working a fire together someday and if we do, it's because they struck a shitload of alarms, so it'll be a bad one. If that happens, I swear to God I will not get in your way. I'll worry about you. Hell, I'll be scared shitless for you, but I won't ever disrespect you again."

"I want to believe that. I want to so badly."

"I've mourned, Jamie. I lost you and I've grieved for you and I hate that it was my own damn fault. I lost my mom to something she couldn't control, but she fought it. And we've lost brothers who were doing what they were called to do. I didn't even give you that. I thought it wouldn't hurt as much to lose you now, but it's even worse because I wasted what we had. I want to make memories with you. I want to grab every single day we can together."

The tears shining in her eyes ripped his heart to pieces, but he forced himself to stand where he was and not try to wipe them away. "I want that, too."

"We can do it, Jamie. We'll make a life together and we'll figure it out. We can have kids and they'll have days with me and days with you and then we'll have, what, three days a week all together? And we can chat and text and video chat during downtime. We can have it all."

She laughed, the sound a bubble of happiness through her tears. "I can almost see it."

"I *can* see it. And we'll worry about each other, but we'll be strong." He moved toward her, unable to help himself. "I'll go see the therapist that Ashley and Danny go to if you want me to. If we have a problem, we'll figure it out together. I don't ever want to walk away from you again."

"You better not." She looked him in the eye as she

closed the distance between them. "Don't ever push me away like that again."

Burying his hands in her hair, he rested his forehead against hers, blinking against the tears that blurred his vision. "I swear I won't. I love you, Jamie."

"I love you, too."

Scott felt like all the broken pieces inside of him knit back together again, and he kissed her. Slowly and tenderly because he wanted to savor this gift he'd been given. Then he wrapped his arms around her and squeezed.

"You're everything to me," he whispered. "I'm going to spend the rest of our lives making sure you know it."

"I can't wait." She tilted her head back to smile at him. "It's still early. What do you say we take a drive down to this little place I know on the South Shore and catch up. They have great seafood."

Three months later...

THE FLAMES GREW taller as smoke billowed around them. The smoke was thick and black, smelling like burnt meat and barbecue sauce.

"Turn the gas off," Jamie yelled.

"Hey," Scott said, turning and waving a spatula at her. "You're not in charge of *this* company."

"Obviously not, because if I was, that grill wouldn't be sending up smoke signals to the neighbors to call 911 right now."

"This is like a bad joke," Lydia said. "How many firefighters does it take to put out a grill fire?"

There were half a dozen of them standing around the grill, so more than six, Jamie thought. Grant and Gavin were just laughing but the others ignored them.

"Maybe I should get a fire extinguisher," Ellen Porter said.

"We'd never get that taste out of anything we cooked after that," Aidan argued.

"Turn the gas off," Jamie repeated.

"If we turn the gas off," Scott said, "then the fire will go out."

"I can't believe they haven't let you skip the exam and just made you an honorary officer," Jamie said.

He waved the spatula at her again. "You're going to pay for that later, funny lady."

"If the fire goes out, how will we cook off the gunk so we can make the steaks?" Aidan shook his head, and then jumped back when something—probably leftover fat stuck to the grill plate—sizzled and popped. "Joey, you always man the grill when we do charity cookouts. Explain this to her."

Joe, one of the guys from Ladder 41, shook his head. "Hell, no. I'm not here to explain anything to my LT. I'm just here for the beer and the steak, and it's probably a good thing I like mine more on the well-done side."

"If you turn the burners on full, that shit'll burn off faster and we can eat sometime today," Tommy said from his lounge chair in the shade.

"Dad!" Ashley walked out onto the back deck, one

hand on her baby bump. "You of all people should know better than to say that to them."

Jamie laughed and turned back to the folding table that was practically groaning under the weight of potluck food. They'd all come together to christen Aidan and Lydia's new house with a backyard barbecue, and all she could do was hope the guys didn't burn down their backyard. That would just be embarrassing, both personally and professionally.

Jess stepped out onto the deck, carrying a tray of condiments. "I don't even know if there's room for these on that table."

"We'll make room." Jamie started shifting dishes around. "I heard you officially opened the Boston branch of Broussard Financial Services last week."

"I did!" Jess set the tray down in the clearing Jamie had made. "It's scary, but so exciting. And I'll still fly to San Diego now and then, but being home with Rick all the time is amazing."

"How are your grandparents doing?"

"They're doing great. They love where they're living and they've made a lot of friends there. I swear, they're always doing something. And my dad's going to fly out later this month."

"Really? That's awesome, Jess." Jess's father had been estranged from his parents for all of her life, so getting him to Boston was a big deal.

"I'm nervous, but I think it's going to be good. Seeing the office is an excuse, but part of rebuilding their relationship is him facing where he came from. We're going to have them all over for dinner, of course."

"That'll be good because it's the house he grew up in, so the memories will be there, but you guys have changed it enough so they won't be overwhelming."

Jess smiled. "Exactly. I think after this visit, if it goes well, we'll probably start planning our wedding. It won't be at Kincaid's Pub, but we'll try to make a decent party."

"Cavemen cooked dinosaur meat over open fires, didn't they?" she heard Rick say. "Why can't we just throw the damn steaks on?"

"Evolution," Jess called to him. "Embrace it, honey."

Inevitably, the flames ran out of caked-on food to burn off and the guys were able to throw steaks and chicken on the grill. Aidan and Lydia didn't have a lot of outdoor furniture yet, but they all stood around or perched on whatever they could find to eat. There was a lot of laughter, and Jamie basked in the glow of more happiness than she'd ever believed she'd find.

This was an amazing family she'd found for herself. It was unfortunate that Joey was the only guy from her company who'd been able to make it, but they'd all been together for a charity half marathon the month before. There was great chemistry between the companies and she didn't think it would be too long before she'd be looking at another promotion. And the separation from Scott was just right. They had the common bond of their career, but each had the space to do their jobs without distraction. Everything was perfect.

Once everybody had eaten, she helped carry the leftover food inside. Luckily, they'd eaten almost all of it and the dishes had been brought in disposable containers, so there wasn't a lot of cleanup. But she took the time to wash up the few dishes and barbecue tools they'd used.

She heard the footsteps behind her just a few seconds before Scott's arms wrapped around her waist. He kissed the back of her neck and then she leaned back against him.

"Nice party," she said.

"Yeah. They've got a nice place here. Worth having to drive to work for them, I guess."

"It's not that far to drive. And it's definitely worth it."

He hugged her close, resting his chin on her shoulder. "Are houses something you think about?"

She'd finally given up her apartment a few weeks ago. After spending a couple of months practically living together, it hadn't taken much for her to officially move in with him. "Not really. I like our place, and I like the fact we can walk so many places. And being around for Tommy so he's not alone."

Her personal life was as perfect as her professional one, finally. She and Scott were happy. He'd gone home to Nebraska with her in July, and her family had loved him. Her niece had been fascinated by his accent and made him repeat things over and over so she could laugh. *Say* car *again! Say* park*!*

"I already have everything I want," she said, turning her head so she could kiss his cheek.

"Everything?"

"Well, I still don't have a car with heated seats but other than that, yes."

"Don't think I haven't noticed how often you take my truck because it's easier to get out of the driveway. Or so you claim."

Laughing, she pulled the plug in the sink and dried her hands on the towel so she could turn and wrap her arms around his neck. "It's not my fault your big truck hogs all the space. My poor car barely fits in the corner."

"Why do I feel like I'm going to start getting links to property listings with big driveways?"

She laughed and gave him a quick kiss. "I'm serious about being happy where we are. You're all I need."

"And maybe this?" He held up his hand, the diamond ring between his fingers sparkling under the overhead light.

Her breath caught in her throat, and she couldn't speak.

"I love you, Jamie Rutherford. Will you marry me?"

She nodded, hating the tears blurring her vision because she couldn't see the ring. While he took her left hand and slid it onto her finger, she used her right to swipe at her eyes. "It's beautiful."

"You're beautiful."

She kissed him and then looked into his eyes. "I love you so much."

"Let's go tell everybody."

Jamie knew as soon as they walked out the door that at least some of them had known this moment was coming. If not today, then soon, because Aidan and his sisters all turned to look in their direction and Lydia's eyes went directly to her left hand.

She held it up so the stones could sparkle in the light, and there was a lot of squealing and hugging from the women and backslapping from the guys. The tears came back when Ashley squeezed her extra hard before handing her over to Lydia for the same treatment.

"I told you," Ashley said, "that Jamie is our perfect third."

She had, the day they'd shopped for dresses for Lydia's wedding. Smiling, she looked at the guys, who were standing with Scott and saying who knew what to make him laugh. Then Tommy pulled her into his arms for a hug that almost squeezed the air out of her.

"Welcome to the family," he said, his gruff voice choked with emotion. "You're everything I ever wanted for my boy."

She probably would have cried some more, but Ashley clapped her hands for everybody's attention. "This seems like a perfect time to bring out the desserts, doesn't it?"

There were cheers and Lydia waved her hand at her husband. "Hey, come help me cut the carrot cake."

As the cheers died abruptly, Scott leaned close to whisper in her ear. "You sure you're ready to be a part of this forever?"

"I can't wait."

* * * * *

AUTHOR NOTE

THE PROCESSES AND organizational structures of large city fire departments are incredibly complex, and I took minor creative liberties in order to maintain readability.

To first responders everywhere, thank you.

To find out about other books by Shannon Stacey or to be alerted to new releases, sign up for her monthly newsletter at bit.ly/shannonstaceynewsletter.

ACKNOWLEDGMENTS

As always, a huge thank-you to Angela James and to the Harlequin and Carina Press teams for your constant support and encouragement.

Go back to the beginning with
HEAT EXCHANGE,
book one in New York Times *bestselling author*
Shannon Stacey's
BOSTON FIRE series.

ONE

Lydia Kincaid could pull a pint of Guinness so perfect her Irish ancestors would weep tears of appreciation, but fine dining? Forget about it.

"The customer is disappointed in the sear on these scallops," she told the sous-chef, setting the plate down.

"In what way?"

"Hell if I know. They look like all the other scallops." Lydia had a hairpin sticking into her scalp, and it took every bit of her willpower not to poke at it. Her dark hair was too long, thick and wavy to be confined into a chic little bun, but it was part of the dress code. And going home with a headache every night was just part of the job. "Ten bucks says if I wait three minutes, then pop that same plate in the microwave for fifteen seconds and take it out to her, she'll gush over how the sear is so perfect now."

"If I see you microwaving scallops, I'll make sure the only food you ever get to touch in this city again is fast food."

Lydia rolled her eyes, having heard that threat many times before, and accepted a fresh plate of scallops from the line cook. The sous-chef just sniffed loudly and dumped the unacceptable batch in the garbage, plate and all. She was pretty sure the guy spent all his off time watching reality television chefs throw tantrums.

Three hours later, Lydia was in her car and letting her hair down. She dropped the bobby pins and elastic bands into her cup holder to fish out before her next shift and then used both hands to shake her hair out and massage her scalp.

She hated her job. Maybe some of it stemmed from the disparity between the cold formality of this restaurant and the warm and loud world she'd come from, but she also flat-out wasn't very good at it. The foods perplexed her and, according to the kitchen manager, her tableside manner lacked polish. Two years hadn't yet managed to put a shine on her. The tips were usually good, though, and living in Concord, New Hampshire, cost less than living in Boston, but it still wasn't cheap.

She'd just put her car in gear when she heard the siren in the distance. With her foot still on the brake, she watched as the fire engine came into view—red lights flashing through the dark night—and sped past.

With a sigh, she shifted her foot to the gas pedal. She didn't need to hold her breath anymore. Didn't need to find the closest scanner. Nobody she loved was on that truck so, while she said a quick prayer for their safety, they were faceless strangers and life wasn't temporarily suspended.

And that was why she'd keep trying to please people who wouldn't know a good scallop sear if it bit them on the ass and taking shit from the sous-chef. That job financed her new life here in New Hampshire, including a decent apartment she shared with a roommate, and it was a nice enough life that she wasn't tempted to go home.

Her life wasn't perfect. It had certainly been lacking in sex and friendship lately, but she wasn't going backward just because the road was longer or harder than she'd thought. She wanted something different and she was going to keep working toward it.

Thanks to the miracle of an apartment building with an off-street parking lot, Lydia had a dedicated parking spot waiting for her. It was another reason she put up with customers who nitpicked their entrées just because they were paying so much for them.

Her roommate worked at a sports bar and wouldn't be home for another couple of hours, so Lydia took a quick shower and put on her sweats. She'd just curled up on the sofa with the remote and a couple of the cookies her blessed-with-a-great-metabolism roommate had freshly baked when her cell phone rang.

She knew before looking at the caller ID it would be her sister. Not many people called her, and none late at night. "Hey, Ashley. What's up?"

"My marriage is over."

Lydia couldn't wrap her mind around the words at first. Had something happened to Danny? But she hadn't said that. She said it was over. "What do you mean it's over?"

"I told him I wasn't sure I wanted to be married to him anymore and that I needed some space. He didn't even say anything. He just packed up a couple of bags and left."

"Oh my God, Ashley." Lydia sank onto the edge of the sofa, stunned. "Where did this even come from?"

"I've been unhappy for a while. I just didn't tell anybody." Her sister sighed, the sound hollow and discouraged over the phone. "Like a moron, I thought I could talk to him about it. Instead, he left."

"Why have you been unhappy? Dammit, Ashley, what is going on? Did he cheat? I swear to God if he stepped out—"

"No. He didn't cheat. And it's too much for me to talk about now."

"If you had been talking to me all along, it wouldn't be too much now. You can't call me and tell me your marriage is over and then tell me you don't want to talk about it."

"I know, but it's…it's too much. I called to talk to you about the bar."

Uh-oh. Alarm bells went off in Lydia's mind, but there was no way she could extricate herself from the conversation without being a shitty sister.

"I need you to come back and help Dad," Ashley said, and Lydia dropped her head back against the sofa cushion, stifling a groan. "I need some time off."

"I have a job, Ashley. And an apartment."

"You've told me a bunch of times that you hate your job."

She couldn't deny that since a conversation rarely passed between them without mention of that fact.

"And it's waiting tables," Ashley continued. "It's not like I'm asking you to take a hiatus from some fancy career path."

That was bitchy, even for Ashley, but Lydia decided to give her a pass. She didn't know what had gone wrong in their marriage, but she did know Ashley loved Danny Walsh with every fiber of her being, so she had to be a wreck.

"I can't leave Shelly high and dry," Lydia said in a calm, reasonable tone. "This is a great apartment and I'm lucky to have it. It has off-street parking and my space has my apartment number on it. It's literally *only* mine."

"I can't be at the bar, Lydia. You know how it is there. Everybody's got a comment or some advice to give, and I have to hear every five minutes what a great guy Danny is and why can't I just give him another chance?"

Danny really *was* a great guy, but she could understand her sister not wanting to be reminded of it constantly while they were in the process of separating. But going back to Boston and working at Kincaid's was a step in the wrong direction for Lydia.

"I don't know, Ash."

"Please. You don't know—" To Lydia's dismay,

her sister's voice was choked off by a sob. "I can't do it, Lydia. I really, really need you."

Shit. "I'll be home tomorrow."

"WE GOT SMOKE showing on three and at least one possible on the floor," Rick Gullotti said. "Meet you at the top, boys."

Aidan Hunt threw a mock salute in the direction of the ladder company's lieutenant and tossed the ax to Grant Cutter before grabbing the Halligan tool for himself. With a fork at one end and a hook and adze head on the other end, it was essentially a long crowbar on steroids and they never went anywhere without it. After confirmation Scotty Kincaid had the line, and a thumbs-up from Danny Walsh at the truck, he and the other guys from Engine 59 headed for the front door of the three-decker.

Some bunch of geniuses, generations before, had decided the best way to house a shitload of people in a small amount of space was to build three-story houses—each floor a separate unit—and cram them close together. It was great if you needed a place to live and didn't mind living in a goldfish bowl. It was less great if it was your job to make sure an out-of-control kitchen fire didn't burn down the entire block.

They made their way up the stairs, not finding trouble until they reached the top floor. The door to the apartment stood open, with smoke pouring out. Aidan listened to the crackle of the radio over the sound of his own breathing in the mask. The guys from Ladder 37 had gained access by way of the window and had a woman descending, but her kid was still inside.

"Shit." Aidan confirmed Walsh knew they were going into the apartment and was standing by to charge the line if they needed water, and then looked for nods from Kincaid and Cutter.

He went in, making his way through the smoke. It was bad enough so the child would be coughing—hopefully—but there was chaos in the front of the apartment as another company that had shown up tried to knock down the flames from the front.

Making his way to the kid's bedroom, he signaled for Cutter to look under the bed while he went to the closet. If the kid was scared and hiding from them, odds were he or she was in one of those two spots.

"Bingo," he heard Cutter say into his ear.

The updates were growing more urgent and he heard Kincaid call for water, which meant the fire was heading their way. "No time to be nice. Grab the kid and let's go."

It was a little girl and she screamed as Cutter pulled her out from under the bed. She was fighting him and, because his hold was awkward, once she was free of the bed, Cutter almost lost her. Aidan swore under his breath. If she bolted, they could all be in trouble.

He leaned the Halligan against the wall and picked up the little girl. By holding her slightly slanted, he was able to hold her arms and legs still without running the risk of smacking her head on the way down.

"Grab the Halligan and let's go."

"More guys are coming up," Walsh radioed in. "Get out of there now."

The smoke was dense now and the little girl was doing more coughing and gasping than crying. "My dog!"

Aidan went past Kincaid, slapping him on the shoulder. Once Cutter went by, Kincaid could retreat—they all stayed together—and let another company deal with the flames.

"I see her dog," Aidan heard Cutter say, and he turned just in time to see the guy disappear back into the bedroom.

"Jesus Christ," Scotty yelled. "Cutter, get your ass down those stairs. Hunt, just go."

He didn't want to leave them, and he wouldn't have except the fight was going out of the child in his arms. Holding her tight, he started back down the stairs they'd come up. At the second floor he met another company coming up, but he kept going.

Once he cleared the building, he headed for the ambulance and passed the girl over to the waiting medics. It was less than two minutes before Cutter and Kincaid emerged from the building, but it felt like forever.

They yanked their masks off as Cutter walked over to the little girl and—after getting a nod from EMS—put an obviously terrified little dog on the girl's lap. They all smiled as the girl wrapped her arms around her pet and then her mom put her arms around both. Aidan put his hand on Cutter's shoulder and the news cameras got their tired, happy smiles for the evening news.

Once they were back on the other side of the engine and out of view of the cameras, Kincaid grabbed the front of Cutter's coat and shoved him against the truck. "You want to save puppies, that's great. If there's time. Once you're told to get the fuck out, you don't go back for pets. And if you ever risk my life again, or any other guy's, for a goddamn dog, I'll make sure you can't even get a job emptying the garbage at Waste Reduction."

Once Cutter nodded, Kincaid released him and they looked to Danny for a status update. They had it pretty well knocked down and, though the third floor was a loss and the lower floors wouldn't be pretty, the people who lived in the neighboring houses weren't going to have a bad day.

Two hours later, Aidan sat on the bench in the shower room and tied his shoes. Danny was stowing his shower stuff, a towel wrapped around his waist. He'd been quiet since they got back, other than having a talk with Cutter, since he was the officer of the bunch. But he was always quiet, so it was hard to tell what was going on with him.

"Got any plans tonight?" Aidan finally asked, just to break the silence.

"Nope. Probably see if there's a game on."

Aidan wasn't sure what to say to that. He didn't have a lot of experience with a good friend going through a divorce. Breakups, sure, but not a marriage ending. "If you want to talk, just let me know. We can grab a beer or something."

"Talk about what?"

"Don't bullshit me, Walsh. We know what's going on and it's a tough situation. So if you want to talk, just let me know."

"She doesn't want to be married to me anymore, so we're getting a divorce." Danny closed his locker, not needing to slam it to get his point across. "There's nothing to talk about."

"Okay." Aidan tossed his towel in the laundry bin and went out the door.

A lot of guys had trouble expressing their emotions, but Danny took it to a whole new level. Aidan thought talking about it over a few beers might help, but he shouldn't have been surprised the offer was refused.

He'd really like to know what had gone wrong in the Walsh marriage, though. He liked Danny and Ashley and he'd always thought they were a great couple. If they couldn't make it work, Aidan wasn't sure he had a chance. And lately he'd been thinking a lot about how nice it would be to have somebody to share his life with.

A mental snapshot of the little girl cradling her dog filled his mind. He wouldn't mind having a dog. But his hours would be too hard on a dog, and he wasn't a fan of cats. They were a little creepy and not good for playing ball in the park. He could probably keep a fish alive, but they weren't exactly a warm hug at the end of a long tour.

With a sigh he went into the kitchen to rummage for a snack. If he couldn't keep a dog happy, he probably didn't have much chance of keeping a wife happy. And that was assuming he even met a woman he wanted to get to know well enough to consider a ring. So far, not so good.

"Cutter ate the last brownie," Scotty told him as soon as he walked into the kitchen area.

Aidan shook his head, glaring at the young guy sitting at the table with a very guilty flush on his face. "You really do want to get your ass kicked today, don't you?"

"MAYBE I SHOULDN'T have called you. I feel bad now."

Lydia dropped her bag inside the door and put her hand on her hip. "I just quit my job and burned a chunk of my savings to pay Shelly for two months' rent in advance so she won't give my room away. You're stuck with me now."

Tears filled Ashley's eyes and spilled over onto her cheeks as she stood up on her toes to throw her arms around Lydia's neck. "I'm so glad you're here."

Lydia squeezed her older sister, and she had to admit that coming back was about the last thing she'd wanted to do, but she was glad to be there, too. When push came to shove, her sister needed her and when family really needed you, nothing else mattered.

When Ashley released her, Lydia followed her into the living room and they dropped onto the couch. About six months after they got married, Danny and Ashley had scored the single-family home in a foreclosure auction. It had gone beyond *handyman's special* straight into the rehab hell of *handyman's wet dream*, but room by room they'd done the remodeling themselves. Now they had a lovely home they never could have afforded on their salaries.

But right now, it wasn't a happy home. Lydia sighed and kicked off her flip-flops to tuck her feet under her. "What's going on?"

Ashley shrugged one shoulder, her mouth set in a line of misery. "You know how it is."

Maybe, in a general sense, Lydia knew how it was. She'd been married to a firefighter, too, and then she'd divorced one. But the one she'd been married to had struggled with the job, tried to cope with alcohol and taken advantage of Lydia's unquestioning acceptance of the demanding hours to screw around with every female who twitched her goods in his direction.

That wasn't Danny, so other than knowing how intense being a firefighter's wife could be, Lydia didn't see what Ashley was saying.

"He's just so closed off," her sister added. "I feel

like he doesn't care about anything and I don't want to spend the rest of my life like that."

Lydia was sure there was more to it—probably a lot more—but Ashley didn't seem inclined to offer up anything else. And after the packing and driving, Lydia didn't mind putting off the heavy emotional stuff for a while.

"I should go see Dad," she said.

"He's working the bar tonight. And before you say anything, I know he's not supposed to be on his feet that much anymore. But you know he's sitting around talking to his buddies as much as being on his feet, and Rick Gullotti's girlfriend's supposed to be helping him out."

Rick was with Ladder 37 and Lydia had known him for years, but she struggled to remember his girlfriend's name. "Becky?"

Ashley snorted. "Becky was like eight girlfriends ago. Karen. We like her and it's been like four months now, which might be a record for Rick."

Lydia looked down at the sundress she'd thrown on that morning because it was comfortable and the pale pink not only looked great with her dark coloring, but also cheered her up. It was a little wrinkled from travel, but not too bad. It wasn't as if Kincaid's was known for being a fashion hot spot. "And Karen couldn't keep on helping him out?"

"She's an ER nurse. Works crazy hours, I guess, so she helps out, but can't commit to a set schedule. And you know how Dad is about family."

"It's Kincaid's Pub so, by God, there should be a Kincaid in it," Lydia said in a low, gruff voice that made Ashley laugh.

Even as she smiled at her sister's amusement, Lydia had to tamp down on the old resentment. There had been no inspirational *you can be the President of the United States if you want to* speeches for Tommy's daughters. His two daughters working the bar at Kincaid's Pub while being wonderfully supportive firefighters' wives was a dream come true for their old man.

Lydia had been the first to disappoint him. Her unwillingness to give the alcoholic serial cheater *just one more chance* had been the first blow, and then her leaving Kincaid's and moving to New Hampshire had really pissed him off.

Sometimes she wondered how their lives would have turned out if their mom hadn't died of breast cancer when Lydia and Ashley were just thirteen and fourteen. Scotty had been only nine, but he was his father's pride and joy. Joyce Kincaid hadn't taken any shit from her gruff, old-school husband, and Lydia thought maybe she would have pushed hard for her daughters to dream big. And then she would have helped them fight to make those dreams come true.

Or maybe their lives wouldn't have turned out any different and it was just Lydia spinning what-ifs into pretty fairy tales.

After carrying her bag upstairs to the guest room, Lydia brushed her hair and exchanged her flip-flops for cute little tennis shoes that matched her dress and would be better for walking.

"Are you sure you want to walk?" Ashley asked. "It's a bit of a hike."

"It's not that far, and I won't have to find a place to park."

"I'd go with you, but…"

But her not wanting to be at Kincaid's was the entire reason Lydia had uprooted herself and come home. "I get it. And I won't be long. I'll be spending enough time there as it is, so I'm just going to pop in, say hi and get the hell out."

Ashley snorted. "Good luck with that."

It was a fifteen-minute walk from the Walsh house to Kincaid's Pub, but Lydia stretched it out a bit. The sights. The sounds. The smells. No matter how reluctant she was to come back here or how many years she was away, this would always be home.

A few people called to her, but she just waved and kept walking. Every once in a while she'd step up the pace to make it look like she was in a hurry. But the street was fairly quiet and in no time, she was standing in front of Kincaid's Pub.

It was housed in the lower floor of an unassuming brick building. Okay, ugly. It was ugly, with a glass door and two high, long windows. A small sign with the name in a plain type was screwed to the brick over the door, making it easy to overlook. It was open to anybody, of course, but the locals were their bread and butter, and they liked it just the way it was.

Her dad had invested in the place—becoming a partner to help out the guy who owned it—almost ten years before his heart attack hastened his retirement from fighting fires, and he'd bought the original owner out when he was back on his feet. Once it was solely Tommy's, he'd changed the name to Kincaid's Pub, and Ashley and Lydia had assumed their places behind the bar.

After taking a deep breath, she pulled open the heavy door and walked inside. All the old brick and wood seemed to absorb the light from the many antique-looking fixtures, and it took a moment for her eyes to adjust.

It looked just the same, with sports and firefighting memorabilia and photographs covering the brick walls. The bar was a massive U-shape with a hand-polished surface, and a dozen tables, each seating four, were scattered around the room. In an alcove to one side was a pool table, along with a few more seating groups.

Because there wasn't a game on, the two televisions—one over the bar and one hung to be seen from most of the tables—were on Mute, with closed-captioning running across the bottom. The music was turned down low because Kincaid's was loud enough without people shouting to be heard over the radio.

Lydia loved this place. And she hated it a little, too. But in some ways it seemed as though Kincaid's

Pub was woven into the fabric of her being, and she wasn't sorry to be there again.

"Lydia!" Her father's voice boomed across the bar, and she made a beeline to him.

Tommy Kincaid was a big man starting to go soft around the middle, but he still had arms like tree trunks. They wrapped around her and she squealed a little when he lifted her off her feet. "I've missed you, girl."

She got a little choked up as he set her down and gave her a good looking over. Their relationship could be problematic at times—like most of the time—but Lydia never doubted for a second he loved her with all his heart. Once upon a time, he'd had the same thick, dark hair she shared with her siblings, but the gray had almost totally taken over.

He looked pretty good, though, and she smiled. "I'm glad you missed me, because it sounds like you'll be seeing a lot of me for a while."

A scowl drew his thick eyebrows and the corners of his mouth downward. "That sister of yours. I don't know what's going through her mind."

She gave him a bright smile. "Plenty of time for that later. Right now I just want to see everybody and have a beer."

A blonde woman who was probably a few years older than her smiled from behind the bar. "I'm Karen. Karen Shea."

Lydia reached across and shook her hand. "We really appreciate you being able to help out."

"Not a problem."

Lydia went to the very end of the back side of the bar and planted a kiss on the cheek of Fitz Fitzgibbon—her father's best friend and a retired member of Ladder 37—who was the only person who ever sat on that stool. She supposed once upon a time she might have known his real first name, but nobody ever called him anything but Fitz or, in her father's case, Fitzy.

There were a few other regulars she said hello to before getting a Sam Adams and standing at the bar. Unlike most, the big bar at Kincaid's didn't have stools all the way around. It had once upon a time, but now there were only stools on the back side and the end. Her dad had noticed a lot of guys didn't bother with the stools and just leaned against the polished oak. To make things easier, he'd just ripped them out.

About a half hour later, her brother, Scotty, walked in. Like the rest of the Kincaids, he had thick dark hair and dark eyes. He needed a shave, as usual, but he looked good. They'd talked and sent text messages quite a bit over the past two years, but neither of them was much for video chatting, so she hadn't actually seen him.

And right on Scotty's heels was Aidan Hunt. His brown hair was lighter than her brother's and it needed a trim. And she didn't need to see his eyes to remember they were blue, like a lake on a bright summer day. He looked slightly older, but no less deliciously handsome than ever. She wasn't surprised to see him. Wherever Scotty was, Aidan was usually close by.

What did surprise her was that the second his gaze met hers, her first thought was that she'd like to throw everybody out of the bar, lock the door and then shove him onto a chair. Since she was wearing the sundress, all she had to do was undo his fly, straddle his lap and hold on.

When the corner of his mouth quirked up, as if he somehow knew she'd just gone eight seconds with him in her mind, she gave him a nod of greeting and looked away.

For crap's sake, that was Aidan Hunt. Her annoying younger brother's equally annoying best friend.

He'd been seventeen when they met, to Lydia's twenty-one. He'd given her a grin that showed off perfect, Daddy's-got-money teeth and those sparkling blue eyes and said, "Hey, gorgeous. Want to buy me a drink?"

She'd rolled her eyes and told him to enjoy his playdate with Scotty. From that day on, he had seemed determined to annoy the hell out of her at every possible opportunity.

When her brother reached her, she shoved Aidan out of her mind and embraced Scotty. "How the hell are ya?"

"Missed having you around," he said. "Sucks you had to come back for a shitty reason, but it's still good to see you. I just found out about an hour ago Ashley had called you."

"She just called me last night, so it was spur-of-the-moment, I guess."

"It's good to have you back."

"Don't get too used to it. It's temporary."

She'd always thought if she and Scotty were closer in age than four years apart, they could have been twins, with the same-shaped faces and their coloring. Ashley looked a lot like both of them, but her face was leaner, her eyes a lighter shade of brown and her hair wasn't quite as thick.

Scotty was more like Lydia in temperament, too. Ashley was steadier and liked to try logic first. Scott and Lydia were a little more volatile and tended to run on emotion. Her temper had a longer fuse than her brother's, but they both tended to pop off a little easy.

They caught up for a few minutes, mainly talking about his fellow firefighters, most of whom she knew well. And he gave her a quick update on their dad's doctor not being thrilled with his blood pressure. It didn't sound too bad, but it was probably good Ashley had called her rather than let him try to take up her slack.

Then Scotty shifted from one foot to the other and grimaced. "Sorry, but I've had to take a leak for like an hour."

She laughed and waved him off. "Go. I'll be here."

He left and Lydia looked up at the television, sipping her beer. She only ever had one, so she'd make it last, but part of her wanted to chug it and ask for a refill. It was a little overwhelming, being back.

"Hey, gorgeous. Want to buy me a drink?" What were the chances? She turned to face Aidan, smiling at the fact she'd been thinking about that day just a few minutes before. "What's so funny?"

She shook her head, not wanting to tell him she'd been thinking about the day they met, since that would be an admission she'd been thinking about him at all. "Nothing. How have you been?"

"Good. Same shit, different day. You come back for a visit?"

"I'll be here awhile. Maybe a couple of weeks, or a month." She shrugged. "Ashley wanted to take some time off, so I'm going to cover for her. You know how Dad is about having one of us here all the damn time."

His eyes squinted and he tilted his head a little. "You sound different."

"I worked on toning down the accent a little, to fit in more at work, I guess. Even though it's only the next state over, people were always asking me where I was from."

"You trying to forget who you are?" It came out *fuh-get who you ah*. "Forget where you came from?"

"Not possible," she muttered.

He gave her that grin again, with the perfect teeth and sparkling eyes. They crinkled at the corners now, the laugh lines just making him more attractive. "So what you're saying is that we're unforgettable."

She laughed, shaking her head. "You're something, all right."

Aidan looked as if he was going to say something else, but somebody shouted his name and was beckoning him over. He nodded and then turned back to Lydia. "I'll see you around. And welcome home."

She watched him walk away, trying to keep her eyes above his waist in case anybody was watching her watch him. Her annoying brother's annoying best friend had very nice shoulders stretching out that dark blue T-shirt.

Her gaze dipped, just for a second. And a very nice ass filling out those faded blue jeans.